NO ORDINARY HATE

WHITNEY DINEEN

MELANIE SUMMERS

Published by 33 Partners Publishing and Indigo Group

First edition

E-Book ISBN: 978-1-988891-49-1

Print Book ISBN: 978-1-988891-53-8

This is a work of fiction. Names, characters, businesses, places, events, and incidents are either the products of the authors' overactive imaginations or used in a fictitious manner. Any resemblance to actual persons, living or dead, or actual events is purely coincidental. And we don't mean maybe.

Made in the United States.

May 2022

Cover by: Becky Monson

To all the single mothers who do the cuddling, cleaning, and cooking,
You are our heroes!
XO Whitney and Melanie

Books by Whitney Dineen and Melanie Summers

The Accidentally in Love Series

Text Me on Tuesday
The Text God
Text Wars
Text in Show
Mistle Text
Text and Confused

A Gamble on Love Mom-Com Series

No Ordinary Hate
A Hate Like This (Coming Soon)

Also by Whitney Dineen

Romantic Comedies

The Mimi Chronicles

The Reinvention of Mimi Finnegan

Mimi Plus Two

Kindred Spirits

Relatively Series

Relatively Normal

Relatively Sane

Relatively Happy

Creek Water Series

The Event

The Move

The Plan

The Dream

Seven Brides for Seven Mothers Series

Love is a Battlefield

Ain't She Sweet

It's My Party

You're So Vain

Head Over Feet

She Sins at Midnight

Going Up?

Love for Sale

Conspiracy Thriller

See No More

Non-Fiction Humor

Motherhood, Martyrdom & Costco Runs

Middle Reader

Wilhelmina and the Willamette Wig Factory

Who the Heck is Harvey Stingle?

Children's Books

The Friendship Bench

Also by Melanie Summers

ROMANTIC COMEDIES

The Crown Jewels Series

The Royal Treatment

The Royal Wedding

The Royal Delivery

Paradise Bay Series

The Honeymooner

Whisked Away

The Suite Life

Resting Beach Face

Crazy Royal Love Series

Royally Crushed

Royally Wild

Royally Tied

Stand-Alone Books

Even Better Than the Real Thing

WOMEN'S FICTION

The After Wife

Chapter 1

Harper

Dear Readers,

Is it just me or are you hankering for the next Hollywood scandal too?
This town has become so dull, I can barely drag myself out of bed in the morning.
Enough with the plastic surgery mess-ups. Hard pass on who's a pain in the bootay to work with. Spoiler—everyone is.
Daddy needs some real drama, so somebody out there better give it to me before I shrivel up and die from boredom.

Dish,
Ferris Biltmore

~

You know how you can have a nightmare so vibrantly bizarre that you're one hundred percent certain there really *is* an axe murderer looming over your bed, about to serve you pigs in a blanket before he kills you? That's how I feel right now, except in reverse. I'm currently trying to convince myself that what I'm witnessing is nothing more than a horrific dream.

Standing in the doorway of my Mediterranean-style living room—lovingly decorated in earth tones, with pops of orange and rust reminiscent of the Tuscan sunset—I'm watching my husband bone the nanny. I realize *bone* is a word that lacks class, but believe me, there is nothing classy about what's occurring over the back of my cocoa-colored leather sofa. A couch I must now burn. Possibly while they're still on it.

I should be devastated and rocked to my core, but sadly, this is not the first or even the second time I've caught my husband in a compromising position.

"Oh. My. GOD. Right there!" Justine yells.

Brett responds with, "You're so tight I can barely hold back!"

I'm about to insert myself into the conversation with something along the lines of, "*You* give birth to two children who inherited your giant head and see if you bounce back to normal." Instead, I glance outside to make sure my kids are safe in the backyard. Thankfully, they are.

"Oh, yeah, Brett, you're so … sooooo …"

"Scummy? Deplorable? Clichéd?" I suggest loudly.

Brett jumps off Justine and scrambles to pull up his pants. Unfortunately for him, there's no blood left in his brain, which obviously messes with his equilibrium. He staggers around for a few moments before falling, his butt making a slapping sound against the terracotta tiles. I think of all the wonderful sounds I could make hitting him with an assortment of art pieces around the room.

Justine mumbles, "Oh, Mrs. Kennedy, I'm so sorry. I was just … I mean … I was choking … and Mr. Kennedy was giving me the Heimlich maneuver."

"He needed his pants down for that?"

She opens her mouth, then closes it.

That's right. Shut it. "Justine, you're fired," I say with a superhuman calm I do not feel. "Get out now, and don't bother to pack your bags. I'll have your things delivered to the agency."

"Please don't tell them," she begs, pulling up her underwear. Which look suspiciously like my underwear—Agent Provocateur, Taisia. At nearly $700 a pair, I'm pretty sure they aren't in my nanny's budget. And while I can certainly afford them, I would never waste that kind of money on underwear. Which means they were a gift. Likely from my idiot husband. "They won't find me another position if they know that—"

"You needed my husband to give you the Heimlich maneuver with his penis?" This girl is about six eggs short of a dozen.

Brett finally gets to his feet. "It isn't what you think, Harper."

I'm pretty sure it's *exactly* what I think. My movie star husband has a major problem keeping it in his pants. In the past, he's assured me he was seeking professional help for his lack of impulse control, but I don't even care anymore.

Every time he's promised it's the last time, he's moved one step closer to being permanently expelled from my life. I've tried to forgive him for the sake of our children, but now that he's brought his philandering into our home—my safety zone—it's the last straw.

"You can go with her, Brett. You no longer live here."

"You can't kick me out!" He's hopping around on one foot while he attempts to tug his jeans up. "I paid for this house."

My spirit shoots out of my body and hovers somewhere around the ceiling. I'm seriously experiencing a *Twilight Zone* moment here. "I had a hit television show for six years, Brett. I assure you a good deal of *my* money has gone into this house as well."

"What about the kids?"

It's a question that hits so close to the cavity of my heart that I feel an almost electric shock of pain course through me. "Do you mean the two innocent children currently playing in the yard? The ones who could easily have walked in to watch as you dogged the nanny?" I'm pulling out *all* the unsavory terms now.

"I knew they weren't going to come in," he says, sounding surprisingly offended for someone still sporting a chubby.

"Because kids are so predictable?"

"Because I told them if they got an hour of fresh air, I'd buy them hoverboards."

In lieu of launching myself at his neck, which, let's face it, is just begging to be snapped, I let out a long, disgusted sigh.

"Sounds like an absolutely fool-proof—and highly premeditated—plan. Not to mention, stellar parenting there, Brett. Now get the hell out before I bludgeon you to death with my Emmy."

"You're being unfair. I have an addiction and you know it." His eyes narrow as though *I'm* in the wrong.

"*Oh, please*, that's about as plausible as every celebrity who's ended up in the hospital for 'exhaustion.'" I do air quotes for good measure, then glance at my Emmy—my fingers itching at the sight of the heavy statue. If I don't get out of here now, I'm going to have some impulse control issues of my own.

Turning around and walking out of the room, I lay some truth on myself—my lying sack of crap husband isn't worth one night in prison for misdemeanor battery, let alone several years for murder.

I somehow manage to make my way through the enormous white kitchen, stopping at the French doors that lead to the backyard. Taking a long deep breath, I realize the nightmare is just getting started. It could be months, if not years, before any kind of normalcy comes back to my life. But right now, I have to get through the next few hours until my kids go to bed so I can eat an entire box of truffles and process what just happened.

Putting on my best "everything is wonderful" smile, I open the door and call out, "Hey, munchkins!"

My sweet four-year-old, Lily, spots me first and shouts, "You're home!" She runs at me like I'm a quarterback with the ball and she's a three-hundred-pound front lineman. "I missed you! What did you eat for lunch? Did you bring me a double-chocolate chunk cookie? Did you know it's impossible to lick your own elbow? Did you know Charlie likes to eat his own poop?" Charlie is the neighbor's black lab and Lily is known for her machine-gun fire ability to shoot out questions. She rarely waits for the answers.

My son Liam, on the other hand, is the quiet type. At eight years of age, he reminds me of a tiny grandpa, with his love of socks in sandals and his collection of WWII memorabilia. He also prides himself on being far more grown-up than his "way younger" sister. "Hi, Mom. How was lunch?"

"Great, buddy. Auntie Kay said to give you each a big squeeze from her, but I know how much you don't like big squeezes, so I'm just telling you instead."

"Thanks," Liam says with a serious nod. "I appreciate

you respecting my boundaries. I know a lot of moms aren't comfortable doing that."

I chuckle while ruffling the back of his blond hair. Across the yard, in our hen house, our four chickens cluck away to each other. The chickens were one in a long stream of attempts to give my kiddos a "regular life," back when I was certain that emulating the simplicity of farm-living would help counterbalance the oddities of growing up with famous parents.

My heart squeezes again. "I thought maybe you and your sister might be in the mood for some ice cream."

"From the freezer or the Purple Cow?" he asks, like it will make any difference. Liam will eat *any* frozen sweetened milk product put in front of him, any time of day, in any kind of weather. I'm pretty sure he'd suck on frozen milk cubes if I made them for him.

"The Purple Cow, of course," I say, as though any other option would be insane. "I don't think I can get through the rest of the day without one of their root beer floats."

"Ooh! Let's see if Daddy can come! And Justine!" Lily says, her blue eyes sparkling with

love for the man who has just humiliated me for the last time.

"You know what?" I ask, somehow managing to keep my tone light. "Let's make it just the three of us. Your father has to get back to the studio and I told Justine she could have the afternoon off. But you've got me for the rest of the day."

For longer, actually. Now that the nanny has been fired, I'm going to have to cut back on my commitments. I can't stomach the idea of another person moving into my home. Especially at the same time the whole world finds out Brett and I are separating.

We'll have to get our PR people together to come up with some benign blanket statement that says, "While we love and respect each other and will always remain great friends, we've simply grown apart." That's about as honest as the exhaustion BS they try to sell people, but it's all I've got. I would like to retain a modicum of dignity during what is sure to be a horror show chapter of my life.

If Brett and I didn't have kids, I would have pulled out my camera and filmed him banging Justine, then sold it to TMZ to pay for the divorce lawyer. I have no desire to protect his image for his fans. As far as I'm concerned, they should know the truth about the man they worship—that he's a cheating lothario. But I will walk the walk and safeguard his sorry hide for the sake of my kids. Liam and Lily should *not* have to hear the sordid details of their parents' split.

"Come on, guys, what do you say we hoof it?" I ask with a bright grin that could not be more forced.

"*All* the way to the Purple Cow?" Lily asks. "That's a far way, Mommy. Can we drive instead?"

"We'll make it, baby," I say, tearing up a bit. "We. Will. Make. It." Of course, I'm not talking about ice cream.

Liam narrows his eyes at me like he suspects something is wrong. "Come on, Lil, it's not that far."

I kneel next to my little girl, who is the spitting image of me at that age, then I pull both of my kids into a group hug. "I love you so much," I tell them. "You're my world, you know that?"

"Um, Mom, boundaries. My guts are going to pop out if you don't let go."

I release them with a quick apology, then stare at my two perfect humans. I wish more than anything I could stop time for them right here on this gorgeous early-summer day. As much pain as I'm in right now, my kids are still blissfully unaware of what's coming. A soft breeze ruffles their still-baby-fine hair; the sun reflects against their white highlights, reminding me of fairy children from a storybook.

"Come here." I motion to them, unable to resist the temptation to pull them back into my arms. I'm going to do everything I can to make this the best afternoon of their lives because, far too soon, their entire world is going to come crashing down.

Chapter 2

Digger

"Did you enjoy the trip?" I ask, reaching up to help Mrs. Baker down from the float plane. The middle-aged woman, decked out in what I'm guessing is a tennis outfit, says, "I suppose. I'm just really disappointed we didn't come face-to-face with a grizzly bear. The lady on the phone said we'd see one."

"That would be Evie, our receptionist, who should not be making promises like that." Evie Cantrell is young and *extremely* sarcastic, and although most people catch on that she's not actually promising a "face-to-face grizzly encounter" (on account of it being one hell of a bad idea), there are those who take her at her word. Case in point: Mrs. Baker.

Fancy resorts would never put up with Evie's attitude, but in Gamble, Alaska, you make do with what (or who) you've got. With a population of one thousand eight hundred and forty-six (technically eight hundred forty-seven, but everyone considers the Dickerson twins one person—mainly because it's never occurred to anyone to count them twice), it's not exactly easy to find help. Especially when you need that person to be a Jack (or Jill) of all trades.

Here at the Whistler Lake Lodge, Evie not only takes reservations for our family's lodge, cabin rentals, and flight-seeing tours, she also cleans rooms, waits tables in our dining room (that doubles as a bar), and does the books.

Narrowing her eyes, Mrs. Baker says, "We *paid* for an interaction with a grizzly bear and I'm not going to be satisfied until I get one."

"Tell you what, we'll give you a free supper out at Best Eats tonight as an apology." My sister, Moira, owns the only diner in town. She'll hate me sending a customer like Mrs. Baker in, but I'm heading over to her house tomorrow night to change the oil on her truck so it's not like she won't get paid back for her trouble.

Mr. Baker sighs. "Rita, it's not Digger's fault there weren't any grizzlies around." He forgoes my assistance and hops onto the dock on his own. "I had a terrific time. I've never seen salmon that size before. Oooh-wee! I can't wait to show the boys at the golf club these pictures."

"Glad you had fun, sir," I tell him as I lock the passenger door of the Cessna 360.

Clearly not ready to let the matter go, Mrs. Baker makes a loud *tsk*ing sound. "We came all the way from Coral Gables because we were guaranteed a grizzly encounter. We spent three hours up in that plane, and then two hours at that stream without even seeing *one.* Not even from the air. I'd like to speak to the manager."

Of course she would.

"Let's head up to the lodge," I say evasively. Grandpa Jack will be there. He's used to pretending to be the boss, as well as being the head baker, bartender, and, on occasion, shotgun-wielding bear frightener.

We stroll up the wide path of fallen leaves and pine needles from the shore of Whistler Lake to the expansive one-story log cabin that houses the reception desk, the guest rooms, and our small restaurant/bar (which serves the best plate of bacon and eggs in Alaska, thanks to me). I'm not only the pilot, I'm also the chef, the handyman, the accountant, and the part-time dentist (but only when one of my nephews needs a hand pulling out a tooth).

"What time of day is it anyway?" Mr. Baker asks.

It's June so the sun stays high in the sky so long, it's easy to lose track of time. "Four fifteen," I tell him. Now he's going to say something about how it looks like early morning.

"Gosh, it might as well be breakfast time. I absolutely love Alaska," he gushes. "Rita, we should move here. Think of how much we could do in a day!"

"While it might be fine in the summer, come winter, it's twenty-four hours of night. What are you going to do then?" she asks her husband.

With a waggle of his overgrown graying eyebrows, he says, "Stay in bed." Mrs. Baker looks like she's just sipped from a glass of spoiled milk. "I don't think so."

Here we go … another miserable couple proving that marriage is the worst idea anyone has ever had. I've always been anti-commitment and lucky for me, I see enough unhappy couples to stay true to my beliefs.

As we come around the corner, Moose, my dark gray Great Dane, lifts his head from his favorite spot on the covered porch where he's been basking in the sunlight. As soon as he sees me, he scrambles to get up, clumsily makes his way down the steps, then bounds toward us with his tongue hanging out to the left.

Mrs. Baker shrieks, "Sweet Jesus, save me, I'm going to get eaten alive!"

I hold up one hand to Moose and he stops running. I point down and he drops into a sitting position on the grass. "Wait there," I tell him.

He does as he's told, even though his hind-end is in a full wag of excitement. "That's just Moose. He's big, but he wouldn't hurt a fly holding a shotgun."

Mr. Baker shakes his head at his wife's histrionics. "For God's sake, Rita. It's a dog. He's not going to kill you."

"I see that *now*, Rodney," she bristles. "But from back there, I thought it was ...something else."

"A bear, perhaps?" her husband says.

"Oh, shut up." She doesn't wait for him to say anything else; she just storms off toward the lodge.

"Maybe it's a good thing we didn't have that grizzly encounter," I murmur when she's out of earshot.

Mr. Baker starts laughing while I pat my leg to release Moose. I wait while he trots up to me and butts his head into my thigh—which is his version of a high-five—then he walks stride-for-stride next to me as we make our way to the porch.

The smell of freshly baked buns hits my nose, reminding me it's almost time to fire up the grill. Grandpa Jack whips up bread, cakes, and cookies so good, you'd think he'd been trained in Paris, France. But he wasn't. Everything he learned was here at the Whistler Lake Lodge.

Mr. Baker and I jog up the ten wooden steps to the double front doors. I open the one on the right for him, and follow him in, glancing over my shoulder at Moose resuming his place on the porch. I look around inside to see what Mrs. Baker is up to. Evie has left a "back in five minutes" sign on the front desk. That means she's out cleaning one of the cabins that was vacated this morning. I sigh in relief. Evie's tough, but at the moment, my money is on Mrs. Baker if those two come to blows. Our discontented guest is currently trailing Grandpa Jack as he lights candles at each of the ten tables. And surprise, surprise, she's complaining about not seeing a bear.

I overhear my grandfather tell her, "I bet if you slept out on the front porch tonight you'd have yourself a grizzly encounter. Want me to make up the hammock for you?"

"You can't be serious." She sounds totally appalled.

"I'm just trying to figure out how badly you want to see a bear," he says with his lopsided grin. "How 'bout a glass of whiskey? You look like you could use one."

"I really could," she replies. "I was almost knocked over by a giant wild dog. My heart is racing like a rabbit."

"I bet," he tells her, gesturing for her to sit down on one of the stools. "Let's have a couple of drinks to help calm your nerves, then you can tell me all about how my grandson disappointed you." He flashes me a conspiratorial smile, letting me know he's going to make everything all right with Mrs. Baker.

I hold up one finger to my grandpa. He has a heart condition which means he shouldn't be drinking scotch, but I won't complain if he has one. He flicks his fingers under his chin mobster-style to indicate what he thinks of my opinion, then pours two generous servings of the amber liquid.

Chuckling to myself, I make my way over to the fridge to grab a beer, then take my cold Bud out to the deck and wait for the grill to heat up. Moose is lying nearby, watching a dragonfly dive down near his head to catch a mosquito. I take a deep breath of warm summer air, happy that I get to live here in the most beautiful place in the world—and one of the last few places on Earth where a guy can truly be free.

Mrs. Baker comes out onto the porch with her cocktail and a *People* magazine in hand, all thoughts of bear sightings forgotten. "Can you believe Harper and Brett Kennedy are getting divorced? I'm completely devastated. They're the perfect couple." She stares at the page she's reading, and amends that to, "*Were* the perfect couple."

"I don't have the first clue who they are, but if they're famous, I'm not all that shocked that their marriage is on the rocks."

"You don't know who they are?" She looks personally affronted by my lack of Hollywood knowledge. She shakes her magazine at me, and demands, "Haven't you seen the *Helioman* movies?"

"Can't say I have." *What the hell is a helioman?*

"What about the TV show *Conspiracy*? Harper played the double agent for the CIA."

Now *her* I remember. If the woman who starred in *Conspiracy* is Harper Kennedy, wow. She has a face you won't forget. But even I know that looks alone aren't enough to keep a marriage together, especially a Hollywood one.

Mrs. Baker continues to lament the end of the Kennedys' marriage like they're close personal friends of hers as she makes her way to the far side of the deck. She finally settles onto a lounge chair to flip through her magazine, leaving me alone with the sound of a pair of Arctic loons calling to each other as they search for their dinner. Thank God I live in Alaska instead of in LA. where all the phonies of the world like to congregate. Up here, we're so far removed from the entitled veneer of that world, we wouldn't know what to do if we came face to face with it.

Not that we ever will …

Chapter 3

Harper

Dear Reader,

Ask and ye shall receive!

Just when I thought Tinsel Town had given up on scandal, Helio-hunk Brett Kennedy gets caught with his pants down, quite literally!

He's not servicing his wife, the ethereally lovely Harper Kennedy, either. Word on the street is that he's sticking it to the nanny!

I know what you're thinking, that's SO last summer. It's so Ben, Arnold, and Jude. But men never seem to learn, do they?

A note to Hollywood wives: Stop hiring cute nannies. Think

Mrs. Doubtfire and Nanny McPhee. If you keep letting Mary Poppins into your house, you're tempting the fates. Even I would bang Mary and she lacks all my favorite body parts!

The question on everyone's lips now is, what is Harper going to do about it? Is she going to turn a blind eye, or can we look forward to some fireworks?

Dish,
Ferris Biltmore

I haven't been in love with my husband for years. It's hard to give your heart to a man who's busy sharing his man parts with other women. Having said that, I've been grieving hard for the last six days since the boinking heard around the world.

Every night, the second I get the kids off to sleep, I crawl into bed, dead tired. But I can't turn my brain off long enough to actually sleep. I wind up staying awake watching the Home Shopping Network until the wee hours. Not only is this an enormous waste of time, but I've purchased some pretty dicey stuff. It's only two in the morning and I've already bought a toaster oven, an Ab Rocket, and an automatic apple peeler. But no more. I'm done for the night. The credit card is going back in the wallet until tomorrow.

Oh! Meat Shredder Claws are half-off for the next twelve minutes. No, Harper. No good could come from owning shredding claws, not now. The temptation to misuse them would be too great. My cell phone buzzes. It's Prisha Choudree, my best friend on this planet, and maybe on Mars too. She's also my PR manager and—other than my lawyer

—the only person in this town I actually trust. I answer with, "I know why *I'm* up. Why are you still up?"

"I need to tell you something."

"Is it 'don't marry Brett?' Because you're a tad late on that," I say, before flopping back onto the mountain of pillows I'm using to fill up his side of the bed.

Before my friend has a chance to answer, I add, "Oh, Prish, the family I envisioned my children growing up in is no more. Christmases will now be every other year; probably the same with birthdays unless Brett and I can figure out how to be civil around each other. The best we can hope for is one slightly-awkward, yet all-encompassing, party instead of two half-assed ones."

"Or even worse. Two huge parties." Prisha is very big on helping me remember the perils of spoiling my children and I love her for it.

I kick my feet out of the covers and dig my heels into the mattress. "Poor Liam and Lily are going to end up with entitlement issues. You know that jackass went ahead and bought them those hoverboards? He had them sent to the house yesterday."

"You mentioned that earlier today. Twice. Listen, sweetie, I don't want to keep you. I know you're probably just about to sleep, or, you know, put in a bid on the Hope Diamond …"

"I won't fall asleep for another four hours," I tell her, dreading another night of insomnia.

"You're not buying anything else on the Home Shopping Network, are you?"

"Not with *my* credit card," I say with satisfaction. "I figure I need to find a way to make Brett really pay. Did I tell you that I ordered forty pizzas to be delivered to his hotel room at midnight?"

"Do you feel better?" she asks with her signature calmness.

"I did for about ninety seconds." I sigh like I'm trying to blow out a hundred birthday candles. "What if he marries Justine? That would totally screw the kids up."

"Don't even think like that," she answers in a firm voice.

"I have to, because it might happen."

"It won't be Justine. Brett will get bored of her now that the fun of sneaking around has disappeared," Prisha says.

"How did I marry that man? Also, are you sure you don't want me to buy you some fur-covered toilet seats? They look really soft."

"Gross, on so many levels. I'll text you my wish list when we get off the phone, but please be assured that anything with fur will not be on it."

"Oh, right, on account of Sheila and her PETA membership."

Sheila is Prisha's lovely wife—an artisan who has an adorable pottery shop in Old Town Pasadena.

A wall of grief suddenly hits me. "I'm going to miss half of Liam and Lily's childhoods. Half, Prish," I say, tears filling my eyes. "I feel like someone wearing meat claws just dug into my heart."

"Oh, honey, I'm so sorry. If I weren't so scarred by my recent binge watch of *Orange is the New Black*, I would totally offer to knock him off for you."

I bet she'd still do it if I said pretty please.

"After everything I gave up for him. I could have been Daenerys Targaryen on *Game of Thrones*, Prish. The freaking mother of dragons," I moan. "In hindsight, I'm glad I didn't, since she went all burn-the-entire-city at the end there, but still. Until season eight, it would have been an incredible ride. But did I take that ride? No. Because Liam was on the way, and I wanted to put my children first. Not that I regret having my kids. I don't. I just want to know why Brett gets it all."

"You're a wonderful mom," Prisha tells me.

She's used to me doing most of the talking, but even so, I'm barely letting her get a word in edgewise. I punch the pillows lined up to represent my errant spouse. "I *am* a good mother. People judge me for having a nanny, but she was only there for times when I had to make publicity appearances for Brett." I'm talking like she doesn't know this firsthand. "Yet unbeknownst to me, in addition to some light housework, she apparently took over servicing my husband." Punch, punch, punch. "We treated her like a little sister. Well, I did. Brett clearly didn't see her that way, the lying sack of hemorrhoids."

"He really is, hun. For real. It's the reason I called so late—"

"How could I have fallen for that slick line about being the other half of his star? The first time we went away together to Cancun—do you remember that? You warned me not to go, but did I listen? No, I did not."

"Harper, you need to listen to me *now*."

"Instead, I just hopped on that private jet with him and let him pull the wool over my eyes with his 'Harper, I don't shine nearly as brightly when you're not around. Will you marry me?' I thought he meant his love for me made him shine brighter, when in fact, he meant that my love for *him* made him shine brighter. What kind of an idiot was I? All Brett ever wanted was to see his own reflection in my eyes."

"Yeah, he's a real bastard, Harp. Now quit talking. TMZ broke the story about him and the nanny ten minutes ago. It's going to be all over town by noon, and I'm guessing by twelve-oh-one every reporter from here to Santa Barbara is going to be sitting at your gate."

Panic slams into me like a bucket of ice to the head. It's a full thirty seconds before I say anything. "How did they find out? Brett said he'd keep their relationship under wraps until we worked out the details of the separation."

"Well, if by under wraps he meant a picnic at the Hollywood Bowl with champagne, caviar, and a load of cameras pointed at them, then hopping on a jet to Hawaii, kudos to Brett."

Shock vibrates through my bones until my teeth nearly start to chatter, although the only thing that should shock me is that I didn't see this coming. Thank God for Prisha. She's been the tether in the storm of my marriage. She has kept me focused and calm in times where I wanted to do nothing more than run Brett over with that stupid Hummer he bought himself. Talk about over-compensating. *Nothing* says tiny wiener like a man with an oversized vehicle.

Prisha and I moved to LA within months of each other. We met while waiting tables at Pinot Bistro in Studio City. We were both aspiring actresses, but at the time there was a serious lack of roles for people of color in the industry, so instead of being in front of the cameras, my friend found a home for herself in Tinsel Town public relations.

"I guess I'm a prisoner in my own home now," I practically whimper.

"I just packed a couple suitcases," she tells me. "I'll move in and make sure to keep the wolves at bay and go for regular ice-cream runs."

"I love you, Prish," I tell her, meaning it with my whole heart. "Why couldn't you have been a man?"

"Why couldn't you have been a lesbian?" she asks. "I don't have the answers, so let's focus on the matter at hand, okay? Sheila wants to come along, but I told her she'd better not. The last thing you need is for the press to report on your being part of a queer love triangle."

"That sounds much more appealing than being the wife of a husband who cheats on her with the nanny."

"Hang tough, my friend. We'll get you through this. I have a meeting at nine that I can't reschedule, but I'll come straight there as soon as I'm done. Hopefully, the vultures won't have arrived yet."

My stomach lurches as my entire body goes weak. "Oh, God, this is it. This is really happening."

"Get some sleep, sweetie. I'll be there as soon as I can." Her words are so warm and caring, they feel like the hug I need.

"Okay."

"And go ahead and buy yourself something really nice since it's Brett's credit card."

"I will," I sniff. "There's a set of gold-plated shotgun ammo for almost four hundred thousand."

"So long as you don't buy the gun to go with it."

"No promises."

When I hang up, I toss my phone across the bed and cry until I finally drift off to sleep. I don't wake up again until I hear, "Mommy ... Mommy ... Mommy ... MommyMommyMOMMY!!!"

"Lily, what?" I roll over in bed, so sore I feel like I've just run a full marathon in an hour.

Grief hurts. Unfortunately, unlike actual running, there are no health benefits from it that I know of.

"There's a man in a tree taking pictures of us!" my daughter yells while wedging a finger so far up her left nostril, I'm afraid she's going to accidentally give herself a lobotomy.

This news propels me out of bed in record time. "What man? What tree?" I demand, following her into the living room.

There I find my son on his knees in front of the large bay

window. He's staring up at something. "Liam, honey, come back here by me, please." I'm hoping he detects the urgency in my voice without getting scared. Brett and I may not have been a good couple, but we did shield our children remarkably well from the scum-sucking paparazzi.

"I've got this, Mom," my sweet son says while standing up. Then, as if speaking for us all, he turns around, drops trow, and moons the photographer trespassing on our property. I can just see the front page of the *Inquisitor* now. Luckily, they can't print a picture of my child's bare bottom smooshed against the glass without breaking all kinds of child pornography laws. But still, somewhere out there someone will have an image of him doing that and that is *not* okay.

Hurrying to the front door, I take a quick glance in the gilded mirror hanging above the trestle table. I gasp in shock. The dark circles under my eyes make me look like I've taken up boxing and am using my face to stop the punches. I quickly run my fingers through my straggly light brown hair before telling my kids to wait on the couch and decide what they want for breakfast. Then I step out my front door wearing nothing more than my shortie white nightgown.

The man formerly lounging in my Magnolia tree jumps down and starts taking rapid fire pictures while shouting questions like, "Harper, do you have anything to say about your husband taking your ex-nanny to Maui with him? Have you already filed for divorce?" and my favorite, "Are you worried you'll never love again?"

With my arms crossed in front of my chest to protect any last vestiges of modesty, I smile disingenuously. "Brett can vacation with anyone he wants. The end of our marriage was a mutual decision, and no, I have no current interest or concerns involving my own love life."

I take a deep breath before adding, "What does concern

me is that you just took photographs of my children without my consent while they were in the privacy of their own home. If you don't want a giant lawsuit, you'll hand over your SIM card right now before the police get here."

Mr. Scruffy Beard, (who also has the beginning of dreadlocks), glances toward the street and back to me like he's trying to decide if he should make a run for it.

"My friend called me from the road," I tell him. "She saw you sneak in. I'm pretty sure she's slashed your tires by now." I have no trouble lying to this scumbag.

"What? Dude, Harper, that's not cool. I have bills to pay." Why do paparazzi always try to make you feel guilty for not letting them violate your privacy? "I'm just doing my job here."

"And I'm just doing *my* job." At his look of confusion, I add, "I'm protecting my children from douchebag creeps who think it's okay to sneak onto private property and photograph them without their pants on." With his camera hanging around his neck and hands stretched out in front of him like this is a holdup, he promises, "I won't use those pictures. I swear."

"What's your name?" I ask, using my least-hostile tone, which still sounds pretty menacing. When he doesn't answer, I add, "My friend already has your license number."

"Tony. Tony Watkins."

"Well, Tony. Tony Watkins. Here's how this is going to go down. You are going to hand me your SIM card and then you're going to walk down the driveway through the gate. If your tires haven't been slashed, you're going to drive away. If they have, you'd better figure out how to get out of here before the cops show up."

"That's it? I don't get anything for my troubles?" Once again, he's acting like he's the wronged party, which is really chapping my ass.

"Hand me the camera and I'll give you something good." I hold my palm out for his Nikon. "What are you going to give me?" he asks dubiously.

"The camera first." Once it's in my possession, I turn it on and do a mass deleting of the whole card. Then I flip the lens and screw my face up in a panicked expression. I take one selfie before handing the camera back.

"That's it? You're giving me a selfie?"

Nodding my head, I answer, "Yup. That's it." As he walks away, I call after him, "Oh, and Tony, I categorically deny the accusation that Brett has ever hit me. Those dark circles under my eyes are from lack of sleep and nothing more."

The smile that consumes his face is blinding. "Dude, nice! That ought to bring in enough serious coin to pay my rent for at least a year."

I don't respond. Instead, I turn around and walk back into my home, relieved that I was able to garner some control of the situation. Brett hasn't been gone a week, and already the vultures are circling.

In the living room I find my two beautiful babies huddled together on the couch looking as sad as orphans from a Charles Dickens novel. *Bleak House* comes to mind. "I want Daddy to come home," Lily sniffles with a giveaway hiccup that makes it clear she's been crying.

"Me, too," Liam adds with some heat.

Sitting on a footstool in front of them, I reach out to take their hands in mine. "Daddy had to go to Hawaii on business."

"What?" Lily looks wild-eyed. "He didn't tell us!"

"It was all very last minute, honey." I will lie like a dog to protect my children's hearts, even if it means covering for their father.

Liam looks skeptical. "Dad's never gone away without telling us before."

"It can be a little awkward at first when a mommy and daddy decide to divorce," I tell them softly. "I bet your dad was just nervous about calling."

"Is Daddy divorcing us, too?" Lily asks as the pools shimmering in her baby blue eyes spill over and run down her cheeks.

"No, sweetie, no." I pull her toward me and hold her tightly. "Daddy isn't divorcing you. He loves you very much."

"Does Dad want us to go live with him?" Liam asks. He's only eight, and he must be hurting every bit as much as his sister.

"Daddy and I will be working out a schedule so you can spend time with both of us, but he absolutely wants to see you as often as possible." I force a brighter tone as I open my eyes wide in excitement. "I have a great idea! Let's go on vacation, too!"

"You said Dad was away for work," Liam says, narrowing his eyes.

Nothing slips by these kids, and for a split second I wonder what life would have been like for them had they grown up in a small midwestern town like I did. A place where no one knew them because of their parents' fame. Where they could ride their bikes around town and hang out with their friends without moms or nannies always hovering.

"I mixed up my words." I pull my laptop off the coffee table. Opening it, I ask, "Where should we go? Peru? Greenland? Antarctica?" I fire off the first three places that come to mind where no one would look twice at us.

"I want to go to Hawaii and see Daddy," Lily pouts. *Wouldn't that be a fun surprise for Brett.* I'm almost tempted. Then she asks, "Is Justine home from her emergency yet? Can she come with us?"

I might have told my kids that Justine was called away on a family emergency. I couldn't tell them their dad and I were getting divorced *and* tell them that I've fired Justine. There's only so much heartache a kid should have to handle at once.

"No, honey, Justine's still visiting her family." Before she can say anything, I ask my son, "What about you, Liam? Where do you want to go?"

"Normandy, France," he says without skipping a beat.

"I promise I'll take you to Normandy someday so you can visit your favorite battle site, but let's do something a little more fun this time."

"We could go see Nana and Papa," Lily suggests.

While I would love to see my parents, I don't particularly need to hear a passive/aggressive "I told you so." Neither of my parents liked Brett, and they both warned me about Hollywood marriages, but I didn't listen. I was too blinded by love for a man I thought I knew, a man that never really existed.

"I bet there are a lot of cameras at Nana and Papa's house right now. Let's go someplace exotic and private where we can have loads of fun and no one will know we're there."

"The North Pole?" Lily asks.

And that's when it hits me. "How about Alaska? Remember how we were talking about taking a vacation there last year?"

"That was with Dad." Liam's voice cracks, confirming that he's not as unaffected by the current drama as he wants me to think.

I type away frantically, hoping the perfect place will pop up.

Do you yearn for a simple life? Do you need a break from the outside world? Do you want to escape to the quiet tranquility of the beautiful Alaskan wilderness?

Hm, let me think. Yes, yes, and yes.

I start to read the advertisement out loud to the kids. "Come to Whistler Lake Lodge where you can catch salmon bigger than your dog, camp along the shores of the crystal-clear lake, and, if you're lucky, you might even have the chance to see a grizzly bear. We offer three rustic cabins as well as a few rooms inside the lodge. Book now and fall off the face of the earth like a true Alaskan!"

"A grizzly bear?" Lily asks nervously.

"I'm sure they'll only introduce us to the nice ones," Liam tells his sister, sounding more than a little interested.

"We're going to Alaska!" I tell my kids excitedly. Personally, I'm less enthused about the grizzly bears than I am about falling off the face of the earth. The thought of being someplace where the press can't find us feels like just about the best thing that could ever happen.

Chapter 4

Digger

"Hunter said Mom's a floozy because she wears V-neck T-shirts instead of crew necks like his mom, and that was it, Uncle Digger," my nine-year-old nephew Wyatt says with the most earnest expression a kid can put on. "I couldn't let him get away with that."

Wyatt is the oldest of my sister's three boys, and unfortunately for Moira, he's inherited his dad's temper. Not that Everett would have ever hit anyone without a good reason, but he was known to get into his share of fights. "Hand me that wrench," I tell him from underneath Moira's Bronco.

While fetching my tool, he says, "I know I shouldn't have punched him in the beans but, gosh darn it, he had it coming."

I loosen the drain plug, then slide out from under the vehicle to let the oil pan empty into a bucket. "Hunter was wrong to say that, and you were wrong to punch him in the

… beans. But I understand you were just protecting your mom, and I applaud you for that."

Moira, who is currently watering the garden next to the driveway where I have her SUV jacked up, is leaning in our direction, pretending not to listen. I'm one hundred percent sure she's making sure I set Wyatt straight. I've taken over the role of de facto dad since her husband was killed in a crabbing accident.

Hunter's mom and Moira's nemesis, Sissy Sinclair, screamed at her that Hunter will probably never be able to have kids because of Wyatt. If you ask me, it wouldn't be the end of the world if the Sinclair line died out. Hunter's dad, Travis, was my own personal demon in childhood.

After Moira got off the phone with Sissy, she went up one side of Wyatt and down the other—and then called me.

Standing up, I wipe my hands on my overalls before glancing at my sister. I predict she's about to hit the roof because I haven't laid into her son properly. I hurry and ask my nephew, "Do you know what integrity means?"

Wyatt nods and out of the corner of my eye, I see Moira smiling.

"When men fight, they don't hit each other below the belt. That's called a low blow …"

"Nowadays, it's called a nut cruncher," Wyatt interjects, with a gleeful expression covering his freckled young face.

"Whatever you call it," I tell him, "It's a move that lacks integrity. You don't want anyone to accuse you of that." I hold up my hands and make fists. "You want to aim for the chin, the cheek, or the eye. The stomach's good too. Now show me how you make a fist. I want to make sure you're doing it right, so you don't break your—"

"Are you kidding me right now?" Moira snaps.

"What? The boy called you a floozy," I tell her. "Wyatt can't let him get away with that."

Planting both hands on her hips, Moira says, "Digger, you're supposed to tell him *not* to fight, not teach him how. This is the twenty-first century, and we have much better ways to resolve conflicts than resorting to violence."

Wrinkling up my nose, I ask, "Do we, Moira? Do we really?" Then I turn to Wyatt. "Come here, Wy, let me show you how real men hug it out." My nephew bursts into laughter which really ignites my sister's anger. Come to think of it, maybe Wyatt inherited her temper too.

"That's it. You get in the house and write that apology letter," Moira tells her son. "And no screens for a week."

His skinny shoulders drop. "See you later, Uncle Digger."

"See you, buddy."

With his head down, Wyatt shuffles toward the back door with his golden retriever, Juno, following close behind. Moira glares at me, before yelling after him, "And forget what your idiot uncle just told you about fighting. There will be *no* fighting!"

I wait until the screen door slams before muttering, "You've got three boys, Moira. I hate to tell you this, but there's going to be some fighting."

"Jackass," she says, tugging the hose as she stalks over to the peas to give them a drink. "You're supposed to have my back."

To the whole world, my sister is one tough nut. She's raising three sons alone, she owns and runs the only diner in town, and she can shoot a grizzly between the eyes before single-handedly tanning its hide to use as a rug. All that said, I know how much she struggles to keep that "nothing's gonna get me down" attitude going strong. This is not the life she thought she'd have.

"I do have your back," I tell her. "But I also need to have Wyatt's, Ash's, and Colton's. Like it or not, a boy has to learn to fight. Out here in the wild, it's possible he'll wind up in a situation where his life depends on it."

"You big dope. Calling me a floozy isn't exactly a life-or-death offense."

"It's good practice for whatever comes next. And believe me, where there are men, there will be fights. In case you haven't noticed, this is Alaska. The boys have to learn how to defend themselves."

"You act like you grew up in the Old West, Digger. This may be Alaska, but that doesn't mean we have to be uncivilized."

"Boys will be boys, Moira," I tell her with a wry grin that fades as soon as I see the stress lines etched in her forehead.

My sister has had a real time of it. Not only did she grow up without a mom to be a role model for her, but then she lost her husband when Wyatt was three and she was eight months pregnant with the twins. Unfortunately for Moira, instead of everyone in town rallying around her, a lot of the married women started to see her as a threat. Single, young, pretty, *and* she runs the diner? Most of the men in town would have a crush on her for the food alone. "If you don't like what I'm teaching the kids, maybe it's time to think about finding someone who'll do a better job?"

"Been there, done that, didn't like how it ended."

"Husbands don't usually die so young," I tell her gently. "It's been six years. It's okay to find happiness again."

"For someone who's dishing out relationship advice, I don't see you jumping in line to get married." Forgetting the hose is still turned on, she accidentally sprays herself. "Crap," she mutters, looking down at her soaked jeans.

"I never wanted a family. You did," I remind her.

"And I have one, and my life is more than full. Three boys, two cats, one dog, and five fish are more responsibility than any woman needs. The last thing I need is a man to look after, too."

"So don't find a man that you'll have to look after. Relationships are a two-way street. If you do it right, you can find someone who will help you, and who you can help in return. And you know, all that other mushy stuff."

"There isn't a man on the face of the earth who'll want to take on my ready-made family. Especially, out in the middle of nowhere," Moira says. "Present company excluded."

"There's got to be at least one other good guy on the planet, Moira."

"If there is, he doesn't live here in Gamble, I can tell you that much."

"He'll come." Maybe. I hope so, for her sake, anyway.

"Tell you what. You fall in love and get married first. If that works out, I'll consider it."

"I guess the boys are stuck with me," I tell her, crouching down to see if the oil is still draining.

"It looks like it, so if we could try not to send mixed messages, that would be awesome." My sister skillfully brings the conversation back where she wanted it in the first place. Then she shuts off the hose and walks toward the house. "I need to get Ash and Colton into the shower. When you're done out here, maybe you could come in and read them a bedtime story."

"You bet, but they're probably going to end up getting more wound up than anything. Robin Hood is about to give the Sheriff of Nottingham what for."

"As long as you don't suggest slitting people's throats when they're rude to you."

"Deal," I tell her. Then, after I hear the screen door slam, I add, "But I'm still going to teach them how to fight."

Chapter 5

Harper

Dear Readers,

Until I learn more about what's going on with Brett and Harper—*but don't worry, I have my ear to the pavement*—I'm going to dish some history.

You might remember that over the years, Brett Kennedy has been linked to such starlets as Holly Wooshwiller, Julia Fletcher, and Monica Thompkins. While I've always loved to report on his many affiliations, no one was as happy as me when he settled down with Harper.

I loves me a lady! And Harper is that through-and-through. She's beautiful, classy, and just plain perfect. She's Audrey Hepburn for the millennial generation and I cannot get enough.

I just knew that she was the gal to tame that bad boy, but

alas, things are looking grim. Rumors of Brett's past philandering have run amok.

Harper, doll, you need to put on your thigh-highs and crack that whip. Don't put up with any more nonsense!

Dish,
Ferris Biltmore

~

"The woman on the phone said they have one cabin left," I tell Prisha excitedly.

"But Alaska? There's nothing there other than wilderness and grubby men with three-foot-long beards. They'll probably make you eat seals and wear raccoon tails on your head."

I throw a couple of sweaters into my suitcase. "Where do you get your information?"

Kicking her feet up on the footstool in front of my reading chair, she replies, "That show *Wild Men* on Netflix. It's downright terrifying."

Turning back to packing, I tell her, "I'm going to a lodge. You know, a place where they not only house you, but feed you as well?"

"A-L-A-S-K-A," my friend enunciates slowly and loudly like she's trying to teach me a new language. "Not only that. It's a place called Gamble. Is that even real? It sounds like something you'd see in a romantic comedy movie." She tilts her head, then adds, "Or a horror film."

"Prisha, we'll be fine. But if you're so worried, come with us."

The startled look on her face causes me to laugh for the first time in weeks.

"As much as I'd love to do that, someone has to stay here and represent you when the tabloids get the wrong info. By the way, that 'Brett has never hit me' photo is causing all kinds of trouble for him with the studio." She pulls the *Inquisitor* off the stack of rags on her lap and holds it up for me to see.

"Can you blame me? I'd just found out my loser husband had made his relationship with the nanny public. What was I supposed to do?"

"Harper, no one hates Brett as much as I do," my friend says in her placating fashion. Then, noticing the look on my face, she quickly adds, "Except you, obviously. But you should know by now that his reputation is directly tied to yours. I've taken more calls than you can count from battered women's groups asking you to be their spokeswoman." Before I can respond, she says, "You need to keep a low profile and quit spreading false rumors."

"Yes, Mom," I say with an abundance of sarcasm. "I'll just be a good girl and let my husband cheat on me with the free world and not say a word."

"Harper ..." Prisha cautions, running her hands through her thick, dark curtain of hair. "All I'm saying is that you need to let me oversee the PR. The more money Brett is worth, the more you'll get when the divorce is final."

"I don't want anything from him," I spit with righteous indignation.

She sighs loudly. "The more he gives you, the less he'll have to spend on other women."

Rolling my eyes, I say, "Fine, I'll keep quiet, but I want a hefty animal maintenance budget added to whatever child-care he has to pay. I'm talking five hundred a month per chicken."

Prisha laughs. "You do realize that having free-range

chickens isn't exactly the celebrity way of doing things, don't you?"

"Maybe not, but charging your ex-husband five hundred a month to keep their pedicures up sure is."

She looks alarmed.

"Just kidding. But I might make those mealworms they love so much an everyday affair instead of a biweekly one."

"You're not expecting Sheila and me to feed them while you're gone, are you?"

"Aren't you going to feed the cats?" I retaliate.

"Of course, we'll take care of the cats. But they're cats. Sheila loves cats."

"But as a card-carrying member of PETA, shouldn't she also love chickens?"

"Yeah, but from afar."

"You are aware that if you give them food, they'll return the favor by giving you eggs for breakfast."

Big sigh. "Fine, but just so you know, I might have to consult with Ethan about adding an animal tending stipend, depending on how long I'm here."

As well as being my lawyer and godfather to my kids, Ethan Caplan is my only other true friend. Brett pretended he didn't mind Ethan in my life—I mean, how could he when he was so busy telling me that all his relationships with other women were platonic—but the truth is, my husband was jealous of my close friendship with another man. Probably because it's not possible for him to befriend a woman without wanting to screw her. He assumed Ethan must be the same way.

"I'll make sure to tell him to give you whatever you want." Then I ask, "Do you and Sheila mind being here for so long?" *Please say no, please say no, please say no.*

"Not at all," Prisha answers. "Your place is six times bigger than our bungalow in Pasadena. We'll treat it like a vacation—except for the chickens. I've never vacationed at a place with live poultry."

"You're lucky I didn't get those pigs and that cow I had my eye on," I tell her with a challenging lift of my left eyebrow. My mom calls it my power brow.

Waving her hands in front of her face like she can't absorb the horror of actual farm animals, my friend demands, "Stop." Then she adds, "You're lucky the agency is lending their jet. Speaking of which, you'd better hurry because you're scheduled to take off in just over an hour."

Zipping up the last suitcase, I tell her, "We really need this, Prish. I've got to get the kids out of this circus. Plus, I'm so sick of this Hollywood life I could spit."

"Well, now you can spit all day long in the middle of nowhere." She jumps up and grabs two of my bags while I get the other two. We carry them out the back door where a fake gardener is waiting. He puts the suitcases into garbage bags and then drives them around the front on his golf cart. That's where he'll load them into his pickup before following us to the airport.

Prisha is going to drive me and the kids in her SUV. That defensive driving class she took two years ago has saved many of her clients from being tailed. While we may be vomiting our guts out by the time we get to the private terminal at the Santa Monica airport, we will get there without anyone following us.

Liam and Lily are sitting in the living room looking like a little prince and princess ready for a drive in the country. My son is wearing sharply creased khakis and a button-down shirt. Lily is wearing a light-yellow summer dress with a matching bow in her hair.

My mom always believed in the importance of dressing up when you travel, even if you're going by bus. I've taken her lead. While no one else will be on the plane with us, I want my kids to grow up knowing that you have to make an occasion out of things.

Going on vacation is definitely an occasion, more so if you're flying in a private plane.

We don't even crouch down to hide in Prisha's SUV. Instead, the kids wave to all the reporters waiting outside our gate. I merely keep my eyes on the road. As predicted, several vehicles follow closely behind.

When we hit the 405 Freeway, four similar SUVs join us. They are all being driven by employees of Prisha's. As soon as we pull out ahead, they each take a lane and slow down to a crawl, effectively blocking anyone from getting too close. "I was prepared for you to go all NASCAR on us," I tell her.

"Not with the kids in the car."

"I appreciate that." We all sit quietly for the rest of the drive. The kids are busy playing a game with their stuffed animals; Prisha stays focused on the road; and I fantasize about how pleasant it's going to be spending the summer in Alaska, where people are nice and friendly, and, with any luck, will have no idea who I am.

Three hours into our five-and-a-half-hour journey, the flight attendant serves us a lunch of quesadillas, fruit salads, and hot fudge sundaes. They were obviously told to prepare for children.

Four hours in, the kids are both fast asleep. By the time we land in Anchorage and get off the plane, I inhale a deep breath of the freshest air that's ever hit my lungs. The dead weight that's been in the pit of my stomach is immediately replaced by a flicker of optimism.

Prisha has arranged for a ride to the docks where a float plane is waiting to take us to Gamble. The driver, a young man who introduces himself as Gib, clearly recognizes me. I know this because his jaw is currently having a meeting with his neck. Happily, he doesn't do the usual, "Oh, my God, you're Harper Kennedy! Can I get a selfie? No one is going to believe I met you!" thing. Instead, he recovers quickly and holds the back door of the SUV open for us. "Welcome to Alaska, the last frontier."

"I thought space was the last frontier," Liam tells him, looking skeptical.

Gib chuckles. "Space is the *final* frontier. Totally different."

"Hmm, I don't know about that," Liam says as he climbs into the backseat.

I find myself smiling as the kids point at the mountains in the distance and the ocean to our left. "It's so pretty here, isn't it?" I ask Lily.

She nods excitedly and the three of us chatter about all the fun things we're planning to do while on vacation.

"If you want to see something really amazing, we could stop up ahead at Crow Creek and pan for gold," Gib says.

"Gold?! Like real gold?" Lily asks, her entire face lighting up.

"Yup, real gold. They have a place there where you're guaranteed to come out with some real gold flakes," he tells her.

I glance at both my kiddos, a wave of relief washing over me as I see the expressions of excitement on their faces, then I remember we're due at the float plane. "How long will it take?"

"About half an hour," he answers. "You're a little ahead of schedule so you've got time. Besides, you're the only passengers on your next flight so you can rest assured they won't leave without you."

"The pilot won't mind?" I ask.

Shaking his head, Gib says, "You'll find people are a lot more laid back here than in most places."

"Please, Mom," Liam whispers. "It would be SO cool."

I love seeing my son so happy. It's been far too long. "Sure. We're here for an adventure, so let's have one."

Chapter 6

Digger

"Evie, are you sure this name is right?" I ask, pointing to the booking for the guests I'm picking up this afternoon.

She gives me the stink eye from behind all that black eyeliner she wears. Evie has the blistering confidence only the young possess. She also hates when I dare to question her competence.

Evie made her way up to Gamble three years ago, when she was fresh out of high school—and fresh out of fricks to give—as she so poetically puts it. Also, she doesn't say frick. She pulled up in a beat-up ancient Volkswagen camper van, and I hired her immediately.

It takes grit to drive all the way from Virginia to Alaska by yourself when you're forty. You have to be made of much tougher stuff to do it at eighteen. If there's one thing a person needs to survive here, it's a strong backbone.

"I got the woman on the phone to repeat it twice. Marge

Simpson and her two children. I'm assuming she's bringing Lisa and Maggie. Bart has probably been sent off to military school or something."

"Hardy har har." I rub the bridge of my nose. "This better not be a joke because I'm going to feel like a jackass standing on the dock with a sign that says Marge Simpson."

She wrinkles up her nose. "*Right*, because there'll be so many people on the dock this afternoon."

"I could do without the sarcasm," I tell her, taking the lid off the Sharpie and writing my guest's name on the piece of card stock.

"Sarcasm is my love language," Evie tells me with the closest thing she's got to an actual smile.

I answer with a half-grin. Popping the lid back on the felt tip, I grab the cooler of refreshments Evie prepared for Marge et al, and start for the door. "We've got a full house, so we're going to have to stay on top of our game today. I should be back in time to make supper for our other guests, but you know the drill if I wind up running late."

"I'll get Jack to fire up the grill on account of me not having a set of testes," she says.

"On account of you nearly burning the lodge down last year ..." I remind her.

"Yeah, yeah, yeah," she says, rolling her eyes. "You start one little fire ... Jack does the grilling, I prep the salad and pop the baked potatoes in the oven, and if you're still not here by the time the garlic bread is supposed to go on the grill, I'll put it in the oven with the potatoes, so Grandpa can't drunkenly char the bread."

"It happened one time!" Grandpa Jack yells from behind the bar.

"See you two later." I push open the screen door and walk out into the sunshine. I take a long, deep breath, then send Moose back into the lodge to hang out with Evie where he'll pout the entire time I'm gone.

I'm a little more stressed than usual. It's the Bakers' last night at the lodge, and Mrs. Baker has been wandering around scrawling things onto a notepad, while hinting she's going to be writing up reviews on Yelp, Trip Advisor, and on her ladies' golf club's Facebook page. If you ask me, this is the problem with the world today. Whatever happened to people just experiencing life for themselves instead of reading about other people's opinions to make their decisions for them?

When I was growing up, we did our best to make our guests happy because it was the right thing to do. They worked hard to pay for their trip and our job was to make it the best vacation we could.

People understood that coming up here meant leaving the comforts of home behind. Rustic means just that. There was no such thing as "glamping," no expectation that no matter how far out in the wild you were, you were owed a strong Wi-Fi connection. But every year it seems like our guests show up a little more pampered and a lot less ready to experience Alaska the way it is. This makes my job a heck of a lot more demanding. We now cater to the whims of a bunch of whiners, while living in fear of the dreaded bad review.

A few minutes later, I've fired up the engine on the Cessna. I take off trying to remind myself to enjoy the day. At least I'll have a couple of hours in the sky to myself. The pure pleasure of flying hasn't changed one bit since I was a kid.

Glancing back at the lodge from above the lake, I spot Mrs. Baker out on a lounge chair sunning herself. I hope like hell I can get back in time to cook dinner. As great of a baker as Grandpa Jack is, he's not exactly a Michelin-star chef when it comes to the barbecue. Looking down at the clock, I realize I should have plenty of time. After all, when I last checked the arrivals, the flight had made up time in the air. If anything, I'll be getting back early.

Chapter 7

Harper

Dear Readers,

While I eagerly await some news, I've been poring over old photographs of Harper Kennedy. Harper at the Oscars, Harper at the Emmys, Harper at movie premieres ... The woman never disappoints in her selection of wardrobe and accoutrements.
But it's got me thinking ...

When you become such a paragon of beauty and taste, it's kind of hard to see you as human. Maybe Brett had to go spelunking in nastier caves to feel like the hero.

I know, gross metaphor, but apropos, no?

Brett if you're reading this, it's time to pack up your junk and return to the light. Harper is not going to give you many more chances.

Dish,
Ferris Biltmore

~

We're almost an hour behind schedule when we pull up at the dock. The kids had a fantastic time, but I hate being late. It reeks of disrespect and entitlement. I'd be a nervous wreck, but Gib has assured me several times that our pilot won't mind—once again citing the laid-back Alaskan way.

"You're going to get the same warm welcome everyone gets here in the land of the midnight sun." He sounds very sure of himself.

"I thought it was the final frontier," I tease.

"Last frontier," he corrects me. "And don't worry, Alaskans are known for their hospitality."

When we finally get to the dock, I see a small plane bobbing on the water.

"That's your lift to Gamble," he tells us, before getting out to unload our suitcases. He leaves them on the cement sidewalk. I quickly slide out of the backseat and tell the kids to grab their backpacks so we can get going. They're both clutching their tiny vials of gold like they house magic.

As I hand Gib his tip, I see an extraordinarily tall, well-built guy hop down from the plane. His hair is as dark as his scowl. His aviators are hiding his eyes, but I can tell by the way his jaw just tightened that he's not too happy. He slams the door shut before lifting his sign that says "Marge Simpson" on it.

Urgh. It's because we're late. Why didn't I just say no to the gold panning? I'm sure we could have found another place to do it. The way he's striding up the ramp is not at all what I'd call friendly.

Whatever. I'm not going to let some grumpy pilot ruin the first day of our freedom. We'll be rid of him in about two hours anyway. I can certainly put up with a surly man for that long—look how long I lasted with Brett.

Offering him a polite smile, I say, "I'm sorry we're running a little behind."

"A little?" he asks, his head snapping back. "You were supposed to be here an hour ago. I was just about to leave without you."

He pauses and even though his eyes are covered, I can tell he suddenly knows who I am. I offer him my best Hollywood smile, hoping he'll forget all about being grumpy now that he knows who he's going to be flying to Gamble today. I don't like to rely on special treatment because of my status, but there are times when it comes in handy. Right now seems like it could be one of those times.

Only the pilot doesn't smile back. With a terse nod, he says, "Marge Simpson, huh?"

I nod, biting the inside of my cheek. "I have to travel under an assumed name. My real name is Harper."

"Digger McKenzie. I run the Whistler Lake Lodge."

Crap, I'm not going to be rid of him in two hours. "*And* you're the pilot?"

"Yes, ma'am. Pilot, guide, cook, and maintenance crew all rolled into one package, which means I have a lot of people who rely on me."

That must be another shot at me for being late. "That's a lot of stuff for one person to do."

"In Hollywood maybe, but up here we learn to fend for ourselves." He dismisses me and turns to the kids. His face immediately breaks out into a broad smile. "I'm Digger."

He holds out his hand to each of them for a fist bump

while they introduce themselves. "You two ready to explore the wild?"

They both nod, little grins lifting their cheeks.

"Good. We're going to go up in my float plane so you can get the best view of the most beautiful place on earth. But first you've got to grab your bags and lug them over to the plane."

Both kids hurry to wheel their suitcases toward the dock. Digger looks over at me and gruffly asks, "You coming?"

Excuse me? "I can't carry four suitcases all by myself," I tell him.

Without saying another word, he picks up the two largest and leads the way to the float plane. So much for my warm Alaskan welcome …

Chapter 8

Digger

Forget social media, *Harper Kennedy* is everything that's wrong with this world. Entitled with a capital E. She may have apologized for being late, but people who respect other people's time show up when they're supposed to. The end.

Now, I've got to sit here hoping Jack and Evie manage to pull off a meal fit for a king (or worse, a cranky guest with an axe to grind). But there's nothing I can do about it now. We won't arrive until after supper is served.

The sad thing is that Miss Fancy Movie Star is going to raise her two adorable children to think the world revolves around them. She's got them all dressed up, even though she had to have known they were coming to a place where the only tuxedos you'll see are of the Canadian variety (denim up top and on the bottom). If I had to guess, I'd say she's trying to show everyone she thinks they're better than we are.

Although, maybe that's not entirely fair. Her attitude doesn't exactly say "stuck-up," and so far, the kids seem nice enough—lots of pleases and thank yous when I opened the cooler for them. They probably learned those manners at school.

"See that, kids?" I ask, pointing to the right at a pair of juvenile bald eagles mid-flight.

"Are those hawks?" Liam asks, his headset askew as he cranes his neck for a better view. He's sitting next to me in the front, while his mom and sister are in the middle row.

"Bald eagles," I tell him.

"But they don't have white feathers on their heads."

This kid is sharp. "That's because they're teenagers. When they grow up in another year or so, their heads will turn white. Same with their tails."

"I had no idea they started out looking so different," Harper inserts herself into the conversation.

"Well, they do." My level of enthusiasm is losing altitude quickly.

I peek in the rearview mirror at her, only to be hit with the same irritating reaction I had when I first set eyes on her. Apparently, my body hasn't gotten the message that I don't like her.

According to Mrs. Baker, Harper has been named one of the world's most beautiful women by *Hollywood Style* magazine every year for the last six years. She *really is* something. She's got the physique of a dancer—long, lean limbs, perfect posture, and a sense of grace that any guy would find alluring. Add to that, she's got a smile that can light up a room—not that I've been trying too hard to make her smile.

Based on her children's tow-headedness, that blonde hair of hers must be natural. Although, I wouldn't put it past some phony in La La Land to dye their babies' hair just so they can keep up the illusion.

Having said that, she looks pretty natural. Hardly any makeup that I can see. She's pointing to a yacht on the ocean below and telling her kids that "Uncle Steven has one like that."

I force my eyes not to roll as I pretend not to listen.

"Can we go for a ride on it sometime?" Lily asks her.

"Maybe," Harper tells her. There's something sad in her tone.

"He's *dad's* friend," Liam says. "So, *he'd* have to take us."

"But Mom could come too," the little girl protests.

"She might not want to," Liam says.

"But you would, right, Mom?"

"Umm ... well ... I'm not sure," she answers, her smile faltering just the tiniest bit.

"When couples get divorced, they don't go on trips together anymore," Liam announces. "They don't do anything together anymore because they hate each other."

I glance back in time to see Lily's eyes fill with tears. "Is that true?" she asks, her little voice nearly a whisper.

"No, baby." Harper pulls her in for a hug. "Your dad and I don't hate each other. In fact, we'll always love each other because we love you so much." She drops a kiss on her daughter's head, then gives her son a little glare that says *that's enough, mister.*

"If you'll always love each other, why don't you stay married?" Lily gives her a hopeful look that could break even the most hardened of hearts.

"The thing is ... sometimes people can love each other but they can't make each other happy anymore. That's what happened with Daddy and me. But we'll always want the best for each other, and we'll always be good friends."

I'm not buying it. According to Mrs. Baker's *People* magazine, her husband has already moved on. I'm guessing that's the reason she filed for divorce.

The kids clearly aren't buying it either because her son just rolled his eyes so hard, they could've gotten stuck back there. When I glance back, I see Harper is looking out the window, blinking back tears. The sight tugs at my heart a little. But just as quickly as the tears come, she manages to shake them off. She forces a bright smile as she looks down at her daughter and points in the direction of town. "Is that Gamble, Digger?" she asks.

"Yes, it is," I answer, doing my best to sound friendly. "See that big lake behind town, kids?"

They answer in the affirmative.

"That's where the lodge is—it's the long building with the red roof. We're going to land at the dock next to it. Your cabin is the one farthest down the shore."

"The one with the green roof?" Lily asks.

"No, that's my place. Next to it is my grandpa Jack's house, but if you look to the other side of the lodge, you'll see three cabins—all with red roofs. Yours is the last one. It has the biggest bedrooms and the prettiest view of the lake."

"Can we swim in the lake?" Lily asks.

"Sure can. It's cold, so you may not last too long in the water, but it's safe and clean."

I look back again to see Harper offering me a grateful smile. If I had to guess, I'd say she's pleased that I'm distracting her kids. I give her a little nod in return.

She may be entitled, but she's also a woman in pain who's trying her level best to appear happy for her children. I've spent enough time around my sister to know what that looks like when I see it.

Chapter 9

Harper

Dearest Readers,

I have dish! Word in the Hollywood jungle is that Harper Kennedy has abandoned ship and left the domestic nest she shared with Brett Kennedy, a.k.a., the nanny screwer. I don't blame her for a hot second, either.

My dog walker's sister's boyfriend's chiropractor saw Brett and Justine (that's *her* name) out at Pink Wiener on Sunset having lunch.

Not only should Helio-humper not be dining at such a suggestively named restaurant given his recent exploits, but he should be lying low in hopes that his lovely wife will see her way clear to taking him back.

Harper, you deserve better!

Dish,
Ferris Biltmore

Gamble looks exactly like it did on the internet—postcard perfect in its wild beauty. The sky is such an intense blue, it's like someone painted it that color. But it's really just that blue, and there's something about standing under it that makes me feel like anything is possible. How fanciful is that?

I turn on my phone while Digger takes our luggage off the plane. Part of the reason for getting away was so that I didn't have to pay attention to the constant stream of messages being sent from my agent, manager, and all the people who pretend to be my friends but are really only looking for the inside scoop.

Gossip is currency in the lives of the Hollywood elite. If you have the latest dish, then you get to wear the crown until the next scandal dethrones you. I'm not interested in feeding the beast.

I check to see who sent the messages before deciding if I want to read them. I click on the last one that came in. It's from Prisha.

Girl, we got you to the airport just in time. Lady Gaga was flying out right after you and she was being trailed by a whole parade of paparazzi. Don't bother messaging until you get settled. I just wanted you to know that I love you and I'll take care of everything on this end. Get some rest.

"Ahem." Digger clears his throat right next to me. "If you're done checking your phone, I can show you to your cabin." He doesn't wait for me to answer, he just starts walking toward a golf cart at the end of the dock.

"Can I drive?" Liam calls excitedly while running after him.

Digger turns around. "How old are you?"

"He's only eight," Lily answers before her brother can.

"Yeah, but we have a golf cart at home and Mom lets me drive it. I'm a good driver." It's important to Liam for adults to see him as responsible. It's like the kid came into this life in the body of a baby, but his mind was already thirty.

"If you're allowed to drive in LA, who am I to say you're too young to drive here?"

"Seriously?" To say my son is shocked would be a massive understatement.

Digger shoots me a quick glance. "If it's okay with your mom."

"Fine by me," I say.

"But Moooooom." My daughter's whining is a clear sign she feels like she's being left out of something cool.

Before I can find a way to make it up to her, Digger says, "It's a good thing you're four."

"Why?" she wants to know.

"Because I don't carry kids on my shoulder after that age. There's a lot of walking to do here and it's nice to have a ride."

"Hear that, Liam? Digger's gonna carry me and you have to walk. What do you think about that?"

Liam ignores her and runs straight for the driver's side on the cart. Once our luggage is loaded in the back he asks Digger, "Which way?"

"Follow the signs marked Guest Cottages. And watch out for grizzly bears."

Lily lets out a shriek while Liam says, "Cool!"

Not only does my son sound and dress like an old man, he also drives like one. "You can speed up if you want," Digger tells him.

"I'd prefer to take it nice and slow until I'm used to your

roads." Digger's shoulders start to move up and down slightly as he tries to hide his amusement.

"When do we get to go swimming?" Lily demands. "I want to go now!"

"I won't be able to show you where the best swimming spots are tonight," Digger tells her. "I'm late helping with supper up at the lodge. I'm the grill master, so there's no telling what our guests were given to eat tonight."

"I'm sorry again for being tardy," I tell him. "Our driver assured us you weren't in any rush."

He doesn't respond to my apology. Instead, he asks, "Are you all hungry?"

"Starving," Lily tells him.

"Why don't we drive up to the lodge and I'll get you fed. Then someone can take you down to your cabin."

"Are there a lot of other guests?" I don't like the idea of being on display. The whole reason we chose Alaska was to avoid people.

As though reading my mind, he answers, "There won't be at this hour, but if you're worried, there's a small private room I can seat you in."

"Thank you." Maybe Digger isn't as bad of a guy as I'd originally thought. He's wonderful with the kids and being nice to my children is always a good way to get on my good side. Unless you're nice to them at the same time you're banging my husband. Then all bets are off.

"Abort mission, Liam. Start following the signs to the lodge."

"Aye, aye, captain." My son salutes Digger before taking a hard left. "What's for supper? Can we have cheeseburgers?"

"Cheeseburgers are my specialty," he tells him. "How do you feel about blueberry pie, Miss Lily?" he calls back to my daughter.

"Would this pie have any ice cream on it?" she challenges.

"Any pie worth eating has ice cream on it."

My daughter reaches over and takes my hand. "I'm happy we came here, Mommy," she tells me quietly.

"No more worries about bear attacks?"

"Mom, Little Bear is a bear. I bet any nasty bears will leave us alone." My sweet little girl is trying hard to make the best of our being here and Digger seems to be making that a whole lot easier for her.

"Do I get a cheeseburger and pie too?" I ask, suddenly feeling lighter than I have in days.

"You can have whatever you want." Somehow his response doesn't seem that hospitable.

"If my kids are having cheeseburgers, then so am I." I don't know why this guy has a chip on his shoulder regarding me, but I'm not some princess he has to cater to.

Digger points at a red traffic cone. "Park there."

Liam pulls over and we all get out. "What about our luggage?" I ask. "Should we take it with us?"

"No one's going to take your stuff," he says. "And I'm guessing you don't want to schlep it yourself."

"I don't, but I'm not really comfortable leaving it."

"Up to you." He turns to Lily and says, "You ready for that ride?" He lifts my daughter effortlessly onto his shoulders.

Well, shoot, I guess it really is up to me if he's carrying Lily. I decide my purse has all the important stuff in it, so that's all I take. Walking behind Digger and the kids, I listen to his easy conversation with them.

"When I was a kid, I used to dream about visiting LA. Do you guys like it there?"

"It's okay," Liam tells him. "We have a great house and a nice school …"

"There are lots of people with cameras hanging around our house," Lily interjects. "We don't like them very much."

"They're called paparazzi," Liam says authoritatively. "I mooned one of them."

"Nice!" Digger says with a little nod. "What did your mom think of that?"

"She went after him and deleted all of his pictures." Then my son asks, "Did you ever get to LA when you were little?"

Digger shakes his head.

"Why not?" Lily wants to know.

"It's kind of hard to pick up and leave the lodge. There's always a lot going on."

"Surely your parents could have taken you at some point?" My son is like a dog to a bone.

"My mom is the reason I wanted to go."

He doesn't elaborate, but it would be clear to a blind person there's a story there. Before Liam can press the issue, I hurry up the steps to the lodge in front of them and open the door.

"After you," I tell them with a flourish.

Digger narrows his eyes a little, looking confused. If I had to guess, I'd say he's surprised that I know how to be thoughtful. Taking Lily off his shoulders, he offers me a small smile while at the same time reaching up above me to push the door open a little wider. "Thank you, but that's my job."

I can't help but notice how big he is when he's up this close. I'm a little taken aback by it. It occurs to me that I haven't stood this close to a man in a very long time—even Brett. I don't know if it's the fresh air or this gruff guy in front of me, but I'm suddenly reminded of what it feels like to be a woman. Not a mom. Not a friend. Not a daughter. A woman. A single one.

Because that's exactly what I am now.

Chapter 10

Digger

A quick glance into the dining room tells me the Bakers must have finished supper already. They're probably back at their room, packing for their early flight in the morning. I breathe a little sigh of relief that they're gone so I don't have to run interference between Harper and her biggest fan/most upset person on the planet about Harper's divorce.

Grandpa Jack comes out from the kitchen to greet us. He clearly has no idea who Harper is. Looking over at me, he says, "We were just about to send out a search party."

"No need. We're here," I tell him, avoiding beating a dead horse by bringing up the reason we were late. "This is Harper, Liam, and Lily." Turning to the kids, I say, "This is Grandpa Jack. Be sweet to him because he's the guy who does all the baking around here."

Evie walks in from the patio carrying some dirty dishes. She's got her usual bored look on her face until she sees Harper. Her mouth drops open and she loses her grip on the plates, causing several pieces of silverware to crash loudly to the floor. "You're … you're …"

"Marge Simpson," I tell her.

Harper smiles at Evie and says, "I'm Harper, but I don't want anyone to know that." She gestures toward her children. "These are my kiddos, Lily and Liam."

Evie seems to recover herself a little and smiles up at the kids as she picks up the silverware. "Hey, I'm Evie."

"You're pretty," Lily announces.

Evie rolls her eyes but also blushes a little. "It's the make-up."

"I love it," Lily tells her. "Mom, you should do your make-up like hers."

Harper grins down at her daughter. "Do you think so?"

"Yup!"

"Well maybe while we're here, I can get Evie to show me how she does it."

"I'd be happy to," Evie says, looking far more enthusiastic than I've ever seen her. She glances at me excitedly, then seems to remember she doesn't like anything. She shrugs. "Or, you know, whatever."

"You get the whole restaurant to yourselves. Where would you folks like to have dinner?" Grandpa asks. "Out on the deck with Moose or inside where it's boring?"

"Outside!" both of the kids yell at once.

He winks at Harper. "Thought that might be the answer."

He picks up a carton of crayons and two paper placemats and leads them out the back door.

"I'll bring some drinks out," I tell Harper. "What would the kids like?"

"Do you have chocolate milk?" she asks.

"Yup. And for you?"

"Something cold, wet, and boozy."

"Beer, okay?"

"Perfect," she says before disappearing outside.

As soon as the door closes behind her, Evie rushes over to me. "What's *she* doing here?"

"If I were to guess, I'd say she's hiding from the current shitshow that's her life."

Evie nods her head sagely. "I saw Mrs. Baker's *People* magazine. Just so you know, I'm not going to go all fangirl, if that's what you think," she says. "I'm not even a fan. I was just surprised to see her here."

"Sure," I say, following her into the kitchen to get the drinks.

"We're going to have to hide her from Mrs. Baker," Evie tells me as she sets the dishes down next to the industrial stainless-steel sink.

"Just for tonight though. They're leaving first thing tomorrow."

"Thank God."

I'm grateful not to be flying them. They've decided to take the scenic route and rent a car. Mrs. Baker is determined to see a bear if it's the last thing she does.

I take the tray of drinks outside, only to find Grandpa Jack sitting at the table with our new guests. He's telling them about the time he wrestled a grizzly over a salmon. It's not true—he dropped that salmon fast when he saw the bear coming—but it's a funny story.

Moose has also joined in and has his big head resting on the tabletop while making puppy eyes at Harper, hoping for some attention.

"Moose, go lie down," I tell him while handing out the drinks. He does what he's told, but not without a sigh of resignation. "Sorry about that." I look over at Grandpa Jack. "Some people aren't as strict as they should be about reminding Moose of his table manners."

Harper offers me a warm smile. "No trouble. He's sweet."

"He also drools a lot," I tell her. Looking at Lily, I ask, "Do you have a dog at home?"

"Nope, but we have two cats, five chickens and one rooster," she says proudly.

"Really?" I ask, shocked that a famous actress like Harper would have chickens.

"Why does that surprise you?" Harper asks.

"It just doesn't fit the picture," I tell her.

"People aren't always what they seem." She doesn't seem very pleased by me making assumptions.

If I had to guess, I'd say there's a deeper meaning behind her words. It probably has to do with finding her dirtbag husband with the nanny. "I agree with you totally. People aren't always what they seem."

Three hours later, Moose and I are finally walking through the front door to my cabin. He makes a beeline for his huge dog bed that sits beside the sofa, and I head to the fridge for another beer. It's well after ten o'clock and I should be wiped, but instead, I'm completely wired. I'm old enough not to let myself get all twisted up in knots over a woman. Yet, I'm also self-aware enough to realize that Harper Kennedy is no ordinary woman. Thank God she'll only be here for a few weeks.

Twisting the cap off the bottle, I take the beer with me to my bathroom. Turning on the shower, I down half of it while I wait for the water to warm up.

After I get in, I squirt some shampoo in my hand and start to lather it into my hair. How is it that I'm still thinking about Harper? She's just another guest.

It's guilt. That's it. My chest tightens when I think about the hard time I gave her for being late. She's clearly here to escape from her troubles—troubles that feed the public's appetite for gossip. Imagine not only having to go through the pain of a divorce, but also trying to protect her children from the media. Not to mention all the ugly things people are saying about her and her ex. And then when she gets up here, she winds up facing a grumpy jerk who does his best to make her feel like she's not wanted here…

Rinsing my hair, I decide that tomorrow morning I'm going to make up for today. I'll make sure the Kennedys have the best time possible while they're here because if there's one thing those kids deserve, it's an escape from their sad lives. Harper too, by the looks of it. I don't know why it matters to me, but somehow it does.

Chapter 11

Harper

Dear Readers,

Once upon a time travel, I ran into Harper Kennedy on Third Street Promenade in Santa Monica. She was loaded down with shopping bags from the various baby stores in the area—she and Brett had just announced their first pregnancy.

Anyhoo, I was all, "Harper, is that you?" I was a tad green and nowhere near the sorcerer of style and information I am today, but we all start somewhere.

She smiled at me with that thousand-watt smile of hers and said, "It sure is."

I should have asked for her autograph. I should have asked her to have a cup of coffee with me. But all I managed to say was, "If I was born with girl bits, I would have wanted to be you."

She thanked me kindly and went on her way.

In other historical news, my dog walker's dental assistant's gardener once ran into Brett Kennedy on the street and had to get four stitches when he fell off the curb and hit his head on a fire hydrant.

That's all.

Dish,
Ferris Biltmore

~

"The cabin is perfect." I smile at Evie. "Thanks so much for showing us the way."

"Just doing my job," she says. She helps pull our luggage in and walks toward the kitchen. "The hot water takes a good five minutes to heat up, so don't give up on it. Oh, and sometimes you have to flush the toilet twice." She turns to walk away but stops herself. "If something bangs on your window, don't open the door to see what it is. Just call up to the lodge and we'll send someone down."

"Why?" Liam sounds as nervous as I feel.

"It doesn't happen often," Evie tells him. "But sometimes bears stop by to say hi."

"Mommy." I feel Lily's little hand grasp mine. "I'm scared."

"Don't be," Evie assures her. "I sleep in a van all by myself and I'm not scared."

"You should be," my daughter tells her as her eyes fill with worry.

"Here's the thing, Lily." Evie leans down so she's eye level. "Bears have their own busy lives. They don't have time for us. If they come sniffing around it's just because they want something to eat, but if you don't give them anything, they'll go off and hunt for their own food."

Neither Liam nor Lily looks like they're buying it, so Evie adds, "In the cabinet above the sink, there's some bear spray. You can carry that with you, but make sure you don't spray yourself with it. It stings like a ticked off wasp."

"Why didn't Digger come down with us?" Lily asks. "He said he would."

"He had to help some other guests," Evie tells her. "The plumbing in Cabin Four can be a little dicey." Then she looks at me. "Come on up to the lodge any time after six. Breakfast is served until ten."

Once she leaves, we explore the cabin. There are two bedrooms, one with a queen-size bed for me and one with two twins for the kids. "I want to sleep with you," Lily decides after checking out her room.

"Is that okay with you, Liam?" I don't want to offend him by suggesting he might be scared all by himself.

"I don't see why she can't sleep in her own bed." My son scowls at his sister.

"How about if we pull your mattress into my room? I could use a big, strong man to protect me."

Liam shoves his hands into his pockets and nods his head somberly. He looks like a college professor about to explain the fundamentals of time travel via wormholes. "I think that might be for the best, Mom."

"It's getting late," I tell them. "You two go wash up and put your jammies on and then we can read a book together."

"Why don't we watch a TV show?" Lily asks.

"There's no TV," Liam reminds her.

"I forgot." Her shoulders slump dejectedly.

"I brought along two decks of cards," I tell them. "Who's up for a righteous game of War?"

"I am!" they both yell.

While they roll their suitcases into their room, I go into the kitchen and open the refrigerator. There's a fresh pint of cream and a half-gallon of milk. Rifling through the cabinets, I discover the coffee, filters, and a half dozen boxes of individually packaged cereal.

I don't want to eat all our meals up at the lodge—Evie's reaction was enough to remind me that even people up here will recognize me. I'll have to ask Digger where there's a store tomorrow.

Picking up my phone, I send Prisha a quick text.

Me: *I think this trip is just what the doctor ordered.*

Prisha: *Do you have internet access up there?*

Me: *Up at the lodge. Is there something I need to see?*

Prisha: …

Prisha: …

Me: *What happened?!*

Prisha: *Brett and Justine aren't exactly keeping a low profile.*

Me: *Meaning?*

Prisha: *They're behaving very lovey-dovey for the cameras.*

Me: *That son of a bitch. Why is he doing this? He can't actually think it makes him look good.*

Prisha: *If I had to guess, I'd say he's sending you a message.*
Me: *What message is that? That I'm an idiot and should have left him sooner?*

Prisha: *He wants you to see that he's desirable and you made a mistake by filing for divorce.*

Me: *If that's what he thinks, he's delusional.*

Prisha: *No one ever accused Brett of having his finger on the pulse of reality.*

Me: *Let me know if anything earth shattering comes up. I'm going to stay as far away from the internet as I can.*

Prisha: *Give the babies a hug for me.*

I turn my phone off before tossing it into my purse. Even if Brett doesn't care about me anymore, couldn't he at least care enough about his children to quit making such a sideshow of our lives?

Speaking of our children, Liam and Lily walk out of their room looking freshly scrubbed and highly adorable. "On my bed." I point to my room.

As soon as we're all crossed-legged and ready to go, I deal out the cards. "Twos and jokers trump the king and in the case of double-war, the winner gets a pack of gum in addition to all the cards."

"You brought gum with you?" Gum to Lily is about as exciting as cocaine to a crack addict. The girl can't get enough of it.

"You know I did," I tell her with a wink. Then I reach into my suitcase and pull out three mini packs of M & Ms. I toss one to each of them and we make short work of devouring those six little bites.

Twenty minutes into our game, Lily lays her head on a pillow and goes to sleep. "You tired too, bud?" I ask my son.

He shrugs his shoulders. "Mom, are you mad at Dad?"

That's the twenty-thousand-dollar question that I can't answer honestly. If I claim to be mad at Brett, then Liam will want to know why. "I'm not mad, I'm sad. Neither your dad nor I ever thought we'd ever get a divorce."

"Then why does he date other women?"

"Excuse me? Where did you hear that?"

"I'm eight, Mom. I know stuff," he tells me sadly. "Did you do something to make Dad not love you anymore?" *Ouch.*

"First tell me where you heard that Dad was dating other women?"

He inhales deeply before slowly releasing his breath. "I overheard Jason's mom talking about it on the telephone. She said, 'That Brett Kennedy is a real ladies' man.' Then she said Dad was already back in the game. I think that means he's dating again."

You'd think adults would know enough not to gossip in front of the family they're maligning. Not that Delia was lying. In fact, at one time I was fairly certain she was auditioning for the role of the other woman.

"And you fired Justine …" my son says accusingly.

"How do you know that?"

"Dad told us. He said you were jealous that she was so much younger and prettier than you are."

"What?" That bastard.

"I told him you're the prettiest lady in the whole wide world."

"Oh, honey." I reach out and pull my son to my side. "We're going to get through this, I promise."

"I don't want you and Dad to get a divorce. It's not fair."

"No, it's not, honey. It's not fair to any of us."

I'm glad we're in Alaska right now. Because if we were home, I'd be hard-pressed not to give a slew of damning interviews about my loser of a husband. Now that I know he's been bad-mouthing me to my own children, the gloves are off.

Chapter 12

Digger

"That Harper woman seems nice," Grandpa Jack says, waggling his thick eyebrows at me.

"Don't start, it's not even seven a.m.," I tell him, lifting my mug for a sip of coffee. As Evie starts her day later than us, we're in the kitchen alone. As usual, Grandpa Jack is using our time together to help me "see the light," about settling down with a nice girl.

He punches the huge ball of dough for today's rolls. "She's so pretty, she could be a model."

Lifting a bag of flour off the shelf, I set it on the stainless-steel counter to measure out some for waffles. "Only a total sleazeball would try to get a single mom to go for a roll in the hay."

"I'm not talking about a roll in the hay, and you know it."

"Jack, I'm not about to complicate my life unnecessarily. And even if I were, she lives all the way down in LA and I live all the way up here in Alaska. You might remember how well that arrangement worked for my parents."

He opens his mouth to protest, but I shake my head at him. "It's not going to happen, so please give it up."

I'm gifted a few minutes of precious silence while I crack the eggs, add milk, and a splash of vanilla. Just as I start to whisk everything together, Grandpa says, "Did I ever tell you about my friend Carl?"

"No." *Is this a new topic or is it somehow going to loop back to me needing a wife and kids?*

"He used to manage the Alaska Pacific Bank branch here in town back in the seventies. Anyway, he was a bit of a ladies' man when he was in his twenties. He thought he had lots of time to settle down. But then one day, he went for a haircut, and old Harvey Younghusband—do you remember Harvey?"

"No," I tell him, wondering how long this story is going to take.

Grandpa nods. "Before your time. Good fellow. Anyway, Harvey takes one look at him and says, 'Carl, you're losing your hair.' And Carl—who had this thick, wavy, dark brown hair that he kept long—says to him, 'No, I'm not.'"

Grandpa covers the huge steel bowl he put his dough into with a folded tablecloth and continues, "So, Harvey sits him down in the chair, then holds a mirror up so Carl can see the back of his head. And sure enough, the hair at the back on top was thinning pretty bad already. Well, Carl panicked, because his dad had been bald as a cue ball by the time he was thirty-five. Carl figured he had his mother's hair, so he didn't have to worry, but no dice. While he was sitting in the chair, getting his haircut, he realized, 'Holy crap, if I got my dad's hair, I might have inherited the shape of his skull too.' Which would've been bad since his dad's skull was as odd as they come—oblong instead of round, and real bumpy. He realized that without that thick, wavy hair, his chances of finding a pretty wife were going to be slim-to-none. Especially if he *did* have his father's head shape."

Oh, my God. Please stop telling me about Carl's head.

"Anyway, now Carl's got this ticking time bomb sitting right on top of his neck, so he starts getting serious about finding a woman. He goes out every night to the pub, to the library, even starts going to a new church every Sunday—searching for the right girl." Jack walks over to the coat rack next to the screen door and takes his ball cap off it.

"So, did he find one?"

"Two of them actually." He tugs his cap into place. "But up here the options were even more limited back then than they are now, so he had to choose between an ugly-but-nice girl and a nasty-but-hot one." He says this last part as if imparting vital wisdom on me.

"And?" I ask, now fully invested.

Grandpa makes a clicking sound with his tongue, then shakes his head. "I forget which one he wound up with. The point is, he waited too long to find someone who was both nice and nice to look at. Funny thing is, he wound up having his mom's head shape, so he probably didn't have to rush quite that much. Okay, I'm going to go have a nap while the dough rises. I'll see you in a bit."

I stare at him for a second. "Good talk."

"Don't forget Carl, son. You're not going to be young and handsome forever, you know."

Ah, so *that* was the point of the story. I salute him before getting back to work. I'm now a full five minutes behind schedule, all to find out I'm going to age like everyone else on the planet. I mutter to myself while I finish preparing the waffle mix. "I'm glad I'm not going to be this young and handsome forever. Good. Maybe once I get old and wrinkly with a big paunchy stomach people will leave me alone. I like being single and nothing is going to change that. So there, *Grandpa*."

Chapter 13

Harper

Dearest Readers,

PUKE!!!

Brett Kennedy is wining and dining his children's babysitter in a big, bad way. That's right, couple's massages, private catamaran trips, lounging by the pool at the Four Seasons Oahu. Insert full body shiver here.

I have no words. Oh wait, here are a few. Abhorrent, abysmal, repugnant, reprehensible, appalling, horrific, atrocious ...

Dude, you are not going to get the lady back acting like that. Toss the trash on the curb and go home with your tail between *your* legs—not anyone else's.

Harper, I apologize for my species. The hetero variety of man sometimes needs a sharp knock to the head. Let me know if you'd like some help in that arena.

Dish,
Ferris Biltmore

It's been two days since we got to Alaska and I'm starting to think it may be the most relaxing place on earth. Yesterday after a big breakfast of waffles, eggs, and fruit, the kids and I spent the entire day lakeside—swimming, reading, and lying on a big blanket, watching the clouds float by. Evie brought us a picnic lunch. For dinner we meandered up to the lodge for some freshly caught salmon. After that, we all snuggled up in my bed to watch *Cars 2*. The kids have several of their favorite movies already downloaded on their iPad in case of emergency.

The best part is we were left alone the entire time. No one with a cell phone asking for a selfie, no dreaded paparazzi, and, come to think of it, no men—period. Well, except for Grandpa Jack who I won't count, since he's somewhere around eighty—a total sweetheart, though. He served supper last night while Digger was helping his sister's sons build a skateboard ramp at their house.

In retrospect, it was the perfect day. The whole Brett schtupping the nanny thing feels like it's something that happened a long time ago, and to someone who isn't me. I'm hoping to be able to keep the ordeal from the kids for a little while longer. Maybe by then their "relationship" will be a thing of the past, which is highly probable given my husband's attention span.

For the first time since I kicked Brett out, I fell into a

deep sleep as soon as my head hit the pillow last night. The kids must be worn out, too, because we all overslept and missed breakfast.

It's after ten when Lily wakes me, her bare feet slapping against the hardwood floors. "Mom! I'm as hungry as a bear in the springtime." (She got that line from Grandpa Jack who said it to her last night at supper.)

She pulls the blackout curtains open, letting in the sunshine while I yawn and stretch and pray for another week of sleep like this. If I could manage it, I might be back in fighting form.

Liam sits up on his mattress, his blond hair sticking up in every direction as he scratches his Spider-Man-pajama-clad belly. "I'm a starvin' Marvin. I hope they have waffles again."

Throwing my covers off, I stand up. "Me too, but I think we missed breakfast. I'll call the front desk and find out."

Evie answers on the fourth ring and I quickly fill her in on our 'starving' Marvin' status. She confirms that breakfast won't be served again until tomorrow, but that she'll head our way with some supplies to tide us over. After hanging up, I hurry around and get dressed while encouraging the kids to do the same.

A few minutes later, there's a knock at the door. It's Evie carrying a basket that's nearly half her size.

"There are only three of us, you know," I tell her laughingly.

"I know, but Grandpa Jack thought you might need more. Most folks who stay awhile usually go into town and pick up snacks and stuff at the market."

"I'll definitely do that. But what do I do about a car? Is there a place in Gamble to rent one?"

She reaches into her pocket and hands me a set of keys. "These are for the old Toyota pickup. It's parked right next to the golf carts up at the lodge."

"Thank you! Do I just leave it there when I'm done?"

She nods her head. "If you want to go now, I can drive you up. "

"Just let me unload this lovely basket into the fridge." I pull out fresh fruit, more milk, butter, bread, and an assortment of meats and cheese, as well as several pre-made sandwiches. "My goodness, I'm not going to need much with all of this."

"Living in the middle of nowhere Alaska makes it imperative to always have supplies on hand. We had such a bad storm a couple of winters ago that supply trucks couldn't get here for two weeks."

"What did people do?" I can't imagine not being able to get food. While I grew up in Illinois and we always had a garden, we relied on the grocery store for most of our sustenance.

"Everyone's freezer is full of elk, moose, and bear. We got by."

I turn toward her with my face so scrunched up it probably looks like a fist. "Bear?"

"Some of the old folks eat it and swear it's as good as venison. Personally, I'm not a huge fan, but I did eat some that winter."

Shaking my head, I tell her, "This really *is* the last frontier, isn't it?"

"Oh, yeah. If you need a lot of conveniences to thrive, this is not the place to be."

I call out, "Kids, come on! Evie is going to drive us to the lodge."

"Yay!!" They cheer simultaneously while running out to the living room.

"I want pancakes!" Lily shouts.

"I want waffles," Liam tells her.

Evie turns her attention to me. "We're prepping for lunch

up at the lodge, so if you want pancakes and stuff, you'll need to hit the diner in town. Moira serves you whatever meal you want, no matter the time of day."

"That sounds like just the ticket." I grab a light jacket from off the back of the chair, throw my purse over my shoulder and announce, "I want a three-egg omelet with hash browns, bacon, toast, and orange juice."

By the time we get up to the lodge, the kids' and my stomachs are growling so loudly, you'd think we hadn't eaten in a week. Evie gives us directions to town, which aren't exactly essential: turn left at the end of the road and you'll run into it.

"The market is across the street from the diner. The only places on Main Street are a bar, a beauty shop, a gas station, and a hardware store."

I hadn't quite realized we'd be this far removed from civilization, but I'd rather be somewhere without a Starbucks than be back in LA where everyone is surely dissecting the tragedy of my life. I don't know why, but when a famous couple goes through a divorce, everyone treats the woman like she's some sort of Victorian flower that will fall apart with the least provocation. Then they do everything they can to provoke her so they can document it for public consumption. That's why not being there is the only answer for keeping my sanity.

It takes me three tries to get the ignition on the truck to turn over. When it does, I pull out and drive the four miles into town.

"I like it here," Lily says. "Everything is so green and pretty."

Liam offers, "Our lungs are going to clear out, for sure. We breathe in too much smog at home." My little old man.

We're only the third car to park in the lot next to a quaint—and delightfully empty—diner. At first, I worry that the lack of customers might be a bad sign, but then I remember it's too late for breakfast and too early for lunch. In a booth near the front window, three boys that look so alike that they must be brothers, sit squeezed onto one bench, huddled over an iPad.

A very pretty young woman in jeans and a tee looks up from the cash register. "Morning!" she calls out. "Sit anywhere you want, and I'll be right with you."

The kids run across the room and sit at a booth in the back corner. "Do you think they have crayons here?" Lily asks.

I reach into my purse and hand her the emergency pack I keep on hand.

As soon as we're settled, the woman starts our way, while calling to the boys, "Okay, you three. That's enough screens. Get outside and play."

I wait for the arguing to start, but incredibly, the kids do what they're told. The tallest one hands the iPad to her while the other two hang out near the front door. Lily and Liam both wear matching intrigued faces. They're clearly interested in making some friends.

The woman ruffles the boy's hair. "Stay in the park and keep an eye on your brothers."

"Yes, Mom," he tells her before glancing in our direction. His eyes land on a pack of Pokémon cards that Liam has set out on the table. "You like Pokémon?"

"Yeah, I'm really into it. You?" Liam asks.

"Totally," he says, pulling a stack out of his pocket. "If you have time after you eat, we'll be across the street. There aren't a lot of kids to trade with around here."

Liam's eyes light up and he looks at me. "Can I go, Mom?"

I glance across the street and see that I'll have a good

view of the park from here. "Sure, but only if you bring your sister."

"Cool," the boy says. "See you in a bit. Get the pancakes. They're the best in the world."

"That was Wyatt, my eldest," the lovely lady tells me. "And I'm Moira. Can I start you three out with some coffee?"

Lily giggles while Liam tells her, "Thank you, but we're too young for coffee."

Giving him a half grin, she says, "How about some orange juice then?"

"Yes, please," he says.

"Me too, please," Lily adds.

Smiling up at her, I say, "I'll have coffee and juice. Evie told us you were the best place in town to get breakfast at this hour. I think we already know what we want."

Once we're done ordering, Moira walks away to get our drinks. When she comes back, she puts them on the table. "So, you're staying up at the lodge, huh? My family owns that place."

"Really? So, Digger is your …" *Husband, brother, cousin?*

"That goofball is my brother."

Lily covers her mouth while she laughs. "Goofball!"

"Him and his silly dog Moose. Who names an animal after another animal?" she asks Liam, rolling her eyes good-naturedly.

Liam's stomach growls and Moira's eyes pop open. "My goodness. You're as hungry as a bear in the springtime!"

"That's what Grandpa Jack said to me yesterday," Lily tells her.

"Do me a favor and tell him to stop using my best lines," Moira says with a wink. "Now, I'm going to go see if I can get the cook to put a rush on your food before this young man faints."

With that, she disappears into the kitchen, leaving the three of us alone. Liam flips slowly through his cards while Lily decorates a napkin with her crayons. I sip my coffee, enjoying the feeling of being a normal woman doing normal things with my children.

In my handbag, my phone buzzes away, but I ignore it. I'm not ready to face whatever the breaking news is today.

Within minutes, Moira brings three huge plates of food to our table and sets them down. "Happy eating. Let me know if you need anything else."

"Can I get whipped cream for my pancakes?" Lily asks.

"Now that's up to your mom," Moira tells her. "I don't let my boys have whipped cream, but according to them, I'm the meanest mom in the whole world."

"You don't let them have whipped cream on their pancakes?" My daughter is aghast.

"It's like this," Moira says. "If they have whipped cream on their pancakes, they don't get any pie after dinner. I figure life's about choices."

Lily nods her head slowly. "I think I'd rather have the pie, too."

"Good girl. I sent lemon meringue up to the lodge for supper tonight. Make sure you get yourself a piece."

We nearly lick our plates clean. We're so stuffed when we're done, I'm not sure I can move, but the kids are eager to go to the park. I make them wipe their faces, then send them off, leaving myself alone with Moira to sip my coffee in peace.

When she comes by to clear our plates, I say, "So, Digger is your brother?"

"Yes, he is. My crabby big brother who knows everything about everything," she answers with a smile.

I can't help the laugh that bursts out of me.

Moira arches an eyebrow in question, so I tell her, "I got on his bad side by being late to the plane."

"How in the world could you have helped being late? It's not like you were flying the other plane that got you to Anchorage."

I gesture for her to sit down, and she slides into the booth across from me. "Our cab driver suggested we pan for gold first. He said Digger wouldn't mind."

A knowing look crosses her face. "I have a feeling I know who it was. Was his name Gib?"

I nod.

"Yeah, he gets a cut from the guy who runs the gold panning place."

"Ah, that makes sense now."

After a second, she says, "I don't mean to pry, but he didn't recognize you, did he?"

"Recognize me?" I sound surprised. She never let on that she knows who I am.

"Digger stopped by last night after dinner to help my sons with a project. He may have mentioned who you are. But don't worry, he told me to keep it quiet. He's really good about protecting people's privacy."

"I'm hoping that trait runs in the family," I say, narrowing my eyes in concern.

"I don't have too many friends in this town, and I'm certainly not a blabbermouth." There's a sad look in her eyes which suggests a whole story she's not telling.

"Are you new to town or something?"

"Not that." Then, with a deep breath, she confesses, "I'm considered the biggest threat to every marriage in Gamble." My look of confusion causes her to add, "Ever since my husband died."

My gaze follows hers out the window in the direction our children are playing. Lily is on one swing next to one of

Moira's younger sons, chatting away.

I realize that even though I'm going through a tough time, there are a lot of people out there who have it a lot worse. Looking back at Moira, I say, "I'm sorry about your husband. I can only imagine how hard that must be."

She nods. "Thanks. We're through the worst of it. I was pregnant with the twins at the time."

"Oh, wow. That's just … awful."

Shrugging, she offers me a sad smile. "You play the hand you're dealt, right?"

"That you do," I answer.

We're both quiet for a second, before she says, "Look, it's none of my business, but for what it's worth, I'm really sorry about what you're going through, too. I'm sure having your private life splashed all over the internet and every news channel doesn't help matters."

I let out a frustrated chuckle. "A lot of people think celebrities get what they deserve, which I get. I mean, no one forced me to go to Hollywood looking for fame and fortune. But, in my defense, you can never fully comprehend what the fame part really means until you're in it." I shake my head and look out the window again. "And even then, it's not until you have your first child that you really get the impact of what you've done. By then it's too late to take it all back." I look at Moira, expecting to see a look of judgment, but instead, she's wearing an expression of pure empathy.

I hurry to tell her, "I'd give it all up if I could save my kids from living like prisoners in their own home. Save them from the scandal that's erupting."

Nodding, Moira reaches out and puts her hand on mine to comfort me. "I believe you. Digger told me you were a really good mom, and he's not one to hand out praise where it's not due."

I'm surprised by this—more pleased than I should be

that her brother thinks highly of me. "I'm trying, but sometimes it seems like an impossible situation."

"I can only imagine," she tells me, squeezing my hand. "Listen, while you're here, my family and I will do our level best to give you all a break from the chaos at home."

Tears spring to my eyes and I nod at her, unable to express my gratitude while also keeping it together.

The bell above the front door rings and the kids burst into the restaurant, all breathless from running. "Mom! Mom! There's a news van pulling up!" Wyatt yells, his eyes wide.

My heart stops for a second and my blood runs cold.

They found us.

Chapter 14

Digger

I'm leaving one of the guest rooms after fixing a toilet that wouldn't stop running when my cell phone rings. Moira's name pops up on the screen. She sounds out of breath. "Digger, I've got Harper and the kids here. A couple of guys from Channel Six just showed up. Obviously, someone sold them out."

My heart starts to pound at this news, which doesn't make any sense. Harper Kennedy's life is none of my business. Yet, somehow, in a very short period of time, I've started to feel responsible for her and her kids. I tell myself it's no more than I would feel for any other guest, but deep down, I know that's not true. "Who in the hell would have done that?" I ask, stepping up my pace to get to my truck.

"I'm pretty sure it must have been that idiot Gib who picked them up at the airport," she says. "Harper said he took some pictures of them while they were panning. Looks like he sold them to TMZ, before tipping off a news crew about where they are."

"Are they harassing her and the kids?"

"Not yet. I've got them in the kitchen with me hiding, but the reporter and his cameraman have seated themselves in a booth by the window. They're either hungry or hoping to overhear some town gossip."

"I'll be right there," I tell her, dropping my toolbox at the front desk.

I ride the Space Mountain of emotional roller coasters while driving to the diner. I go from worried that those leeches are going to do or say something to upset Harper and her kids to furious that Gib is such a douchebag of a human being.

I did some googling last night and found out that Harper's ex left her for their nanny. If that isn't bad enough, he's flaunting his new relationship for the world to see. Bastard.

As badly as I don't want a bunch of reporters hanging around bothering our guests, I'm not about to go into the diner with guns blazing. This situation has to be handled with the utmost discretion. Parking behind the building, I get out of my truck and walk through the back door. Harper, Lily, and Liam are all crowded around the prep table. The kids are kneading dough while Lloyd, the cook, looks on.

Moira peers through the small circular window into the dining room. Meanwhile, Harper stands frozen looking like a kitten about to be thrown into a lake. Wyatt and the twins are all seated at a small table playing Pokémon, but as soon as they see me, they rush over, all talking at once.

A cacophony of excitement ensues, from "OMG, Uncle Digger, you won't believe this," to "It was so scary. We ran like we were being chased by hungry bears!"

"Calm down, you guys," I tell them, holding one finger over my mouth. "We can't be too loud or those…" *Don't say losers in front of the kiddos*… "People from the news might think there's something going on back here."

My proclamation is met by firmly nodding heads and the old "zip up your lips" move. I give them each a fist bump, then look over at Harper.

In a low voice I say, "So much for your great escape."

I can tell she's trying to be brave, even though she's clearly on the verge of tears. Her vulnerability tugs at my heart. "We're not going to let them win. I have a plan."

"What's that?" she asks, looking skeptical.

"I can get you three somewhere where no one will ever find you. It just depends on whether you're willing to go."

Her eyebrows fly up as Moira says, "That sounds kind of creepy, Digger. In a true crime kind of way."

My face heats up with embarrassment and I shake my head quickly. "That came out wrong is all. There's a fishing cabin I fly clients to sometimes. It's not much, but you can stay up there until this all blows over."

"You're not talking about Thompson Lake, are you?" Moira wrinkles up her nose like she just got a big whiff of old fish.

"You got a better idea?" I ask her.

"Maybe we should just give up and go home," Harper says, rubbing her forehead. "I don't want to put you through a lot of trouble."

I look over at her kids, who are both playing with the dough. "It's no trouble. Jack and Evie can hold down the fort for a couple of days. Moira here can get the word out that you've left town, and we'll be back before we know it."

Harper chews her bottom lip for a second. "You'd stay with us? Why would you be willing to do that for me?"

I nod, feeling a strange urge to pull her into my arms and

drop a kiss on her head. "It's not just for you." *It totally is, but I'm not about to cop to that.* "The last thing I need is for a bunch of reporters to be hiding in the bushes at the lodge. People come up here to get away from real life."

"Right, yeah," she says with a long sigh. "Of course, this is going to affect everyone." She nods contemplatively. "Okay, we'll do it."

I don't give any indication of how relieved I feel by her answer. Instead, I tell her, "The first step is to sneak you all back to the lodge. The quicker we get out of here, the better."

"Where are we going?" Liam asks, coming to stand next to his mom's side.

"There's a little fishing cabin up the mountain," I tell him. "I thought you and Lily might like to see it."

He looks up at Harper. "It's because of those reporters, isn't it?"

She nods, doing her best not to look worried. "But it's mostly about us having our great Alaska adventure."

"Can we come?" Wyatt asks, looking excited.

"No," Moira tells him. "Uncle Digger will take you another time."

"Aww, Mom, but I love it up there, and it's summer and you promised to take us on a trip and we haven't gone anywhere," Wyatt tells her.

I'm just about to tell him no when Harper looks at Moira and shrugs. "Honestly, it's okay with me."

"You sure you want *five* kids to watch after, way out in the bush?" Moira asks, planting one hand on her hip.

Harper smiles at her. "It'll be a lot of fun for my two. Plus, keeping busy is the best way to get your mind off your troubles, isn't it?"

Moira looks at me. "If you're sure it's okay. Having the

house to myself for a couple of nights sounds like heaven on earth."

I tell the kids, "All right, boys, head home and get your camping gear and some clothes. We'll pick you up once we get Harper and her kids packed."

And just like that, I'm about to head into seclusion with someone I instinctively know I should not let myself get any closer to.

Chapter 15

Harper

Dear Readers,

Sit down and hold on tight, I have news ...

Harper Kennedy is in Alaska! I can only assume she'd have preferred the moon, but unless you're Jeffrey Bezos, that's a harder destination to get to. *But kudos on the shape of your rocket, dude ...*

Back to the business at hand, pictures surfaced today of Harper mining for gold with those two darling nuggets of hers.

Buzz is she's staying at a remote lodge in a town called Gamble. Tell me that isn't something straight out of a Netflix series. **Speed dials Netflix.**

The buzzards are circling, so I imagine it's only a matter of time before we have more news. My tummy's in knots. Meanwhile, Brett is hoeing his way through Hawaii. He and the nanny are sucking face and pawing at each other like it's some kind of Olympic event.

While boy/girl love makes me nauseated on a good day, Brett and Justine are making it hard to keep my breakfast down.

LAWDY! What's next?

Dish,
Ferris Biltmore

~

Even though I have a strong sense that Digger is not my biggest fan, I'm more grateful than I can express that he's willing to help us out of this jam. In my experience, most people would be trying to sell us out just like that Gib creep did.

Digger heads to the back door. "I'm going to pull the truck up closer. Come out in two minutes and crawl into the back. There's a tarp you can hide under."

Once Digger is gone, I thank Moira. "You've been a total champ. Thank you so much for everything."

She waves her hand at me. "I'm happy to help. When you get back, maybe we can arrange a girls' night. You know, drink wine, moan about our lives, and watch the kids play."

"I'd really like that." I have friends back in LA, but none of them are unaffected by the Hollywood machine. Prisha is certainly the most normal, but her whole career is based on movie-related drama. It would be nice to hang out with someone as down-to-earth as Moira.

I usher the kids out to the truck and help them climb into the back. When we're all snuggled under the tarp, I say, "This is a pretty cool adventure, isn't it?"

Lily groans. "I'm going to get my dress all dirty."

My son has other thoughts. "I bet this happens all the time during war. Soldiers sneaking away before the enemy even knows they were there."

I hate that my children are growing up feeling like there are enemies around them. It's not right for them to have such worries at such a tender age. An idea—one that I'm not fully comfortable with—pops into my head. Maybe I should contact Ethan and see what he thinks about me going for full custody. I would never keep the kids from their dad, but Brett hasn't exactly shown himself to be a responsible parent. I could cite bribing them with hoverboards while he and the nanny get biblical on the back of the couch.

Shelving the idea for now, I announce, "I'm really excited about camping."

"Will there be bugs?" Lily wants to know. She spent an entire hour of our first morning in our cabin inspecting every corner for creepy crawlies.

"If there are, I will personally escort them outside. How does that sound?"

Instead of answering, she lets out a long pathetic sigh that breaks my heart.

Once we get to the lodge, Digger ushers us into a golf cart and takes us back to our cabin. "Go on in and pack a bag. I'll head over to my place and do the same."

We make quick work of throwing our jammies, swimsuits, and a change of clothes into a bag, then I pack up all the food that Evie brought out earlier. Half an hour later, the seven of us are loaded into the float plane.

As soon as we're in the air, Wyatt says, "Wait until you see the cabin."

"It's tiny!" Ash, one of the twins, exclaims.

Colton, who's sitting next to him gushes, "We're going to be stacked up like cord wood!"

That doesn't sound very pleasant to me, but anything that keeps us from being discovered will be worth whatever discomfort we have to endure.

The kids continue their nonstop chattering, feeding off each other's energy as we get farther from town. Even Lily starts to sound excited.

I lean my head back and take several deep breaths. "How long is the flight?" I ask Digger.

"About a half hour." He flicks one of the switches.

"That far?"

"It's pretty close, actually. If we were going up in a jet at fifteen thousand feet, we'd get a couple hundred miles away in that time. But this baby only flies at a hundred and fifteen miles per hour and we're only going to be a couple hundred feet up."

"So how far in miles?"

"About thirty-five," he tells me. "Flying is the only way to get there."

I close my eyes, letting the sound of the engines and the chattering of the children lull me. I must fall asleep because I don't open them again until we land on the surface of a crystal-clear blue lake surrounded by pine trees. It's like arriving in heaven.

"Holy crow!" Liam shouts. "I've never seen anything so cool. Can we swim here?"

"Of course," Wyatt tells him. "We can take the rowboat out too and go fishing."

"Are there more bears up here than down at the lodge?" I interrupt.

"For sure!" Ash says. "We're totally in the middle of nowhere up here. There's no running water or toilets or anything!" He sounds super jazzed about this, which is a sentiment that neither Lily nor I share.

"No toilets?" Lily gasps. "Where are we supposed to, you know, go potty?"

"We dig holes and do our business. Then we cover it up," Wyatt tells her.

"Mommy," my daughter whispers. "I want to go back." Her eyes are brimming with tears.

"Wyatt's just teasing," Digger says. "There's an outhouse."

Still not great, but *much* better than an individually dug hole in the ground.

As we pull up to the dock, Digger jumps out to tie up the plane. Then he leans his head into the back seat and says, "Princess Lily, your own personal ride awaits you."

She gets out and lets him put her up on his shoulders before nervously saying, "If I don't like it, will you take me back?"

"Not like it?" he exclaims. "That's not possible. This is the most beautiful place on Earth. You'll never see another place like it." He instructs the boys, "Grab whatever you can carry. You'll have to come back to get the rest."

The boys and I pick up backpacks and coolers before following Digger up a narrow path through the woods. I have never been in such a remote place in my whole life, and that includes the time I hiked to Machu Picchu in Peru. While it was certainly isolated there, we were surrounded by other tour groups doing the same thing we were. Out here, we're totally alone.

Once we reach what I suspect is the cabin, my stomach drops. It's nothing like the one we're staying in down by

Whistler Lake. That's more of a rustic house, while this is a shack.

"Um, by any chance, is that the outhouse?" I ask.

"Ahahaha." Wyatt laughs. "That's the cabin! Isn't it cool?"

"The coolest," I say, doing my best to sound positive. It is not in the least bit cool, but I don't want to spoil my son's enthusiasm *or* feed my daughter's trepidation.

"Mooooooommy." Lily runs to me once Digger puts her down. "I don't want to be here. It's not very nice."

Crouching, Digger says, "Lily, my nephews over there are assuming you and your mom will hate it here just because you're city girls. They think you're a couple of delicate flowers who need to live in the lap of luxury. But I think they're wrong. I think you're tough-as-nails and are just as capable of roughing it as anyone else on earth. What do you say? Do you want to prove them wrong?"

Her expression vacillates from "heck no," to "maybe." She ultimately gets a very determined look on her face and gives Digger a firm nod. "Yes, I do."

"Good stuff," he says, offering her a fist bump. "Now, do you want to help me fish for our supper?"

"I want to help!" comes the chorus of young boy voices.

Lily holds up one hand to them. "I got it, boys."

Digger stands up and tucks his lips between his teeth, clearly trying not to laugh. "We should let them come too, though. You know, so they won't feel left out."

"Okay," she says with a shrug.

She gives him the "come closer" gesture with her index finger and when he leans down, she whispers, "I don't have to touch worms, do I?"

"Nah, I'll take care of that for you this time," Digger tells her. "Now, why don't you go check out your castle for the night and I'll bring up another load of stuff from the plane."

He turns back in the direction of the lake and calls over his shoulder, "It's not locked, so you can go right in."

Of course it's not locked. Nobody would willingly want to go in there.

I walk into the two-room cabin and it's all I can do not to burst into tears. It's horrible. There are cobwebs everywhere, and a nest in the corner that could be home to God knows what. It's got one lonely kitchen cabinet, a sink without any taps, a small wooden table with four chairs, and an ancient puke-green colored loveseat that I could never imagine sitting on. It's totally filthy. I'm still standing frozen in place when Digger comes back, his arms loaded with gear.

"Through that door is the bedroom," Digger tells me. "You and Lily can have that, and the boys and I will sleep outside."

I offer him a smile that I'm sure would earn me a Razzie (on account of being so unconvincing). "Super."

Lily tugs on my hand. "It's okay, Mom. We're tough." I walk over to the door and open it. The small room has two double beds pressed up against each wall. They've been stripped down to the mattresses. Digger's voice comes from over my shoulder, "I've got the bedding in the plane, so it'll be fresh. I'll send Wyatt to go get it for you."

"Thanks." I turn around and find him standing closer than I thought he was. The nearness surprises me. He's an imposing figure up close. Handsome, too, if I cared about that sort of thing. Which I don't. Men are the very last thing on my mind and honestly, they may never cross it again.

His eyes flick down to my lips, then he seems to catch himself because his cheeks turn a little red. He clears his throat. "Are you up for some fishing?"

"I think I'm going to stay here for now and try to … spruce the place up a bit."

As we leave the bedroom, he says, "There are some

cleaning products under the kitchen sink. The well is out back if you run out of water in the tank."

"And how does one use the sink?" I ask. "What with the lack of taps and all …"

He points to a large water cooler on the counter. "There's a kettle in the cupboard. I'll set up a camp stove outside if you need to heat it up."

"Ah, okay," I answer, trying not to sound horrified.

"All right, kids, should we go catch some fish?" he asks.

As Digger and the kids disappear down the path, I'm surrounded by silence. I take a deep breath, trying to figure out what to address first. I decide on the nest and the cobwebs. There's a broom leaning against the wall, so I start sweeping. By the time I'm done sweeping, scrubbing, and making the beds, the place seems slightly less wretched. Not good, but at least I don't want to cry.

While this is not home-sweet-home, it's going to have to do the trick. At least until the vultures give up.

Chapter 16

Digger

Five kids is a lot of kids. Especially when you're letting them fish. I rush from one to the other, detangling fishing lines, reminding them not to stand too close to each other, and re-baiting their hooks when they lose their worms. After a couple of hours, Harper shows up on the dock. I'm glad to see her as I'm going to need some help herding the cats.

She's carrying a small cooler that I hope contains at least one beer. With her free hand, she offers a small wave. She looks amused while taking in the scene before her—which can only be described as marginally-managed chaos. "How's it going?"

"It's a little hectic," I tell her, doing my best not to notice how good she looks in her tank top and shorts. She could make a career out of her legs alone.

"Who's thirsty?" Harper asks, causing all five kids to drop their lines and go running.

She chuckles as she sets down the cooler and starts

handing out bottles of soda. Then she pulls out a couple of Bud Lights. She tosses me one. "You look like you could use this."

"Thanks," I tell her, cracking the tab. "Did you manage to make the cabin feel homier?"

She opens her can and holds it up. "Let's just say I earned this." After a long sip, she says, "Tell me about the whole bear situation up here. We're talking grizzlies, yes?"

I nod. "But don't worry, the kids make enough of a racket to keep them far away from here."

She doesn't look convinced. "How about when a person's alone? Like, say, just now when I walked through the brush by myself?"

"I've been coming here since I was a little kid and the only grizzlies I've ever seen have been running the other way." I add, "There's no dump nearby, and we don't leave food in the cabin or around the campsite, so they haven't learned to use humans as a food source. At night, we lock everything up in the plastic tubs to keep the smell in."

She doesn't look convinced, so I add, "But if you're worried, just make a lot of noise, like whistling or singing, or …" *Don't say it, moron.* "Stick close to me."

Dammit, Digger, you said it anyway.

Harper's eyes search mine. I can tell she's trying to decide whether she can trust me or not. Which apparently makes me chatty. "Look, I'm a lot of things, but a liar isn't one of them. And I certainly have no reason to lie to you about this. Knowledge is power, right?"

Her face relaxes a bit as she nods. "I guess I'm just trying to get my bearings." Then she laughs. "Pun intended."

It sounds like she's talking about more than just being out in the wild. If I had to guess, I'd say she's thinking about what her life will be like as a single mom.

The two of us stand side-by-side staring out at the lake

and watching the kids goof around. They're splashing each other and telling fart jokes—which, as I recall, is one of the best parts of childhood.

After a few moments of a comfortable silence, I glance down at her. "You okay?"

"It's just hard to accept that this"—she opens her hands to spokesmodel the wildness—"is what it takes to protect my kids. How did this become my life?" She shakes her head while turning her gaze back out to the lake.

I know her question is rhetorical, so I don't bother answering it. Instead, I have a sip of my beer and give her space to talk.

She watches as Wyatt shows Lily and Liam how to skip rocks. "It's too much. Waking up to some asshole in a tree taking pictures of them in their own house, then overhearing gossip about their dad's extramarital love life …" Looking up at me, she adds, "I know it's doing damage. I just pray it's fixable."

I stare into her blue eyes. "Kids are resilient. Better than us adults." I'm speaking from experience here. "The important thing is that they've got you. At the end of the day, all they really need is one solid parent who cares enough to put them first."

"I hope so," she says with a deep sigh.

"I know so." My mind wanders back to the faded memories I have of my own mother. Even before she left, she was never there for us. Not in the way Moira and I needed her to be. She was only a shell of a person that we couldn't rely on.

"Uncle Digger, can we get back to fishing now?" Ash calls to me from near the shore.

"You bet," I tell him. "You'd better step up your game or we'll be hungry come dinnertime."

~

The sun is still high in the sky as the clock approaches seven, when we're sitting around the campfire, balancing our plates on our laps. Lily managed to catch a good-sized rainbow trout—something she's not likely to let her brother forget anytime soon. I cleaned it, seasoned it, slathered it in butter, and cooked it over the fire in some tin foil. The kids gobble it up, along with some potatoes and carrots.

"This is the *best* rainbow trout I've ever had," Lily announces loudly, proud of her accomplishment.

"It's the only trout you've ever had, you dingus," Liam tells her. While his words are harsh, his tone is playful. It's clear these two love each other.

"Don't call your sister a dingus," Harper says sternly.

"He's just mad because I caught supper and he didn't." Lily is all smiles.

"Am not," Liam says.

"Are too," Lily tells him.

"You know what, Liam? You'll catch one tomorrow," I tell him.

He shrugs "I doubt it. I'm no good at it."

"That's not true, you're just new to it. How about first thing in the morning we all head out on the boat. You're sure to catch something in the middle of the lake."

Liam's eyes light up. "Really?"

"Really," I tell him. "I can help you work on your technique. The trick is in the wrist." I make a flicking motion with my hand.

"I'm not really a morning person," Lily declares. "I think I'll let you men catch tomorrow's supper." I can't help the smile that crosses my face. I'm used to spending time with little boys, but a little girl adds a whole new element to the mix. And it's really nice.

After we finish eating, we work together to get the tent ready for the boys. Once that's done, I show the kids how we wash dishes up here, which is essentially heating a tub of water and throwing the dishes in to sterilize them. They'll be cool in the morning so all we'll need to do is rinse them off and they'll be ready to use again.

Once the kids take a quick sponge bath and are in their jammies, we roast marshmallows to make s'mores until it's time for bed. Of course, we're all sticky again but hey, that's part of the fun of camping out.

By the time the rugrats are all tucked into their sleeping bags, they're so exhausted from the fresh air and sunshine, it doesn't take long for them to drift off.

I watch Harper take Lily into the cabin to put her to bed. I'm torn between wanting her to come out so we can sit by the fire and talk, and wanting her to stay inside, so I can get back to doing what now seems impossible—keeping my distance.

Adding a log to the fire, I open another beer and listen to the sounds of the frogs croaking. An owl hoots in the distance while I remind myself that Harper is not for me. Not that I want anyone. But if I did, it couldn't be her.

I'm not meant for some Hollywood star, especially one who's in the middle of a nasty public divorce. It doesn't matter how badly I want to brush her hair off her cheek and kiss her—how much I want to hold her in my arms. None of that is an option for us.

She's a mom trying to hold it all together for her two kiddos. She's not a tourist looking for some fun. And I am not a man who is about to take advantage of someone so vulnerable.

Chapter 17

Harper

Dear Readers,

I am not a religious man, but I stopped by a Catholic church today and lit a candle for Harper Kennedy.

I just found out from my waiter's dry cleaner's librarian that Harper hopped on a private float plane that took her deeper into the Alaskan outback. These are harrowing times, indeed.

Girl, I have one word for you: bears! Here's another: mosquitos! And while we're on the subject of things that can kill you in the wild ... intestinal worms. Please be careful.

In other news, I've lost five pounds while Brett and "Nanny" continue to flaunt their grossness. Even the double chunk espresso cookies at Marmalade can't entice my taste buds.

I'm contacting my attorney today to see if I have a case for suing Mr. Helio-trash for a new/smaller wardrobe.

Stay tuned ...

Dish,
Ferris Biltmore

~

My friends and I occasionally slept outside in a tent when we were young, but we always wound up inside before the sun came up. This history of mine with the wilderness—yes, I'm including my backyard as the wilderness—makes it particularly surprising that I slept so well out here in the middle of nowhere.

I hurry to the outhouse, carrying a broom to swat any bugs who get in my way. When I come out, I see Digger putting a kettle of water on the fire for coffee. "Are the boys still sleeping?" I ask.

"They get so worn out up here, they always sleep in." He adds, "Unless I wake them up at the butt crack of dawn to go fishing. Which I will probably do tomorrow."

I sit a respectable distance from him. "I can't thank you enough for all you've done for us," I tell him. "I hate being in people's debt, so honestly, if there's anything I can ever do to repay you, just let me know."

"It's no hardship coming up here," he says gently. "I'd live up here if I could, but unfortunately, I'm needed nearly around the clock at the lodge."

"Can I send a text from up here?" We left in such a hurry

that I forgot to let Prisha know that I would be out of reach for a few days.

"One of things I love about being up here is no cell service."

"I can see how that might be a plus. The outhouse, not so much."

He chuckles. "Even *I* don't love the outhouse."

"Have you been coming up here since you were little?"

"My dad built this cabin after ..."

"After what?"

He glances over to me, not waiting long enough to make any discernible eye contact before looking away. "My mother left when my sister and I were young."

"Oh, I'm sorry. I can only imagine how hard that would be on a child. Does your dad still live in Gamble?"

Shaking his head, he says, "He died five years ago."

"And your mom?"

"She died when I was seventeen." I didn't see that coming. Not that it's any of my business, but I want to know, "Did she ever come back?"

He shakes his head. "Nope. We never saw her again."

"That's horrible, what happened?" Again, none of my business, but inexplicably I want to know more about this man.

"She had dreams of becoming an actress, so she moved to La La Land."

"Without you?" I know people do crazy things in hopes of making it big in Hollywood, but leaving a family? "I'm so sorry."

"Don't feel too bad for us. Our dad and grandparents did everything they could to make her disappearance more palatable."

"I can't imagine not seeing my kids again." The thought makes my blood practically turn to ice. "For me, the worst part of getting a divorce is that I won't have full custody of my kids." Talk about oversharing. I don't know why, but I don't want Digger lumping me in with the likes of his mother. Tears prick my eyes, but I blink them back. "I'm going to miss out on half of everything."

His eyebrows knit together. "Divorce is hard on everyone. Especially the kids."

"I don't think anyone gets married thinking that it won't last. At least I didn't."

"The odds aren't exactly in favor of things working out—and I may be wrong, but I've heard they're even worse in Hollywood."

I stare at him for a second, feeling anger bubble in my chest. Is he judging me? I don't need to be judged. Not by some bachelor. "So, from your esteemed position of knowing exactly nothing about my life, you think I should have never gotten married because of what I did for a living?"

Digger shrugs. "It didn't exactly turn out, did it? And now you've got two little people paying the price."

The tears are back, but this time they're hot to the touch as I wipe them away. "How dare you? I'm not the one who couldn't keep my pants on," I grind out. "*I'm* the one who was constantly looking the other way, believing Brett's lies that his current infidelity was the last. I tried damn hard to make it work for the sake of my children." Fury courses through my veins and it's all I can do to keep my voice down so I don't wake the boys.

"I'm sorry, I didn't mean to—"

"To what? Act like some Monday-morning quarterback who knows everything?" I spit out, standing up. "Because that's exactly what you did, and none of those things were accidents!"

With that, I turn and storm off. I wind up sitting on the dock, watching a pair of loons swim past with their babies in tow. What should be a peaceful sight makes me feel more alone, more torn up inside. I want what those birds have—a true partner in raising a family. Someone who will help share the burdens and joys of life, alike. But that has never been Brett. Not even for a day.

After a few minutes, I feel the dock dip a little. I'm guessing it's Digger coming to apologize but I don't bother to look up. I'm still mad.

He clears his throat. "Mind if I sit with you for a minute?"

I look over my shoulder and glare at him. "It's your dock."

He plunks himself down next to me, leaving a space between us. "Harper, I'm really sorry about what I said. You're right. I don't know anything about your life or your marriage. Or *any* marriage for that matter. I've always known I'd never get married and have kids. If you don't have any, you don't have to worry about messing them up."

Yikes. His mother really did a job on him. "No one sets out to mess their kids up."

"I suppose that's true too. Unfortunately, it happens a lot. Selfish people don't care what kind of trouble they leave behind," he growls. He runs a hand through his hair, then sighs. "Look, I'm not saying you're like my mom, because you're not. In the short time I've known you, I can see that you put your kids first, which is how it should be. I'm sorry for what you're going through. All three of you. And I'm sorry for being so hard on you just now."

"It's fine," I tell him. After all, he's not the person I'm truly mad at. I'm obviously pissed at Brett, but deep down, I'm also angry at myself for trusting him so implicitly.

"Your being an actress has probably brought up some negative feelings in me. My mom valued fame over family, and I suppose I painted everyone in Hollywood with the same brush." In case I couldn't figure that out, he clarifies, "You know, a bunch of self-centered dreamers who don't know when to give up the ghost."

"That's us," I say bitterly. Before he can respond, I add, "So you've never been to LA?"

He exhales loudly. "I was planning to go when I turned eighteen. You know, road trip all the way from Alaska to California. Go find my mom and give her a piece of my mind. I wanted her to know how badly she'd hurt Moira, because there's no way I would have admitted she hurt me too. But she died before I could."

I automatically reach out to put my hand on his arm. "You didn't even get a resolution. That's tough." What Digger must have suffered as a child makes my heart ache. Death is hard enough, but to be abandoned without any chance of healing is unfathomable.

"She got into drugs and was found in an alley with a needle still in her arm. I'm guessing that wasn't the life she was hoping for." He grunts bitterly.

"It's a tough town," I tell him. "Not only are good roles hard to come by, but rejection is awful. Even if you make it big, it can be hard."

"Did you grow up in California?" He picks up a stone from a pile on the dock and inspects it before skipping it across the water.

"Central Illinois. The land of corn and beans."

"How'd you wind up in LA?"

"I was in the theater department at the University of Illinois. Occasionally a group of us would drive up to Chicago for open castings. Most of them never resulted in anything, but I got a commercial for Visa once. I made enough money from it that I decided to head to Hollywood after graduation and try my hand at the big time." I shake my fists in the air like a reticent cheerleader.

"It obviously worked out well for you." He sounds like he's accusing me of robbing a bank or something.

"I waited tables for five years before I got my big break."

"Why did you keep trying for so long? You'd think a year or two would be long enough to realize it's not going to happen."

Anger begins to boil, but I quickly remind myself of Digger's experience with Hollywood dreams. "Success is a drug unto itself. If you get enough small doses, you become convinced your big break is right around the corner. I had a few bit parts on television shows and movies. It was enough to keep me on the line. Plus, I *did* hit it big, so it does happen sometimes."

"Do you still act?"

"I haven't done much of anything since the kids were born. I grew up with a stay-at-home mom and I wanted Liam and Lily to have the same experience. Brett kept going though."

"Ah, Helioman."

"Yup. Brett Kennedy, superstar, lover of the limelight, women, and mostly himself."

"Sounds like a real prize," he says sarcastically.

"I once thought so." *What in the hell was wrong with me?*

"Are you going to stay in Los Angeles after you're divorced?" he asks.

His question hits me like a blow to the back of the head. "I never thought about leaving LA. I mean, I wouldn't want to keep the kids away from their father. Besides, I haven't really thought farther than next week, to be honest."

"Survival mode," he says.

"Exactly. I have to find my center again, before I figure out what comes next."

"I'm sure you will," Digger tells me, getting up. "You relax. I'll go get breakfast started."

"Thanks." I stare back out at the water while the dock bobs under his footsteps.

Should I go back to Illinois and raise Lily and Liam near my parents? As much as they would all benefit from that, I'm not a person who relishes the thought of going backward. Unfortunately, moving home would feel like that to me. Also, there would be zero chance of me having a normal life in the town I grew up in. I would be a big fish in a small pond which guarantees eyes would watch my every move and tongues would wag to share every detail.

All I can do is take things one hour at a time. Luckily, I'm in a place where I can do just that. Here in Alaska, I've discovered a sense of peace—if you don't count the paparazzi finding me, that is. For now, I'm just going to relish being away from all the drama of Brett. Hopefully, by the time we go back to the lodge, the press will have given up on me, and we can enjoy the rest of our vacation without worry of being found out.

I inhale deeply. The air is crisp and clean, the view unparalleled. If there ever was a place to heal, I'm starting to think that place is Alaska.

As far as I'm concerned, Brett can say or do anything that he wants. He's no longer my problem. And while that makes me feel bad for Liam and Lily, it's a hundred-and-eighty pounds of weight I'm glad to be rid of.

Chapter 18

Digger

I hope Harper knows my apology was sincere. I couldn't have acted more like a jerk this morning. Even though I wasn't talking about her when I said those things about Hollywood, I should have kept my mouth shut. Clearly, I'm not over my mom's desertion. I'm not sure I ever will be.

We fall into an easy rhythm today, creating fun for the kids and distraction for all. It's such a hot day, we've basically spent it lounging on towels by the lake and playing around in the water. I do my best not to notice how Harper looks in that bikini of hers—it's not super skimpy, but it still shows off enough to up the temperature an extra ten degrees.

I can't be sure, but I may have caught her giving me the once over when she thought I wasn't looking. Not to sound conceited, but the look on her face seemed to suggest she's not oblivious to me, either.

Currently, she's reading while I pretend to doze. The kids are playing cards on a picnic blanket in the shade. The whole scene feels very domestic, which makes it strange that I'm enjoying it so much. The sun goes behind a cloud and the air grows a little chillier, so I open my eyes and sit up. I grab a t-shirt and pull it over my head.

Harper yawns next to me. She looks incredibly relaxed. "What time do you think it is?"

"I'm guessing late afternoon. You hungry?"

"Not yet, but the kids probably are, so we might want to start dinner." She adjusts the big, floppy hat she's wearing.

"Good point. I'll check in with the lodge to see if we're in the clear to head back. If so, we could always eat there." Having said that, I hope she'll want to stay here a little while longer.

"Back to the real world," she says with a sigh. "Yay."

"We don't have to go yet, you know, if being here is what you need."

"Unfortunately, it's just not about me. I need to check in with my publicist. Also, I'm sure Moira's missing the boys by now."

We look back at the kids, only to see the twins wrestling. After a second, I say, "I think Moira would be okay for another month or two."

Harper and I share a laugh, then she shakes her head at them. "She's got her hands full, for sure."

"Tell you what, I'll go call the lodge. If the reporters are gone, we'll head back. If not, we can stay for another night."

"Sounds like a plan."

I slide on my flip-flops, then walk over to the plane and get in. Picking up the radio receiver, I push the button. "Whistler Eagle to Whistler Lodge. Come in, Lodge."

"Lodge here," Evie says. "How's it going in the wilderness? Does it resemble *Lord of the Flies* yet?"

"Not yet, but I'm sure it's only a matter of time," I tell her. "What's happening there? Any unfriendlies?"

"What is this? A war?" she asks.

"Sort of."

"Well, there's good news and weird news."

"Okay …"

"The good news is the reporters are gone. Grandpa Jack managed to bore them into leaving town with all of his stories." She adds, "Plus, he was all, 'Harper who? Never heard of her. Is she some kind of astronaut?' It was really funny."

"Nice work." And while I'm glad the reporters are gone, I still don't want to go back yet. "What's the weird news?" I look back at the beach and watch Harper stretch out on the blanket. Her hat is over her face now, which makes me smile. She looks like she's exactly where she's meant to be.

"Brett Kennedy showed up an hour ago, looking for his family."

That's not what I was expecting to hear. That news feels like a punch to the gut, even though I have no idea why it should. It takes me so long to think of a response, Evie says, "Are you still there?"

"Yup. Just … got a little distracted for a second. You didn't give him a room, did you?"

"He's rented out the McLoughlin's cabin." The only luxury Airbnb in town.

"Of course he did. What does he want?"

"I think he might really want his wife back. He came in all moony and sad, and said how much he was missing his family. I don't think he realizes that we get news up here."

"What did you tell him?"

"That Harper took the kids up the bush for a few days and there's no way to get a hold of her."

"Good job," I say, rubbing the stubble on my chin.

"Are you guys coming back tonight?" Evie asks.

That's the million-dollar question, isn't it? I stare out at

Harper, wondering what to do. She has the right to know her husband is here looking for her. But I'm not sure seeing him is what's best for her. Brett Kennedy is a lying, cheating sack of weeds who deserves to be dropped in the lake wearing a pair of cement shoes.

Plus, Harper didn't exactly sound enthusiastic about going back to "the real world." Maybe another couple of days of being completely disconnected is exactly what she needs right now. Yet, I have a feeling that, if given the choice, she'd insist on going back so her kids can see their dad.

"Boss? Should we cook extra food for supper or what?"

My heart pounds as I answer her, praying I'm making the right choice. "We'll stay here for another night. Harper's not ready to come back just yet. Neither are the kids."

"Okay," she answers. "Have fun. Don't get eaten by any wild animals."

"We'll try not to. Good night, Evie."

"Over and out."

I put the receiver back and sit frozen in place with my hand still on it. Why am I involving myself in Harper's life like this? All I know is that my gut is telling me that this is the right thing to do. The last thing she needs is to let her ex swoop in and confuse her.

She needs to get her head on straight first. She needs to figure out what the best thing is, not just for the kids, but for her too. If I take her back to him right now, I have a terrible feeling she'll let him convince her to give him yet another chance.

Chapter 19

Harper

Dear Readers,

I'm a nervous wreck as I wait for news of Harper's safe return from whence she's hiding. I'm barely sleeping because I can't get that show *Wild Men* out of my mind. Who knows what kind of ruffians our fair maiden may encounter while she's off-grid? I tremble at the thought. I've spent the night outdoors twice myself and both times I nearly met my end. The good news is that I got great seats for both concerts, so ...

In other hot goss, Brett has evacuated from Hawaii *without* the Nanny-goat in tow. Could he be on his way home to beg for forgiveness? Does he even know that his wife isn't there anymore?

My world is shifting on its axis as I await closure. The good news is, I managed to keep down a short stack of pancakes this morning so I should be filling out my clothes again soon.

Dish,
Ferris Biltmore

~

This has been the most perfect day I can remember having, which is not something I ever thought I would say regarding a place where the only bathroom is an outhouse. When Digger comes back from the plane, he announces, "Looks like we're up here for another night, at least."

Relief washes over me as I stretch out my limbs. "So, who's cooking supper tonight?"

"The boys finally caught some fish." He points to a plastic bucket farther down the pier. "How about I do the grilling and you make the salad?"

I nod my head. "We still have cookies left over. We can have those for dessert."

"Hey, Uncle Digger," Wyatt calls out. "If we're staying, we should go up to the falls tomorrow. I bet Liam and Lily have never seen anything like it!"

"What falls?" I ask.

"Copper Creek Falls. It's about a two-hour hike up the mountain. Wyatt is right when he says you've never seen anything like it. It's really amazing."

"Two hours farther up the mountain and away from civilization? Can we fly there?"

"No place to land. We'd have to do it on foot."

I can see the headline now:

Harper Kennedy and Children Slip Off Deadly Falls in the Alaskan Outback

My brain continues to spin as I imagine Brett and the nanny showing up to the funeral all teary eyed and feigning heartbreak. I'm sure their sadness would be real for the loss of the kids, but for me—inner backflips. Maybe a few high fives and fist bumps.

Brett would win the hearts of the world by giving a class-A performance. Maybe he'd read some Bible verse and sob his way through it; he might recall the births of our children—pretending he was there instead of on location during Liam's birth, and in his girlfriend's bed when Lily made her entrance into this world.

The nanny, as I now refuse to dignify her by using her name, would talk about how she was the one who really raised the kids. She'd whisper that I was too busy shopping on Rodeo Drive, lunching with friends, and having five-hour massages at Burke Williams. *I haven't had a massage in over a year.*

"I'm not sure I think that's a good idea," I finally manage to say. "The kids and I aren't really in shape for such a long hike."

"You look like you're in fine shape to me." Digger stares into my eyes before letting his gaze slide down the rest of my body. *Dear God.*

"Come on, Mom," Liam shouts. "We can't miss an opportunity like this!"

"Yeah, Mommy. We gotta go," Lily adds.

"That's a four-hour hike for you, little miss," I tell my daughter. "I don't think you're up for that."

"Digger will carry me, wontcha, Digger?"

He bows to her. "I'm at your disposal m'lady." She giggles in response.

"Is it safe?" I want to know.

"We've been up there at least a dozen times," Colton answers. "The worst thing that ever happened was that Ash tripped on a log and fell into a tree. He cut his head open, but Uncle Digger patched him up and we kept going."

Yeah, that story doesn't instill much confidence. "What about bears?" I've spent my whole life never thinking about bears, and here in Alaska it's almost all I think about.

"Harper, there are bears in Alaska. It's just a fact. But I know how to keep us safe," Digger insists. "Come on, let your kids have this experience. I promise you won't regret it."

After releasing the most dramatic sigh in the history of sighs, I manage, "Fine. But at any point, if I want to go back, we go back."

The kids jump up and down and shout their excitement. I will be the worst villain of all time if I don't let them go all the way. I'd make Cruella de Vil look like a candidate for PETA volunteer of the year.

Grabbing my bag, I stuff my beach towel and book inside, then I pick up the now-empty collapsible cooler. "I'm going back to the cabin to make a salad."

Lily runs up and slips a hand through mine. "I'm glad we're here, Mommy. Digger and the boys are the coolest, aren't they?" My daughter is a social beast, but even so, it normally takes her longer to get so excited about new people.

"Yeah, they're pretty neat." The truth is, they're unlike the other people of our acquaintance. I can see how that might make them glamorous in the eyes of a four-year-old. "I'm glad you're having a good time." I give her hand a squeeze.

"It's a good thing Daddy's not here. He would hate it," she says. "I mean, I miss him like crazy, but he would be a total Grumpy Gus if he couldn't have his cell phone. Good thing he's in Hawaii, right? I bet he's a lot happier there."

My chest tightens. "Yeah, good thing." I hate that our family is breaking up. The kids are so young, they deserve to have the innocence of childhood last longer. Damn Brett's inability to remain faithful—barring that, at least discreet. But he couldn't even manage *that.* I will do almost anything for my children, but how good of a mother could I be if I'm miserable? If I let myself be played for a fool? They deserve a better role model than that.

But then I think about what Digger said earlier, about people being selfish and their kids paying the price. Am I being too selfish? Does my happiness really matter if my kids have both parents at home? Although, if Brett were here right now, I'd want to slather him in peanut butter and leave *him* out for the bears. I'm guessing that's a sign our marriage really does need to end.

The boys join us shortly after we get back to the cabin. We eat supper in record time because Digger laid down the law—if we're hiking tomorrow, we're going to bed early so we can make the most of the day. After tucking the kids in, I make a quick pit stop in the outhouse before falling asleep myself. I'm out the second my head hits the pillow.

Nothing in this world could have prepared me for the loud clanging that jolts me out of bed. What in the hell is that? My brain is so foggy from sleep, I'm not even sure where I am. Lily, on the other hand, jumps out of bed and cheers, "Yay, we're going to the falls!"

I lie still for another minute until all the pieces of the puzzle fall into place. We're in Alaska, someone is clearly banging a metal spoon on a pan, and we're hiking to God-knows-where to see waterfalls today. I flip my pillow over and let the coolness help encourage consciousness.

Lily runs outside and shouts, "I'm ready!"

I'm only a few steps behind her. As soon as I leave the cabin, I'm greeted by the smell of bacon and fresh coffee.

"Are you going to wear your pajamas, or would you like to get dressed first?" Digger asks her from his position in front of the camp stove.

"I suppose I could get dressed." My daughter runs past me and goes back into the cabin. The boys are already sidling up to various trees to take care of their morning business.

Digger offers me a smile that makes my stomach flutter a bit. He hands me a plate full of bacon, eggs, and pancakes. "Good morning."

"Morning. You must have been up at the crack of dawn to make all this," I tell him. "Well, metaphorically speaking, since the sun doesn't set around here."

"I figured I'd better make sure we're all well-fed. Nothing makes kids hate hiking more than being hungry."

I take a seat on a log, and as soon as I start eating, Digger walks over and places a mug of coffee on the ground next to me. With my mouth full of fluffy, sweet pancakes, I say, "Thank you."

"You're welcome."

"Maybe I can help make lunch to take with us," I say, picking up my coffee and having a sip.

"Already packed. Protein bars, apples, rice cakes and peanut butter." He opens his backpack for me to look inside.

"I'll pack the toilet paper," I tell him.

"Why?"

"Why do you think?"

"There are plenty of leaves on the trail if you need them."

Eww. "And yet, I'm going to bring toilet paper anyway." The kids and I make short work of breakfast, then we stick the dishes in the tub, and I quickly gather my own bunch of supplies. I throw in my traveling first aid kit, a roll of toilet paper, six chocolate bars, and a ball of yarn—I have this vision of us needing to fashion a rope bridge.

As Lily and I walk out of the cabin, I see Digger handing out small packages to the boys. He walks over to us and does the same. "Life straws. This way we won't have to carry a lot of water and can just drink from the falls."

"I think I'll carry my water."

"The life straws filter out any impurities," he tells me. "But you don't even need them. The water up here is some of the purest on the planet."

I take the straws out of his hands and put them in my backpack without comment. I can't tell if he's purposefully trying to make me feel like a prima donna or not, but either way, he's succeeding and that is not a picture I like to have of myself.

It turns out the hike is positively breathtaking. We take a path through a field of tall grasses, then make our way through a forest of pines, birch, and poplars, which successfully provide cool air and shade as we walk along. The kids veer off the path more than they're on it, jumping on fallen logs and climbing trees as we go.

Digger keeps a careful eye on them, but he stays at my side. Something about this feels so easy, so right. I don't have to pretend to be someone I'm not with him, and I know I don't have to worry about impressing him. I can just be me, which is a feeling I'm not used to. In Hollywood, you always have to pretend to be something you aren't.

"You're quiet," he says.

"I was just thinking how nice it is to be here. To be around you, actually." I glance up at his eyes and notice for the first time how green they are.

"Really?" he asks, looking surprised.

Nodding, I say, "I spend most of my life trying to be the perfect mom, the perfect wife, the perfectly agreeable actress on set. I live in a state of fear that I'll say the wrong thing and offend someone, and it'll end up in some gossip column. But with you, I don't have to do that."

He stares down at me, the hard features of his face softening. "You're safe with me, Harper."

"I know." I don't tell him how badly I need to be with someone who doesn't want something from me. He already hates the world I come from. "Digger McKenzie, you are a breath of fresh air."

His face flushes slightly as he lets out a laugh. "That's one thing I've never been called before."

"Well, it's true. You're honest. Sometimes a little too honest, but I appreciate that about you. Most people just tell me what they think I want to hear."

He gets a strange look for a second and I don't know how to read it. "I'm not one to coddle people. Especially not capable adults." Glancing up ahead, he calls to the kids, "Get back on the path, you guys. There's a swamp coming up that you won't see until you're in it."

I'm hardly aware that two hours have passed. When I hear the boys' shouts of excitement, I know we're just around the corner from our destination.

When we reach the base of Copper Creek Falls, I feel like we've just strolled into the Garden of Eden. The woods open up to the base of a small mountain with a waterfall rushing down into a crystal-clear swimming hole. The trees surrounding it offer a cool shade, but the center of the water is the focus of a golden ray of sunshine that beats down like a heavenly sign. The falls pour right into the center, and it's all I can do not to run so I can stand right under them.

As though reading my mind, Digger smiles at me. "Worth the trip?"

"Definitely," I answer, inhaling the scent of the fresh mountain air.

"Kids, do you want to eat lunch now or swim?" he asks.

The unanimous decision is swimming.

I find a large rock close to the swimming hole and strip down to my bikini. Then I wade out until I'm only a few feet from the falls. Pure joy builds inside of me, and I release a laugh of delight as I feel the cool water pour down on me. It's as though it's washing away all of my worries.

I don't know how long I'm there, but when I finally look up, I see that Digger has taken off his clothes too. In his swim trunks, he wades out with the kids surrounding him. Lily is in his arms as he somehow manages to keep an eye on the other four children. My mind wanders through all the little moments he's had with my kids and his nephews—how patient he is when he teaches them something new, how playful he can be, and how his eyes light up when they call his name. This is what a real dad is like. He's in the moment with the people he cares about. Not a million miles away accepting an award or tapping away on his phone to his agent. My heart squeezes as I watch him and I can't help but think how sad it is that he doesn't want to be a father. He would make a wonderful one. A sexy one, too.

Where did that come from?

The goosebumps that pop up on my skin have nothing to do with the temperature of the water. I should not be thinking about this man in such a way, but even as I admonish myself, I swear I feel an egg drop. Shaking my head harshly, I force that image out of my mind.

I'm already married, but to a man who never should have had kids. I need to divorce Brett before I can even *think* about having another relationship. Not that I really want one. I'm not about to be taken for a fool again.

Digger walks back to the shore and puts Lily down. She waves at me with one hand as she picks up an apple with the other. Then she sits on a rock to eat it. I'm so focused on her that I don't realize Digger is coming toward me until he's practically on top of me.

I let out a squeak of surprise which causes him to chuckle. "You seem to be having a good time." His voice is warm and thick like maple syrup. A tingle shoots from the base of my neck all the way down to more interesting places. It's been so long since I've felt anything remotely like desire, the sensation almost buckles my knees.

"It's beautiful here." My voice is breathy and full of longing as I look fixedly up at him.

Digger glances behind him to check on the kids and then he takes a step closer to me. My whole body feels like an open nerve ending. Reaching out, he takes my elbows in his hands and pulls me closer. "I'm glad you decided to come up here with us."

Releasing a sound like I've just eaten a baguette fresh out of the oven, I swallow hard as the heat rises between our nearly-nude bodies. "Mmmmm … me too."

Digger stares into my eyes and moves even closer. "Harper …"

I haven't made love to anyone in five years. Not since the night Lily was conceived. Five freaking years in the prime of my life! Good lord, I'm about to climb this man like a tree.

"Yes, Digger?" I lean in closer, lifting my chin so I'm at the perfect angle for him to kiss me.

His eyes flick down to my lips, but he doesn't kiss me. Instead, he reaches up and touches my hair. "Don't panic."

"I won't," I whisper. "I mean it's been a while, but I promise I won't panic. In fact, I'll probably enjoy it. Very much."

He narrows his eyes at me for a second, then says, "You had a stonefly in your hair."

"What?!"

"It's gone now." His mouth quirks up in amusement. "But what were you talking about?"

"Nothing," I say, clearing my throat. I'm aflame with humiliation. I cannot believe I thought he was going to kiss me. And I was about to let him. "The … stonefly, obviously. Why? Did you think I thought you were going to kiss me or something?"

He grins down playfully at me. "It kind of seemed like it."

"Dream on, buddy," I scoff.

"So what had been a while then?" he asks, with a skeptical look.

Crap. Why did I say that? "I forget. We should make lunch now. I bet the kids are starving," I tell him, scurrying around Digger as fast as I can.

Climbing out of the water, I wrap myself in a towel. I shouldn't look, but I do. As Digger walks toward me, the muscles in his arms and torso flex in a most delicious way. He runs his hands through his wet hair to get it off his face, then walks over and picks up another towel. He smiles like a cat who just caught a fat mouse. "For the record, I'm really glad you wouldn't have panicked."

Chapter 20

Digger

Well, that was certainly my favorite trip up the mountain. I wore a smirk the entire trek down, and … actually … it's still there. Harper wanted me to kiss her. I would have never thought that a woman like her would be interested in a man like me. I certainly never thought I'd be interested in someone like her. But here we are.

I know she wouldn't want anything serious with all she has going on, but a fling might be the perfect thing to distract her. Not that I have any intention of going down that path. Even though that's normally how I roll, I don't want to do anything that could make Harper's life more difficult than it currently is.

Although, the fact that she's having those types of thoughts might mean she's getting closer to realizing she can do better than some guy who doesn't respect or love her. And if I were able to play some small role in helping her move on with her life, that would be enough for me.

Guilt gnaws away at me as I watch her crouching next to the fire pit, setting up the kindling to make our campfire for the evening. I should have told her that her douchebag husband is at the lodge. But if I'd done that, then we would have never gone up to the falls and that was obviously a journey she needed.

She's chatting easily with Wyatt, who volunteered to help her. She's laughing at something he said, looking completely at ease. To look at her now, you'd never know her entire life is falling apart.

I take a few minutes to go through the food supplies and realize we have enough food for tomorrow's breakfast, but after that, we're going to need to get back to civilization—whether Brett is there or not. I should probably call back to the lodge to see if there are any new developments, but somehow, I can't bring myself to do it. I'd rather not be aware of any more information that I don't plan to share. I just want to enjoy this last evening of peace without the outside world crawling in.

The kids are so worn out, they crawl into their sleeping bags early without any suggestion from me. Once they're asleep, Harper and I sit beside each other at the campfire and sip slightly warm beers. I should have tied the six-pack to the dock and lowered it into the lake like I usually do to keep our beverages cool.

"You're getting really good at keeping the fire going," I tell her as she stokes the burning embers with a long metal poker we keep at the cabin.

"It's sort of addictive, isn't it?" She picks up a small log and tosses it into the flame. "I really appreciate everything you've done for my children and for me, Digger. You've taken great care of all of us, and it means a lot."

"Just doing my job," I tell her.

"I'd say you've gone above and beyond for us." She smiles at me for a second, then her face grows serious.

"What's wrong?" I ask.

"Nothing." She looks stricken before turning her gaze back to the fire.

"There's something on your mind." What's on my mind is the two of us at the swimming hole this morning. If the kids hadn't been there and if she weren't in the middle of a separation, well, let's just say, I would have seen where things might have gone.

"I don't want to ruin anything by saying something you may not want to hear."

What could she possibly want to say? "Go for it. I've got broad shoulders." Having said that, I still take a long pull on my beer to fortify myself.

"It's just … I couldn't help but feel kind of sad today. Watching you with the kids. The way you are with them—patient, fun, firm when you need to be, encouraging …" She trails off, poking at the fire again.

"That made you sad?"

"You would make an incredible dad, Digger. It seems almost like a crime that you're so set against having a family of your own."

"I know it's hard for other people to understand, but I'm happy with my life the way it is. I've got the boys and I'll always look out for them and do what I can to give them the best life possible. It's enough for me." I glance over at her and see an intensity in her eyes that I haven't witnessed before. "It really is enough."

"I'm sure you think it is," she says. "But it's different when you have children of your own. The connection is beyond anything you can ever imagine. It's pure magic, and pure vulnerability. There's no love quite like it."

She turns back to the fire and stares into it like it's a

crystal ball about to divulge its secrets. After several moments, she says, "Brett's a lousy father. He won't put in the time. He just tosses cash and prizes their way instead of being there for them. He doesn't get on the floor and play games with them, he isn't the one who gets up at night with them when they're sick or have nightmares. The kids are like accessories in his life. It's like they're there to make him look good."

She releases a bitter chuckle. "Do you want to know the craziest thing? They love Brett like mad. They don't know what a good dad is, and they absolutely adore any crumb of attention he throws their way."

Turning to her, I say, "They deserve better than that, and so do you. You all deserve a man who wants to protect you, not hurt you. I hope you know that."

Her eyes search mine.

"I mean it, Harper. You're an amazing woman. Just the way you are. Not because of your job or how you look." I lean toward her slightly. "You're thoughtful and caring and the way you look out for your kids, it's … well … it's obvious to anyone who spends more than a few minutes with you that you're a wonderful mother. Your kids are as great as they are because of you. They love their father as much as they do because *you* have made them feel so safe and secure with your love. You're all they really need."

Tears fill her eyes, and she nods. "Thank you," she whispers. "I needed to hear that."

"I'm only speaking the truth. Don't ever forget how incredible you are, Harper." My eyes flick down to her full lips, then back up. "And don't ever let anyone make you feel less than, because you deserve so much more. You deserve the world."

She leans in toward me, lifting her chin a little. "I'll try to keep that in mind."

"Don't try. Do it." My lips hover so near to hers that just the slightest breeze could bring her right to me.

Closing her eyes, she brushes her lips against mine. The feeling of it is perfect, soothing, thrilling, and hypnotic all at the same time. I kiss her back, letting my lips linger on hers for longer than I should before pulling back and resting my forehead on hers. My entire body protests the fact that I'm not kissing her again, but I can't take advantage of someone so recently wounded. I am not that kind of guy.

"We should get some sleep," I whisper.

"Yeah, we should." She leans back, looking embarrassed and utterly dejected.

I lift my hand to her cheek and touch her soft skin with my fingertips. "The fact that I'm not trying for something right now is not a reflection on you in any way."

"That's kind of hard to believe."

"Only a total asshat would try to get you into bed right now, Harper, but believe me, I've thought about it. A lot more than I should have. You're beautiful in every way, and you deserve a true gentleman."

"You are a true gentleman."

Offering her a half grin, I say, "I wish to God that wasn't the case right now."

"When the right woman comes along and manages to change your mind about relationships, she's going to be one lucky girl." With that, she stands up and walks into the cabin.

She might already be here. Which is why I need to get the hell away from her right now.

Chapter 21

Harper

Dear Reader,

My computer is blowing up!

Bennifer is engaged again? It's all so shocking. I mean, seriously, I just dropped two dissolvable melatonin pills into my cup of chamomile tea to help calm down.

It's not like I have anything against the Divine Miss Lo. No sir. She's the bomb-digga-dom. And while I would once have happily supported her marriage to Ben, that was before he married his lovely wife and then left her for, wait for it—the nanny.

Miss Lo's reunion tour with Ben gives me the willies. It's a matter of been there, done that, don't go back. Don't. Go. Back. (I'm talking to you, Miss Harper!)

I don't give a fresh fig what single people do—or who they do—but once you take Beyonce's advice and put a ring on it, remember that it stands for something.

I have to go lie down. My tea is kicking in.

Dish,
Ferris Biltmore

~

As well as I slept the first night up here, that's how badly I slept last night. I tossed and turned and wondered what my life would have been like had I'd met someone like Digger before Brett. Would I have even noticed him enough to see what a prize he is? Probably not, since my whole life back then was about making it big in Hollywood. Being here in Alaska makes me realize how much I despise everything I'd fought so hard to achieve in Tinsel Town.

I love to perform, becoming a variety of people in the various roles I've been cast in, but I *detest* the politics and machinations behind the scenes. With all the egos and insecurities that abound in the movie industry, it's surprising anything of quality is ever made.

When I can't take my restlessness any longer, I get out of bed and walk out of the cabin. I'm the only one up, so I hurry to the outhouse. After opening the door to leave, I'm greeted by none other than a baby grizzly bear.

Holy crap.

The cub looks up at me and tilts his head, sniffing the air while I stand frozen to the spot. You don't have to be an Alaskan to know that where there's a baby, the mama isn't too far behind.

Think, Harper, think! Or you're going to get attacked by a mama bear in about a minute.

I try listening for the sound of branches breaking but my heart is pounding so hard, I can hear it in my ear drums.

Oh, God. What did Digger tell us about bear encounters? My brain freezes. *If I scream, will I draw the mother to me faster, or will it chase both the cub and his mother away?*

Whatever I do could mean life or death for the boys, who are sleeping in the tent not far from where I'm standing. Panic sets in while I gasp for air.

Forcing my breathing to slow, I back up into the outhouse again and stay as still as possible as my mind spins out of control.

Did I shut the door on the cabin tightly enough or could it be pushed open? What if Lily wakes up and decides to come look for me? Please stay asleep, Lily. Please.

I hear rustling noises outside the outhouse, so I know I'm not alone. Then a horrible thought occurs to me. How many bears are out there?

I suddenly hear Digger's lecture in my head. Never shout or yell when confronted by a bear—use soothing and low tones. I can hear myself now, *"Hello, fuzzy friend. Please don't maul me."* Never make eye contact or they'll think you're challenging them. Never run because not only are they faster than you, but if you try to get away, they'll assume you're prey. They can, in fact, run downhill, whereas I could only drop and roll while praying for a speedy demise.

Before I can decide how best to proceed, a sharp jolt knocks into the side of the outhouse. One guess as to what that something is. Grasping onto the toilet seat for dear life, I start an inward prayer, *Dear God, if I'm going to die, please don't let it be gruesome. Please don't let it hurt. Please don't let it be today.*

In the distance, I hear Liam call out, "Mom! Where are you?"

Nononononononono!!! If he comes this way, we're going to have a mama bear face-off and there's no wondering who the winner will be. The outhouse bangs again but from in the opposite direction. *Sweet baby Jesus, I'm going to die on the toilet in the wilds of Alaska!* I briefly wonder who will play me in the movie because you know that's a script that will get green-lighted *fast.*

Sharp knocks start to hit the side of the outhouse. What's happening? Before I can conjure a scenario on my own, all sound and movement suddenly stops. Then there's a soft knocking. "Harper, are you in there?"

Bears can't talk.

It's Digger.

I open the door and fly into his arms. "Oh, my god, I thought I was a goner! What happened?"

He puts his arm around me and lets me lean against him. "Sometimes cubs have minds of their own, and don't know enough to stay away. Adult bears have never messed with us up here."

"What did you do to get them to leave?" I look around wildly like I'm expecting to be attacked at any time.

"I threw a couple of rocks."

"So they're still around?!?" *Of course, they're still around, Harper. It's not like the Enterprise beamed them up.*

"They're here somewhere. I think we should pack up the kids and get back to the lodge before eating breakfast. That way the smell of food won't tempt them to linger."

I have no words. I disengage from Digger's side and move so quickly back toward the cabin, he practically has to run to keep up with me. Liam bursts out of the cabin and throws himself into my arms.

"Are you okay? Digger woke us up and said there was a bear nearby! Then he made us wait in the cabin while he looked for you." He's trying to be brave, but he's choking back tears.

I hold my son tight. "I'm fine. It was only a baby bear. Everything is just fine." He eyes me like he doesn't believe me, but he doesn't say anything. I tell him, "I'm just going to pack up and get Lily."

While I'm throwing all of our belongings into a bag, Digger walks through the front door with the tent and other equipment they keep in the cabin. "Don't wake Lily. I'll carry her down, that way we don't have to scare her."

"Good idea. But what happens if we run into the bears on our way to the plane?"

He opens a bag and hands me a canister. "Bear spray. Here, boys, one for each of you."

The boys all clamor to get one, their eyes wild with excitement. My heart is in my throat. How could this magical place that I've come to love be so dangerous? I'm probably better off in LA where I know the kinds of beasts who want to rip my heart out. Heck, I even married one of them, and I'm going to survive that.

We grab our supplies before Digger picks up a sleeping Lily. We proceed down the path silently as our heads spin back and forth looking for any signs of danger. I barely breathe the whole way.

"That was so cool!" Wyatt shouts once we're in the plane.

The twins and Liam join in with a chorus of, "I can't believe it! And wait until I tell my dad!" The last one is from Liam.

"I don't think your dad needs to hear about this, honey," I tell him.

The last thing I need is for Brett to accuse me of putting my children's lives in danger before I get a custody agreement in place.

"Don't you think he'll be excited?"

"I think it would just make him worry. We all have enough on our plates right now without adding to that."

"I guess." My son sounds disappointed, which I understand. But no good can come from Brett knowing anything about what happened this morning.

Lily snuggles deeper into my arms. She doesn't wake up until we're in the air. "Mommy, where are we?"

"We're on our way back to the lodge," I say, while hugging her tight.

"But it was my turn to flip the pancakes over the fire this morning," she whines.

"You can come down to the lodge some morning this week and help me flip them there," Digger tells her.

"No fair!" the twins yell in unison. The rest of the flight is full of child chatter. Digger and I stay fairly quiet. After we land, the kids are the first to jump onto the dock. Digger turns to me and says, "Harper, there's something I should tell you."

I can feel my pulse pick up. Is he going to talk about our kiss last night? Is he going to declare that he has feelings for me? I'm not ready for either of those things.

"Can we talk later?" I ask, hoping to postpone an uncomfortable scene.

"I think it's better if I—"

"Please, Digger. Let's just go up to the lodge and get breakfast. This morning has been exciting enough, and I need to settle down."

He seems reluctant, but ultimately agrees. "Okay, but as soon as you've eaten."

"Sure."

Little does he know that as soon as we're done eating, I'm going back to our cabin and locking us all in. I might even see if I can change our airline tickets to get the heck out of here. "Should we unpack everything now?" Look at me, trying to change the subject.

"It looks like the boys have their stuff. Just grab your bag and I'll sort everything else out later."

My stomach finally settles and I'm starving by the time we get to the lodge. Moose runs down the path to greet us, clearly looking for Digger, but he puts up with attention from the kids first. They form a petting crowd around him before clambering up to the lodge. Digger and I follow behind. "Thank you for saving me this morning."

"I'm just glad I noticed what was going on."

"I don't even want to think about what might have happened if you hadn't," I tell him as a full body shiver overtakes me.

"It's okay, Harper. You're safe now and so are the kids." He smiles like he's trying to be reassuring. It's not working.

I'm about to tell him that, when I hear my daughter shout out the last thing I ever expected to hear in Alaska.

"Daddy, you came!"

Chapter 22

Digger

I watch the entire scene unfold before my eyes. Brett crouching to hug his kids before standing and picking up Lily. He swings her around while she squeals with delight. Liam waits patiently until he's done before introducing him to my nephews. He's clearly proud of his dad. Harper is frozen in place with a myriad of expressions crossing her beautiful face. Shock, horror, happiness, fear … it's all there.

I feel like I'm in a movie, but none of the other characters can see me.

Colton, Ash, and Wyatt trip over each other to shake Brett's hand and ask him questions. While I barely follow Hollywood news, my sister is a different story. Hence, her boys know what a big deal Brett Kennedy is.

Harper finally looks back at me, her eyes wide, her face beet-red. Guilt slams into me. I should have called ahead to make sure Brett wasn't around. Actually, what I really should have done is tell her that Brett was in Alaska. I should have never let her get ambushed like this.

"Uncle Digger! Come on! You gotta meet Helioman!" Ash yells at me, snapping me out of my thoughts.

Forcing a tight smile, I walk up to him and extend my right hand. He does the same and when we shake, we both lock ourselves in a game of who can grip harder while maintaining a phony smile. I win.

"So, you're the man who stole my family away." He narrows his eyes while keeping his tone light.

"Digger's our good friend," Lily says. "He's a pilot and a cook, he knows how to fish, and fight bears. He's the coolest, Daddy."

Brett's jaw tightens, before smiling down at his little girl. "He sounds almost too good to be true. Maybe I should be worried that he's going to steal my kids away from me …"

"That would never happen. Digger's our friend, but you're our dad." Liam's face looks far too serious for a kid his age.

"You can't steal people, silly Daddy," Lily says, completely oblivious to the undertones of what's going on here.

Harper seems to have finally recovered from the shock of seeing her husband. She gives him a hard look. "Come on, kids, let's go see if breakfast is ready." She starts walking again, pushing everyone forward, while making a wide berth around Brett.

"What? Not even a hello for your husband?" he murmurs as she walks by.

She pauses, then keeps going. "Hello, Brett," she grinds out.

Attagirl.

He follows behind. "So, you've come up to the end of the world for an adventure, have you?"

"More like to escape the mess you left behind," she quietly hisses as the kids disappear up the path. I stay far enough behind them that it doesn't seem like I'm intruding, but I'm close enough to do something if Harper needs me to. You know, like beating the crap out of her loser husband.

"Imagine my surprise when I got back home, only to discover you'd taken off with my children," he snaps at her.

"You left them first. I brought them up here to protect them from finding out the truth of what was going on with you in Hawaii."

His shoulders drop. When he speaks again, he seems like a totally different person. One with a conscience. "You did the right thing."

"Damn straight, I did." She picks up her pace.

"Harper, wait," he says.

Keep going, Harper. Just keep on walking.

But she doesn't. She stops. "What?"

"When I found out you left, it really shook me."

She stares at him, seemingly in disbelief.

He turns to me and glares. "Do you mind? This is a private conversation."

"Then maybe you shouldn't have started it while I was here," I tell him while straightening my back. I must be six inches taller than this guy. I could squash him like a bug.

Tempting …

"Seriously, who *is* this guy?" Brett asks Harper.

"He's our guide," she says, adding, "He's gone above and beyond to sneak us out of town when the paparazzi nearly found us."

"I'll just bet he did," Brett sneers.

"What the hell is that supposed to mean?" Harper demands.

Shrugging, he says, "I just can't help but wonder what happened between you two all alone in the wilderness."

"Oh, for ..." Harper starts, rolling her eyes. "Alone? We had five kids with us. Not that it's any of your business if something did happen."

With that she turns around and storms up to the lodge while Needle Dick does his best to keep up.

Before heading off into the kitchen, I text Moira:

> Me: *We're back if you want to round up your boys after breakfast.*
>
> Moira: *Do I have to?*
>
> Me: *Ha ha. Yes. I'm afraid I'm going to have my hands full today.*
>
> Moira: *See you in thirty.*

As I walk through the dining room, I see that two tables have been pushed together. My nephews are sitting with the Kennedys, chatting away excitedly, clearly enamored by Brett. He's lapping up their adoration like a cat with a saucer of fresh milk.

Evie hurries out of the kitchen with a tray full of drinks. "Hey, boss, you hungry?"

"No, I'll eat later."

"Good, then you can grab this and take their order." She hands me the tray before pointing to Harper's table. "Grandpa Jack isn't here this morning, so I've been on my own. I have to take the muffins out of the oven."

"Is he okay?" My heart pounds at the thought of my

grandfather not being well. He's the last of the older generation around here. He's the heart of our family.

"He had a date that turned into a sleepover." She offers me a bawdy wink.

"Of course he did." While I should be happy for him, the last thing I want to do is play server to that asswipe Brett Kennedy, but needs must.

I walk over and start handing out orange juices for the kids and coffees and waters for the unhappy couple.

Harper looks up at me, clearly uncomfortable. "Thank you."

"No problem." Turning to the kids, I say, "Pancakes all around?"

They all answer to the affirmative, then I look down at Harper. "Let me guess: two pancakes, two slices of bacon, and two eggs over easy?"

She nods and offers me a small smile.

"Whoa, you haven't been eating like that every day, have you, babe?" Brett says. "Roles for chubby women aren't all that easy to come by."

I set my jaw so hard, it makes a crunching sound in my ears. Harper stiffens slightly but ignores his comment. "That sounds wonderful, Digger. Thank you."

Swallowing every ounce of pride I have, I look at Brett. "Are you ordering breakfast?"

"No," he answers, wrinkling up his nose. "I already had my protein smoothie this morning. I'm training for my next *Helioman* movie."

"Cool!" Wyatt says.

Brett smiles at him. "Yeah, I think so too."

Oh, my God, I have never wanted to punch someone so badly in my life.

Instead, I turn to Lily. "Hey, Lily, do you want to come to the kitchen and flip the pancakes?"

Her eyes light up, but then she looks at her father whose eyebrows are knit tightly together. "If it's okay with you, I kind of want to stay with my daddy."

I smile at her. "Of course you do. I just didn't want you to think I forgot it was your turn."

"Her turn?" Brett asks, turning to Harper with a bemused expression. "What kind of place have you got the kids staying at, Harper? They have to cook their own food . . ."

"It's fun for them. Plus, they're learning a new skill," she counters.

"One they won't need. Unless you're planning for one of our children to be a line cook." He looks at me smugly as he says this.

"Children should know how to cook for themselves, Brett. It's a basic human need." *Go, Harper.*

Ruffling Liam's hair, Brett says, "Not for my kiddos. In fact, after breakfast, let's pack up your things so you guys can all come stay with me at the house I'm renting."

"Really, Dad?" Liam asks excitedly.

"I don't think—" Harper starts but Brett raises a hand to stop her.

He stays focused on Liam. "You're going to love it there. It's huge. It's got a hot tub, a movie screening room, a PS-5, and an incredible view of the ocean," Brett tells his son.

"Can we go there, Mommy, please?" Lily asks excitedly.

She gives Brett a dirty look. "This may have been a conversation for the grownups to have first."

"Not really," Brett says dismissively. "You're my family. We should be together."

"Can we go too?" Ash says.

"No," I tell him, shaking my head. "Your mom has been missing you."

"Aww, nuts," Colton says. "A *PS-5*, Uncle Digger. I don't know anyone who has one of those."

"Maybe you guys can come over later to hang out with us there," Liam offers.

"Sure, yeah," Brett says with a shrug. "The place is massive. We could have two other families living there and not even see each other." Glancing up at me, he says, "I'm guessing your cabins are pretty rustic."

Harper turns to me and whispers, "Sorry."

"Don't worry about it," I mutter, before heading back to the kitchen before I say something I shouldn't. For the next ten minutes, I focus on the task at hand while trying to calm myself down. How could Harper have ever let herself get involved with a guy like that? Anyone with eyes can see he's a total phony.

Part of me wants to rush right out there and force Brett onto the next plane back to LA, where he belongs. But I have no right to do that. At the end of the day, Harper is a guest and I'm just hotel staff. No matter what happened over the last couple of days that inexplicably makes me feel like we should be together, I know it won't happen.

Even though, for the first time in my life, I can actually understand the temptation of getting serious with someone, of wanting to spend your life with them.

Dropping even circles of batter onto the griddle, I realize that it's probably a good thing numb-nuts showed up when he did. It's snapped me back to reality before I could do something stupid like fall in love.

Chapter 23

Harper

Dear Readers,

My uncle's massage therapist's barista has a second job at Galaxy Studios. She works in the commissary, steaming milk for the stars. *Imagine the things she knows …*

Anyhoo, she had some dish this morning.

The overlords at Galaxy are not impressed by one Mr. Brett Kennedy's new marital status—separated. Apparently, they've issued a warning—get your life together, or get out.

One can only assume that's why Brett left Sneaky Nanny in Hawaii. My travel agent's landlord's cousin owns the house the newly separated couple was sharing, and word is that the nanny of Nannygate has yet to vacate the premises.

As an asexual gay man with a penchant for drama, even I can't understand the need for this kind of chaos.

Dish,
Ferris Biltmore

~

I'm guessing Digger knew about Brett and he was trying to warn me down at the dock. I wish I'd let him talk. Any warning would have been better than the shock I got.

After a very uncomfortable breakfast, we say goodbye to Digger and his nephews. Brett walks with us to our cabin. "Let's get you all packed up and checked out, then I'll show you how to take a real vacation."

The kids run up ahead of us, happily smacking at branches along the path. They're clearly thrilled to have their dad here.

"Where's Justine?" I ask Brett.

"I left her in Hawaii." He shrugs his shoulders. "She's probably still there."

"You should be there, too."

"Harp, I miss you and the kids so much, I couldn't be away from you for another minute."

My husband has become the ultimate fist magnet. Every lie that comes out of his mouth makes me want to punch him.

"Don't even," I say, while screwing up my face into a look of pure disgust.

"It's true. I'm meant to be with you. We belong together." He slouches in an "aw shucks" kind of way that is exactly the kind of overacting he's known for.

"How did you even know where we were?" The only

people I told were Prisha and Ethan. Brett is the last person they'd say anything to.

"You used the agency plane, Harper. Surely you don't think they wouldn't tell me."

Crap.

"So, you left your girlfriend in paradise to come see your children? Forgive me for not believing that." Never in our marriage has Brett put anyone above himself.

"Justine is not my girlfriend."

"My mistake," I say snidely. "The woman you're having sex with then."

"It's over between us, Harp. It was over between us when you … that is to say … when you *saw* us together."

He must think I'm a complete idiot. "It was so over that you took her to Hawaii?"

"In my heart it was. I just … I don't know, freaked out because you kicked me out. I was upset about the possibility of losing my family."

"And the logical choice was to take the nanny on a very public tropical vacay to paradise?"

Brett lets out a deep sigh. "I was out of my mind. I know that now. I'm so sorry, Harper. You can't imagine how torn up I am inside." He kicks his foot in the dirt and hangs his head so low it looks like he's trying to kiss his collar bone. I'm not buying it.

"Save it for the gullible woman, Brett. I'm through believing anything you have to say." I jog up ahead to be with the kids. Happily, for once, he seems to take the hint and doesn't try to catch up.

Once we get to the cabin, the kids rush in and excitedly start to pack their things. Brett follows behind. "How in the world have you managed up here? This place is depressing."

Ignoring him, I go into the kids' room and help them

pack. The entire time, I keep my game face on, even though I'm dying inside. The very last thing I want to do is to be apart from them. Especially not after the scare I had this morning. But going with them now will only confuse them about what the future holds, and there's no way I can do that to them. The sooner they realize their dad and I live apart, the better.

"I can do this myself, Mom," Liam says, staring at me intently. "Shouldn't you be packing your stuff?"

And there it is, he's testing to see if I'm coming or not. He looks so serious that it breaks my heart.

Shaking my head, I tell him, "No, I think it's best if I stay here and let you have some time just with your dad."

"What? No, Mommy, you have to come." Lily's eyes well-up with unshed tears.

I knew this would be hard, but the pain I'm feeling right now is excruciating. "When people get divorced, they don't have holidays together anymore. The three of us have already had so much fun together. Now it's your dad's turn. When he leaves in a day or two, you'll be right back with me again."

"But, Mom, I thought we were going to have family time." Liam sounds as sad as his sister.

Brett appears in the doorway, leaning against the frame. "Yeah, Harper, come on. I came for *all* of you. Let's go have some family time."

Brett is making me madder and madder. I shoot him a glare, then get down on my knees and pull my kids in for a hug. "I love you to pieces and I'll see you soon. Come on, I'll walk you to your dad's car."

With heads hanging low, they stumble out the front door. I'm still too raw from my bear encounter this morning to let them walk along the path without me.

Brett falls in step with me, and I know he's working on

the mother of all speeches. Whatever he plans to say, he's going to get shut down. Hard.

Even though *I* don't want to ever have to see Brett's stupid face again, I still ache to be where my kids are. More than that, I want to give Liam and Lily the family they deserve. But what kind of mother would I be if I let them think it's okay to be treated the way Brett treats me?

My inner voice reminds me that the kids don't know how Brett treats me. As far as they're concerned, Mommy and Daddy decided not to love each other anymore and that's why their family is falling apart. While I want nothing more than for them to know it's not my fault, there's no way I can be part of them hating their dad. Even though he's taking the opposite tack—bending over backwards to make me look like the villain.

As we near the lodge, Moose stands up and bounds toward the kids. They hurry over to pet him, giving Brett a chance to plead with me without the kids hearing—his ego won't allow him to be rejected in front of anyone, even if it is just a four- and an eight-year-old.

"Please, Harp." Brett breaks into my thoughts. "Come with us. I know we can work this out if we really try."

"I've done nothing but try, Brett. I've seen this song and dance too many times to ever fall for it again. It's time for all of us to get used to the new normal. Go and have a nice time with the kids."

Narrowing his eyes at me, he leans in. "Is this because of that guy you took off with? Are you staying here so you can be with him?"

"It's none of your business who I spend my time with, Brett. Just like it's no longer my business who you spend your time with."

"You're sleeping with him, aren't you?" he demands hotly.

I laugh in his face. "I don't know, Brett. Were you sleeping with Justine?" I'm purposefully giving him the wrong impression, but I'm so mad right now I'm half tempted to admit to a string of affairs I've never had just to put him in his place.

He inhales loudly like he's going to yell, but then doesn't. "It's fine. I don't even care if you did. Just, please come with us. Let's be a family again."

He knows the family card is playing dirty pool, yet it seems to be his only strategy. Steeling myself, I lift my chin. "No, Brett. Now, please go before the kids realize we're arguing. And don't forget to feed them."

His head snaps back. "What kind of thing is that to say? Of course, I'm going to feed them."

I ignore his hurt tone. I have never seen Brett prepare a meal for our children in their whole lives. "Bedtime is at eight," I tell him. "Two books and two songs is their routine."

"Harper …"

I spot a Mercedes SUV in the parking lot and know immediately that it's Brett's rental. Walking over to it, I call the kids to hop in as Brett unlocks and opens the doors using the key fob. I oversee the kids climbing in and getting buckled. Then, putting on the bravest smile I can muster, I tell them, "Have the best time ever. I love you to the moon and back and I'll see you soon!"

Brett walks around to the driver's side and gets in without another word to me. Thank heaven for small mercies.

I watch them pull out of the parking lot and onto the road. I feel like I can't breathe. I hear the screen door to the lodge slam shut and I know instinctively it's Digger, who was probably watching the entire thing.

I can't face him. Not right now. Not when I need to fall apart. Because if I let myself, I'll collapse into his strong arms and I'm afraid I'll never want him to let me go. Putting my head down, I run down the path to the cabin before locking myself in. The tears come immediately.

Sliding down the wall, I let my body curl into a fetal position right there on the floor. I feel hollowed out and helpless. I don't know how long I lay there, immobile in my impotence and grief. But when my telephone rings, I finally stir. It might be Brett calling with a question about the kids. God knows, I don't have much faith that he'll be able to handle them for any amount of time without me or a nanny to help.

But it's Prisha's picture that pops up on my screen, not Brett's. I answer with, "You'll never guess who showed up here."

"I already know," she tells me. "I've been trying to get a hold of you for two days to tell you he was on his way. Next time you go camping in the wilderness, make sure there's cell reception."

"That would have defeated the purpose."

"Good point. Just tell me I'm not too late to talk you out of letting that snake back in the door," she says.

"Don't worry. I've finally learned my lesson. Even though it hurt like hell to see the kids so upset," I answer, my voice cracking.

"Oh, sweetie, I know. Just promise me you'll stay strong though, okay? In the end, it's going to be so much better for the kids."

"I know," I whisper before letting out a shaky breath. "It's just so hard. I feel like I'm tearing their whole world apart."

"Hey, you're not the one who made the mess. You're the one cleaning it up," Prisha tells me. "Now, do you want to know why he's really there?"

My heart pounds in my chest. "There's another motive?" I should have known.

"The whole town is abuzz with the gossip that Galaxy is rethinking bringing Brett back as Helioman. He's fulfilled his three-picture deal, and with all his bad press lately, there's talk about having Jeremy Dillard take over."

"Oh, my God, that asshole! I should have known he wasn't coming back for us." Fury replaces the pain I was feeling just seconds ago. "He's just trying to negate his bad press, so he doesn't lose out on a role."

"You know Brett. Always looking out for number one." Prisha hates Brett with a burning hot passion. Every time he cheated, and I took him back, she threatened to unleash the velvet mafia on him. She claims no one knows how to dish out revenge quite like the gay community.

"I can't even right now," I tell her. "I'm so angry, I could choke him."

"Anger is good. It means you're not in danger of letting him worm his way back into your life."

"Don't worry about me. Brett has made me look like a fool for the last time."

"Good, but just in case, Ethan and I are flying out in the morning. We should be there by five tomorrow night."

"You're coming here?" I'm more excited than I should be. It hasn't been that long since I saw them both.

"We need to sit down and work out your strategy. Ethan thinks you need to file for divorce stat, before Brett can try to fix his image. And then we need to hammer out the details of how to present you in the press."

"Are you staying in the same lodge I am?"

"Everything is booked, so we thought we'd bunk in with you."

"Wow, um, okay. While I'd love that, it's pretty tight quarters here. But we can certainly make do until the kids come back." For the first time all day, I feel happy. "I can't wait to see you, Prish. I'm so lucky to have you in my life."

"We're lucky to have each other," she says. "Now go relax because we're about to kick into high gear and your life isn't going to feel like your own for a while."

"Love you. See you tomorrow." I sign off, wondering what to do with the night ahead of me. I want to see Digger, but I know that would be sending the wrong message. I can't let anything happen between us now. Not only would it not be fair to him, but the last thing I need is for the press to cast aspersions on the nature of our relationship.

I suddenly know what I want to do. Grabbing a can of bear spray out of the cabinet, I leave the cabin and walk back up to the lodge. Grandpa Jack is sitting on the porch swing with an elderly woman who is sporting the kind of bright red hair not normally seen outside of the circus set.

"Hello," I call out.

"Hello, yourself," he answers. "What can I do you for?"

"I was wondering if I could borrow the pickup truck?"

He nods his head. "Keys are under the mat."

"Thank you!" I wave before turning around. I'm going to go into town to see Moira. She said we should get together for a girls' night, and I can't think of a better way to spend my evening. While I'm not going to find out anything more about Digger, I can't help but feel a wave of hope that she might talk about him a little.

I'd love to know if there's a reason, other than his mother's betrayal, that he's so dead set against settling down.

Chapter 24

Digger

"There you are," Jack says, walking down the dock where I'm hosing off the Cessna. "I've been looking all over for you."

"You found me," I tell him, shutting off the nozzle. It's a beautiful, calm summer evening, which is exactly the opposite of how I feel. I'm as agitated as a wolf with one foot caught in a trap. I can't seem to think about anything but Harper. Seeing her walk back to her cabin with Brett really did a number on me. I've spent the last few hours staying as busy as possible to keep from knocking on her door to check on her.

"So, anything you want to tell me?" Jack asks, leaving me to assume the rest of the question, which I'm not going to do.

"Not that I know of." I plunge the sponge into the soapy water and get to work on the propellers. A couple of bubbles float out of the bucket and Moose tries to catch them in his mouth. He winds up falling off the dock with a big splash.

Jack chuckles at him and we both watch as he swims to shore so he can resume his post as bubble catcher. "Where were we?" Grandpa Jack picks up where he left off. "Oh, right. Anything happen between you and that lovely actress while you were up at the cabin?"

"Nope," I lie. No good can come from telling my grandfather anything personal. He doesn't understand why I've chosen to live alone, and he certainly doesn't condone it.

"Hmph. Well, you're no fun, But I knew that." He hooks one thumb through his belt loop and stares off into the horizon.

"I see you decided to take your own advice, though," I tell him, referring to the redhead I saw him with earlier.

A smile crosses his face, causing it to wrinkle a little more. "Savannah's quite the looker, isn't she?"

I don't answer on account of not wanting to be rude. "Is she going to be my new grandma?" I tease.

"Ha! She's a tourist." After a long pause, he adds, "A really fun tourist."

"You're a wily old coot, do you know that?" I get started scrubbing the doors.

"Speaking of tourists, any idea where Harper went this afternoon?" Nice segue, Grandpa.

I freeze in place for a second. "Did she go out?" I'm trying to keep my voice casual, but I'm not sure if I'm succeeding.

"She borrowed the Toyota."

"Maybe she had to run into town for something," I answer, hoping like hell she hasn't gone to Brett's. I saw him drive off with the kids earlier.

"She looked pretty excited," he says. "I think maybe she might have been headed to the Steel Trap or something."

The Steel Trap is Gamble's excuse for a nightlife. Call me crazy, but eight bar stools, six tables, and an old jukebox that doesn't play any music after the eighties, doesn't a nightlife make.

My stomach flips at the thought. "I think it's a little early to go out drinking, Grandpa Jack."

"Depends on what's going on in your life. Seems to me Harper has earned herself an extra cocktail or four." Sounds like Evie has caught him up on all the Hollywood dish.

"That she has," I tell him.

"I've been thinking about Shelby lately." Grandpa Jack changes the subject with all the grace of a rhinoceros on roller skates.

Icy fingers of dread crawl up the base of my neck. I will not engage with him on this subject. "You can think about whoever you want to," I tell him. "That's the nice thing about thoughts, they stay in your head." Hint, hint.

"I saw her mom in the market the other day." *And* he's still talking. "She said Shelby's moving home from Minneapolis this summer." I don't respond. "Looks like the big city doesn't suit her after all."

"Hand me the hose, will ya?"

"Did you hear what I said?" he demands hotly. "Shelby Mayfair is coming home."

"Why is that any of my concern?" I finally turn to face him. "Shelby is my past. I couldn't care less if she was moving to Mars."

"You loved her once, Digger."

"I was a kid. Plus, I learned my lesson with girls like her." I don't like feeling bitter, but that's the only emotion Shelby invokes in me.

"Not every gal is like your mother, son. It full-on broke all our hearts when Donna left us to go pursue her dreams."

"While I'm sure it *was* hard on everyone," I tell him,

"Moira and I were the ones who lost our mother. It was only a few years later that Grandma died, then Dad. It seems to me that my sister and I have had about all the loss we can take." I don't mention Moira's husband, or I might cry like a baby for all my sister has had to endure.

Grandpa Jack walks right over to me and wraps his arms around me. Once upon a time, I felt safe and secure in his strong embrace. Now I just feel sad. One of these days he'll be gone, too. That'll leave me as the old man of the family. And that is not a circumstance I can make heads or tails out of.

"You got dealt a bad hand, son," Grandpa Jack tells me. "But to succeed in life, you can't sit around counting the kicks to your teeth. You can't wallow. Every time you're knocked down, you have to stand up and get right back to fighting."

"Insanity is doing the same thing over and over and expecting a different result," I tell him.

"Faith consists of believing when it is beyond the power of reason to believe. Voltaire." He looks at me like there's no way I can top that nonsense.

"Love Bites. Def Leppard."

"Jeff Leopard? Never heard of him."

"Too bad because he was a genius."

"Come sit with me, son." Grandpa climbs into the passenger side of the plane.

I follow suit and settle myself in the pilot's seat. I know a lecture is coming, but I also know there's no putting off Grandpa Jack when he's determined to say his piece. "When your grandmother died, I felt hogtied. I didn't know who I was without her." His eyes are glazed over like he's lost in the past. "Adele was strong and beautiful and feisty as all get out. I don't know what I ever did to deserve her. But it doesn't matter. She picked me. We had a beautiful life together, and I would have never missed out on all we shared, just so I didn't have to mourn her someday."

"Grandma was the best," I agree. "She's pretty much the only mother I ever had. Even when my mom was home, her head wasn't here."

"Love is worth taking a chance on, Digger. I'm not saying you won't ever be hurt again; you might. But you're tough. And once you find the lady for you, you can handle any pain that comes with it, so long as you've known her love."

"That lady will never be Shelby Mayfair," I tell him. And it's true. Shelby and I were high school sweethearts. We talked about getting married and starting a family, but the summer after we graduated, she backed out. She wanted something bigger than Gamble could offer—than *I* could offer.

While she had every right to live her life as she saw fit, she knew firsthand what my mom's leaving did to me. There's no way I could welcome her back into my close circle. "Look, Grandpa, I appreciate everything you're saying. I really do. But I'm good. You have to trust me on this."

"You're lost, Digger. And you're a bonehead. But I love you. I just don't want to see you moldering away like a dead deer."

"That's pretty gruesome," I tell him. "I'm hardly rotting."

"You can't see what's in front of your face."

"And you can?"

"I have the benefit of a much longer life than you. And I promise, if you don't listen to me, you'll regret your choices."

The only way to get him off this topic is to say, "I'll think about it, okay?"

He nods his head once and gets out of the plane. When he's gone, I get back to scrubbing, only with a little more vigor. Once I'm done, I head back to the lodge to tackle the grill, giving it a full servicing even though it doesn't need one. Afterward, I check all the chairs and tables to make sure they haven't developed any wobbles, and then I top off the salt and pepper shakers.

The entire time, I fight to keep my mind off Harper Kennedy, but it's no use. Finally, I have to lay some truth on myself: Harper Kennedy is going to leave Gamble as sure as every other woman I've let myself care for. The only reasonable thing to do is not to become involved.

The only problem is, I think it might be too late for that.

Chapter 25

Harper

Dear Readers,

As the old folks say, it's on like Donkey Kong! My manicurist's street-sweeper's garbageman saw Brett Kennedy boarding a plane for—wait for it—Alaska.

Oh, to be a fly on the wall for that reunion. Was there a reconciliation? Tears? Accusations? Someone on his knees begging for forgiveness? Whatever the scene, I'm sure it was epic.

A teensy bit of advice for Brett: If your angel wife decides to take you back, you might consider offering to have yourself chipped—via the animal shelter.

A little advice for Harper: Gurl, my mama always said, if you lie down with dogs, you're gonna wake up with fleas.

She also said something about not eating where you poop, but I'm not sure that's relevant here. All I know is that if you take him back, you're gonna need to wear a flea collar.

I'm going to go lie down (*sans* the fleas) and meditate now. I'm going to visualize sweet Harper in a bubble of protective light. She's surely going to need it in the days ahead.

Dishingly yours,
Ferris Biltmore

My old life feels like it's a million miles away. Pulling in front of the diner, I turn the ignition off and sit quietly, trying to focus my thoughts. I take slow, deep breaths, endeavoring to feel myself in my body. But at this very moment in time, I can't. My life seems unreal to me, like I'm playing a character in a movie.

I read somewhere that's how grief makes you feel. It's almost like your soul has been transported out of your skin. It just kind of hovers around you, not quite connecting. I naively thought I could outrun it by coming up here, but apparently, it's not possible to leave your feelings at home when you board a plane, especially when your husband—aka your problem—follows you. This new phase, of actually having to hand the kids over to Brett, is almost too brutal to bear.

Grabbing my purse, I get out of the cab of the truck and head into the diner. The restaurant is empty, so I find a booth and sit down.

Moira waves from the table she's bussing. Once she drops a load of dishes into a bussing tub, she comes over to me and sits down. "Honey, it sounds like you had some excitement this morning. It's all the boys could talk about when they came in for lunch."

"I'd almost forgotten about the bear," I tell her. *My mind has been fully on my idiot husband showing up.*

As if reading my mind, she says, "They also mentioned Brett." She reaches across the table and takes my hand. Giving it a squeeze, she says, "I'm sorry. That can't be easy."

If anyone knows how hard life can be, it's Moira. Raising three kids on her own while working crazy hours at her diner, I can't even imagine. "I shouldn't complain. It's not like I'm the first woman who's gone through this."

"You know what the problem is with us strong gals?" she asks while leaning back. Before I can answer, she tells me, "We're constantly telling ourselves that we shouldn't complain. We shouldn't feel bad. We shouldn't be human. It's all a load of horse poop, if you ask me." She slaps her hands against the tabletop hard. "We have got to cut ourselves some slack occasionally."

"Call me crazy," I tell her, "But I get the feeling you don't practice what you preach."

She laughs bitterly. "No time. But I promise you, when the twins go off to college, I'm going to close the diner for a month and let myself have the biggest pity party that's ever been."

"That seems like a long time to wait. What do you say we have that girls' night we were talking about and feel sorry for ourselves tonight?"

Nodding her head, she strolls over to the door and turns over the "Closed" sign. "Let's do it." She walks over to the kitchen window and tells her cook, "I closed up a few minutes early, Lloyd. Go home to your wife and I'll see you in the morning."

She comes back to me. "Let's go over to my place. That

way I can put some supper on the table for the kids and give them at least a sense that they have a parent left." She takes off her apron and throws it on the counter.

"I can't even imagine how hard it is to raise the boys on your own. You're doing a great job though. They're good kids."

"It's sure not the childhood I wanted for them," she says, opening the front door for me.

I wonder again what co-parenting with Brett will look like. It's my guess he'll make the time he spends with our kids one big party while I'm left with the job of actually raising them to be decent human beings. "Should I follow you?" I ask.

"I usually walk to work, so I'll ride with you, if you don't mind," Moira says while heading to the truck. Once we're in the cab, she adds, "So, did that brother of mine drive you crazy?"

I'm not sure how exactly she means that, so I kind of stumble over my response. "Um … no? I mean … I don't know. No, I mean no." *Good lord.*

"So, no?" She laughs loudly.

"He really went above and beyond for us and I'm very grateful. He's wonderful with the kids." What else can I say without tipping my hand that I kissed the guy?

"I keep trying to talk him into finding a wife, but pickings are pretty slim in Gamble."

She points to the left in lieu of giving me actual directions. I pull out onto the road. "You sound like you speak from experience."

"I'd rather be tied to a tree and slathered with honey than get married again." I don't quite know how to react to that. She adds, "I loved my husband and would have happily stayed with him forever. Having said that, I don't have the intestinal fortitude to break in someone else."

"I can't imagine ever wanting to date again," I tell her honestly. Although my face turns hot at the thought of the kiss Digger and I shared. It wasn't a full-on make out session, but it was the sweetest encounter I've shared with anyone in years. I felt so desirable in his arms, which is a pretty novel experience for me. What with my own husband making it abundantly clear he desires everyone but me.

After three blocks, Moira tells me to make a left, which leads onto a picturesque street. Each house is surrounded by a large lot that in LA would cost a small fortune. Tall trees and shrubbery line the road, providing privacy and making it feel like we're out in the woods.

"It's the last house on the right," Moira tells me. "Expect a mess."

I nod. "I couldn't care less about any of that."

The house itself is an expansive log home built into a hill. Huge windows join at the peaked roof, and even though the place looks a bit worse for wear, it also has a homey feel to it.

The boys, along with a bouncy golden retriever, surround the pickup as soon as we pull up the drive. "Mom, we made dinner!" Wyatt calls out proudly.

"And we didn't even burn the house down," Ash adds.

Moira laughs. "So, you made cereal?"

"Cap'n Crunch is the supper of champions," Colton contributes.

Getting out of the truck, Moira pulls her sons in for a hug. "You know the rule, cereal for supper only once a month. You don't get to do that again for a while." She sounds like she's trying to be stern, but I definitely hear relief in her tone.

The dog walks over to me and immediately nudges my hand to pet her. When I comply, Wyatt says, "That's Juno. If you start petting her, she'll never let you stop."

I give him a mock frightened face and say, "Too late."

He makes a *tsk*ing sound. "You're gonna regret that."

Ash picks up a baseball bat off the grass. "Wanna play, Wyatt?"

"Yup," he tells him. "I'll spot you two five points each on account of me being a way better player."

With that, the three boys take off to the far side of the yard. Juno runs after them, clearly eager to join in the fun. Colton calls to his mom, "Can you take her inside?"

"Come on, Juno, let's go," Moira calls before turning to me. "She likes to steal the ball, and if she gets it, she chews it until the hide's off."

Juno follows us up the steps to the house.

"Have you eaten yet?" Moira asks.

"No. But I should let you know, Cap'n Crunch is a favorite of mine as well," I tell her with a grin.

"I should have offered to feed you at the diner." She shakes her head.

Following her through the screen door to her house, I say, "But I haven't had my cereal for dinner yet this month."

"Me neither."

She giggles while leading the way into her kitchen. Moira's house is obviously well cared for, but even so, the furniture is a bit shabby and worn. The paint on the walls looks faded, and a couple of the pictures are hanging crooked.

An older woman walks around the corner. She's dressed in a bright orange pantsuit that looks like it's vintage 1970 (and hasn't fit well in a while). Her hair is halfway down her back and is being held back by a purple handkerchief. I'm pretty sure I love her already. "Ah, that's better. My back teeth were floating," she announces before noticing who she's talking to. She stops walking and looks at me. "I'm Edna, the neighbor. You're that woman from that show about crooked politicians."

I can't help but laugh at her introduction. I hold out my hand to her. "Harper. It's lovely to meet you, Edna."

"You too," she says, adjusting her glasses on her nose. "If you don't mind me saying—"

Moira cuts her off before she can finish that sentence. "Edna looks after the boys for me every morning before school and whenever we need her during the summer. She's a huge help."

Edna grins at me. "That's true. I watch the boys, but I don't cook, and I don't clean. Because the truth is, if you take your eyes off the three of them for even a minute, they'll either start a fight or blow something up." Seeming to realize she's lost track of her charges, she knits her eyebrows together. "Where did they get off to, anyway?"

I tuck my lips between my teeth to stop myself from laughing while Moira answers her. "Outside playing ball."

"Oh, good," Edna says with an approving nod. "I'd best be getting home then. Ed will be starting supper soon and I hate to miss watching him cook."

"Ed's her husband," Moira explains.

"So Edna and Ed?" I ask.

With a twinkle in her eyes, she says, "It was meant to be." Picking up a massive macramé bag that I can only assume is her purse, she adds, "Same name, two halves of the same heart."

"Thanks for watching the boys," Moira tells her as she heads to the door.

"Anytime, sweetie," she answers. Turning to me, she adds, "It was lovely to meet you. If you don't mind me saying—"

"See you, Edna!" Moira yells over her.

"Oh, you. I'm not going to say something mean."

"You sure?" Moira asks, narrowing her eyes suspiciously.

"I was just going to tell her she can do a lot better than that slimy Brett Kennedy."

Moira's shoulders drop. "I don't think she—"

"—You should see if that nice Brad Pitt is still single. Now, he'd never take up with the nanny."

"Just his co-star …" I remind her.

"Damnation, I forgot about that. I don't know how you gals do it these days. If you ask me, men haven't been the same since our president started getting hummers in the Oval Office."

"Okay, Edna, thank you!" Moira says, raising her voice urgently as she guides her toward the door. "See you tomorrow morning."

"What did I say?" Edna demands while allowing herself to be ushered out.

As soon as the door closes behind her, Moira and I both start to laugh.

"Welcome to my circus," she tells me, throwing her hands up in the air. "I'm so sorry about her. She really shouldn't have said anything."

"Don't worry about it. She's right." Looking around I say, "This is a beautiful place. Big too." I lean over and peer up the stairs.

"Everett was a crab fisherman. He did well enough that we were able to buy this place when it went on the market. It used to be owned by a couple who rented out some of the bedrooms to hunters during the season." She smiles at me, but I can see the pain in her eyes is still fresh. "We were planning to knock down some walls and give the kids bigger bedrooms, but then he died and, well, it never happened. As it is, we have eight small bedrooms up there. Crazy, right?"

As Moira pours me a bowl of cereal and pushes it across the counter, I take a seat on the stool. True to Wyatt's word,

Juno has stayed right next to me since we met and is now staring up at me with a hopeful expression.

I glance around the room again and a thought pops into my head. "Have *you* ever thought about renting out some of the rooms?"

"Who in their right mind would want to stay here with my kids running around like wild animals?" she scoffs. "Also, I'm pretty sick of people by the end of the day and I'd hate to have to be polite to more strangers. I need my down time."

"What if you had a friend who had some people coming to town and they needed a place to stay?"

"Harper." Moira sits down at the bar stool across from mine. "Do you have a friend who needs a place to stay?"

"As a matter of fact, I do," I tell her excitedly. "The lodge is full and from what I understand, Brett is renting the only other place in town." I tell her, "My best friends, Prisha and Ethan, are coming up tomorrow night. They'll probably only be here a few days."

"I'd be happy to let them stay," she says with a grimace. "But you better let them know the accommodations aren't fancy and they'll be sharing with three boys, a dog, two cats, and five fish."

"How about if I give you two hundred a night for each of two rooms. Does that sound fair?" I'm sure it's more than Moira would ever ask, but she's doing us such a favor she really ought to make a premium.

"Don't be ridiculous, Harper. I'm not going to charge you."

"Then I'm going to have to keep them in my cabin and we'll be packed in like sardines." I arch an eyebrow in challenge.

Shaking her head, she says, "Fine. But only if they come

to the diner to eat. All their meals will be included in the price."

I reach my hand out to shake hers. "You've got yourself a deal."

After the boys are off to bed, we spend the next several hours drinking too many wine spritzers and talking on her front porch like a couple of old friends. Even though our situations are vastly different, there're enough similarities to bond us together. Grief has a way of doing that.

Eventually, we move on from talking about our sad stories and start talking about men in general. How ridiculous they can be, how much having a husband can feel like having an extra child.

I lost count of how much I've had to drink, but I know it's a lot when I loudly announce, "Digger's not like that."

"Not like what?" she wants to know.

"Not a child. He's a *man*," I tell her, putting extra emphasis on the word man. "A manly man."

Moira screws up her face and says, "Eww!" Then her eyes grow wide, and she gasps. "You like him!"

"Do not!"

"Do too. You *like him*, like him," she says, leaning toward me.

Dropping my shoulders, I ask, "Is it my fault he's crazy hot and I haven't gotten any in almost five years?"

Moira bursts out laughing, stomping her feet on the porch while sitting in her chair. "Yuck, yuck, yuck! He's my brother." When she stops, she grins at me. "But I can see how other women would like him. He's one of the good ones."

"He sure is," I answer with a wistful sigh. "A guy like that could almost make a girl forget she's sworn off men forever …"

Moira narrows her eyes playfully. "What happened up at the cabin?"

My cheeks heat up. "Nothing. Well, just one very light kiss, but it was …" I trail off, then stop when I see her wincing. "Should we change the subject?"

"Let's," Moira answers, then yawns

I suddenly realize it's at least the third time she's done that in the last few minutes. "I've kept you up way past your bedtime, haven't I?"

"I've kept me up past my bedtime. I've just been having so much fun, I didn't want it to stop, but I'd better hit the hay. I have to be up at five a.m."

I jump to my feet to say my goodbyes but then I stumble and sit back down. "I don't think I should drive right now."

"Probably not," she says. "Don't worry, I'll call you a cab."

"Perfect."

She goes in the house to place the call while I sit, listening to the sound of the crickets. Smiling to myself, I realize how very nice it feels to be me at this moment. All the pain of my impending divorce is lost in a boozy blur. And while I don't know how my life is going to turn out, I do know one thing: if I can traverse the waters of change with half of the grace that Moira has, I'll be just fine.

Chapter 26

Digger

I'm just getting out of the shower when my cell phone rings. Wrapping a towel around my waist, I check the screen and see my sister's name. My heart rate starts to beat in double time. She never calls this late unless something is wrong.

"Hey, Moira, what's up?"

"We're drunk," she says, slurring a little.

"Who's drunk?" I ask.

"Harper and me."

"Where are you?"

"My place, you big dope. I can't leave my kiddos alone."

"Right." The news that my sister is tipsy supersedes any knowledge of how responsible she always is. She's had to be. Which is why she's not known to get drunk.

"Harper needs a ride back to the lodge," she says. "I'll drive the truck to the diner in the morning and you can pick it up there."

"Is that right?" The thought of seeing Harper again makes me feel like a little kid. Unreasonably excited.

Ten minutes later, I pull up at my sister's, only to find Moira and Harper lying on the front lawn next to each other, laughing like a pair of hyenas. I get out of the truck and slam the door, but they don't so much as turn in my direction. They finally put two and two together when I'm standing directly over them.

"Digger!" Moira yells.

"Moira. Harper," I say. "What are you doing down there?"

"Pretending to be centipedes," Harper answers, waving her arms and legs in the air. "You should join us!"

"Maybe next time." I hold out my hand to help her up. As soon as our palms touch, a warmth spreads through me that's as exciting and cozy as Christmas morning.

Harper holds out her hand to help Moira up, but instead of joining us on terra firma, my sister nearly pulls Harper back down. Grabbing Harper by the waist, I hold her close, and say, "Don't move." Then I hoist Moira up with my other hand.

They look at each other, then, at the same time, say, "He's one of the good ones." A huge giggle fit ensues.

"We should get going," I tell Harper.

"Right." She attempts to snap her fingers but somehow misses. "'Cause Moira has to be up really early."

"Yes, she does," I answer, not bothering to mention that I do too.

The two hug like long-lost sisters for another two minutes, telling each other things like, "You're the best,"

"No, *you're* the best," and "Let's do this again." They finally disentangle their limbs and say goodbye.

"Good night, Moira," I say. "Maybe have some water before you go to bed."

"Night-night, bro. Brah. Bruh. Bro, brah, bruh! Brobrah-bruh!" She starts to shake her fists in the air like she's cheering the home team on to victory.

"Oh, boy," I mutter. "She's going to be hurting tomorrow."

"Feels too good to hurt," Harper interjects as she marches very deliberately to the truck.

Once she's all buckled in, I walk around to the driver's side, and we start off. "You and my sister seem to have become fast friends."

"She's the best," Harper tells me. "She's just so … strong and sweet and … and strong."

"That she is," I tell her, shifting to third gear now that we're on the main drag.

"I like her. I like it here," Harper says, looking out the window. Then, turning to me, she adds, "I like you, too. More than I should, probably."

"I'm a pretty likable guy." I can't help the smug smile that crosses my mouth.

Putting her hand on my thigh, she says, "You make me feel alive, Digger. Like *really* alive in a way I haven't in years." She closes her eyes for a few seconds, before adding, "You're so strong and sweet … and seeeeeeeeexy."

"So you like me as much as you like my sister, huh?"

Her head lolls toward me. "No, silly. I don't want to do bedroom stuff with Moira."

She closes her eyes and immediately starts snoring. My heart pounds in my chest like it's decided to make a run for it. She can't possibly mean that. First of all, we barely know each other. Second, she's fresh out of a terrible marriage, so whatever she's feeling is probably more like a desperate need to feel wanted again. Which is insane since half the men on this planet want her.

She doesn't wake up for the rest of the ride, or when I pull into the parking lot at the lodge. I walk around and open her door, then lean over her so I can undo her seat belt, trying not to react to the nearness of her.

Moose wanders over and looks in the truck, then up at me. "She's had a few too many," I tell him. Then I turn to Harper. "Come on, Harper, it's time to wake up, okay?"

"Not gonna," she murmurs, snuggling deeper into the seat.

"Please," I counter, knowing there's really no point. "We're back at the lodge. Do you want me to walk you to your cabin?"

"I sleep here. Long day," she answers.

"I guess I'll have to carry you," I mutter, sliding one hand behind her back and the other one under her thighs.

Hoisting her out of the truck, I slam the door shut with one foot. As she lies in my arms, with her cheek pressed against my chest, I can't help but to stare down at her. She's so pretty, it's almost hard to look at her up close like this. It all seems unreal.

"Mmm … you smell nice," she whispers. "Like pine trees and laundry."

"Thank you?" I ask, hoping she means laundry that's been freshly washed.

"Welcome, hottie."

She doesn't say anything else for the rest of the walk to the cabin. I manage to unlock the door and open it while I'm holding her. Moose sneaks in ahead of us and curls up on the rug in the living room while I carry Harper to her bedroom. I carefully take her shoes off and place them on the floor, before covering her with a blanket.

"Good night, Harper," I say, forcing myself not to touch her cheek.

Her eyes open and she smiles at me. "Stay."

Don't say yes. Do. Not. Say. Yes. "I'd better not," I tell her. "Not that I … you're very … you've been drinking and you're in a tender place in your life right now, so no."

"Too tired for that. Just wanna feel arms around me. I need a hug."

I would love nothing more than to lie down next to her, but I'm not sure I could trust myself if she tried to start something. "How about if I sit here while you fall asleep?" I say, rubbing the back of my neck.

"Lie down," she murmurs before patting the bed next to her and closing her eyes.

Plunking down in the armchair on the opposite side of the room, I kick off my shoes and put my feet up on the ottoman. Moose makes his way in and lies down next to my chair.

I stare at Harper until my eyelids grow heavy. I know I should go, but I can't seem to make myself do it. At some point, I give in to the long day I've had and drift off to sleep, wishing I were about four feet away, with her in my arms.

Chapter 27

Harper

Dear Readers,

When I was just a wee lad of twelve, I, too, became embroiled in a love triangle. Me, Stacy Ferndweller, and Landon Post. I loved the sweaters Stacy wore—which at the time I mistook for lust. And Landon filled out a pair of red polyester gym shorts like nobody's business. What was a boy to do?

I eventually decided to ask Stacy if I could borrow a sweater—baby pink with delicate chartreuse hearts all over it. I wore it to Landon's soccer game and cheered him on like a Dallas Cowboy Cheerleader. He was less than impressed.

After the game, Landon searched me out to delicately disclose his rampant heterosexuality. He broke my heart, but alas, not my nose, so I was grateful. I decided to set him up with Stacy.

It's for this reason that I'm so attuned to the "two humans in love with the same man" scenario. But unlike Landon, Brett Kennedy is no hero. He's a cheater and defiler of nannies. He's a wild card run amok in the landmine of love.

I'm not sure there's a gesture big enough for Harper to consider taking him back. Tip: A boombox on top of your car isn't going to cut it, dude.

I'm skipping my workout today in favor of a good, old-fashioned mud bath. My aura needs a righteous cleanse.

Dish,
Ferris Biltmore

I hurt everywhere—my head, my eyes, my belly button. Reaching under the covers I discover that I went to bed in my jeans and the button is digging into me. Popping it open, I roll over and release a world-class groan.

"Ah, you're up." It's Digger's voice but there's no way he's here in my cabin. "I just put on some coffee." *How is he here in my cabin?*

Memories start to filter into my consciousness and the heat of embarrassment washes over me. The question at hand is, how much of what I'm remembering really happened and how much did I dream? I say the only thing that comes to mind. "Hi."

"Good morning to you." He walks fully into the room before sitting on the bed next to me. "How do you feel?"

"I'm … um … not great." Lordy, this is one gorgeous man.

"You and Moira really tied one on last night."

Okay, so the memory about him picking me up and bringing me home is real. Now to figure out what happened after that. "So, did you … uh … that is to say … sleep here?"

He smiles slightly while nodding his head.

"In my room?"

"Yup." Son of a … *did he sleep in my bed?* I can't bring myself to ask. He watches me closely before pointing across the room. "Over there in the chair."

Thank God. "Why exactly?" I'm having a devil of a time meeting his gaze.

"I was getting ready for bed when Moira called, and by the time I carried you here, I was wiped out."

"I'm so sorry," I mumble. "I'm not much of a drinker." I chance a glance at him from under my lashes.

The look on his face is so intense it's practically melting me from the inside out. "Clearly." He stands up and walks out of the room while saying, "I'm putting your coffee in a thermos. You can drink it on your way up to the lodge."

"No, thank you," I call after him. "I think I'll go back to sleep for a while."

He walks back in, shaking his head. "You'll feel like crap all day if you do that. What you need is some fresh air, followed by a giant breakfast to soak up all the…whatever you were drinking last night." He reaches his hand out to me.

I don't want to take it, but I do. As he pulls, I moan. "I never get drunk."

"Sometimes needs must. I'm guessing Brett was the last person you expected to see up here yesterday."

Ugh, Brett. "You could say that." His name alone makes me feel queasy. He's the reason my kids aren't here right now.

Not that I want them to see me in this state, but I feel totally empty without them.

Once I'm on my feet, I stagger into the bathroom to brush my teeth and hair. I gasp when I see my reflection. I look like a ferocious animal, all wild-eyed and mussed. I hurry to make some order out of my appearance before joining Digger in the kitchen.

He hands me the thermos. "I put in two sugars and some cream."

"Thanks." The first sip is pure heaven. "Whatever genius decided to roast coffee beans and grind them before soaking them in boiling water should be canonized."

After pouring a thermos for himself, he says, "Let's hit it. I'm on kitchen duty and I'm running late."

Our hike to the lodge is more of an Olympic speed walking event than the gentle stroll I was hoping for. "Before you crashed last night, you mentioned something about having friends come up today. Was that real?"

Nodding makes my eyes feel like they're bouncing around my head like two rubber balls. "Prisha and Ethan. She's my PR person and best friend, and Ethan is my lawyer and … my other best friend."

"Do they know Brett is up here?"

"That's why they're coming. Word on the street is that he's on the cusp of losing the Helioman contract for not living up to the terms of his morals clause."

"What's that?"

I'm about ready to jump on Digger's back so he can carry me. I can't keep up with him. "Slow down, will ya?" He immediately slows his pace. "A morals clause is something actors sign when the studio is worried they might do something in their personal life that will jeopardize the success of the movie they're working on."

Digger starts to laugh. "That's kind of hard to believe. It

seems to me the entire industry is based on philandering and bad behavior."

"You're not wrong. The rule of thumb is that anything goes as long as you don't get caught. Brett thinks that if he comes crawling back to me, I'll take him, and the studio will forgive all the questionable press he's had lately."

"He can't possibly think you're so stupid as to go along with that." When I don't answer right away, he repeats himself. "Can he?"

My head drops and I stare at my feet while answering, "I've always known about Brett's cheating. Getting pregnant with Lily was supposed to be a renewal of our love and commitment to each other. Unfortunately, that only lasted until the pregnancy test came back positive. After that, Brett started sleeping with his co-star."

"Which, of course, is why you can never go back to him." He stops walking and stares at me pointedly.

Yesterday I had all but decided that nothing could keep me from leaving Brett. He deserves a world of hurt and I was happy to do my part. But this morning, when I woke up in a cabin without my kids, my heart felt like it was being held in a giant fist intent on pulverizing it. Liam and Lily are my whole world and the thought of missing out on any time with them is unbearable.

"I have kids, Digger. They are the most important thing in my life, and they deserve to have their father around."

"Harper …" His tone is stern. "What about what *you* deserve?"

"I'm not saying I'm going to do it. I'm just saying I have to think through my next move very carefully."

Digger reaches out and takes my hand. "You deserve to have someone who loves you and loves the kids, Harper. Someone who puts you first."

"I'm afraid that's not going to happen. The world I'm

coming from is not set up for that." I could never date another actor or anyone that's in a job that requires public adoration. And let's face it, that's pretty much all of LA.

"So move. Leave that world behind and start over someplace else." He says it like it's the simplest thing in the world to do.

I pick up my pace to a jog, hoping that the sooner we get to the lodge, the sooner this conversation will end. "It's not that easy. My kids have friends there, that's where Brett lives when he's not on location. Plus, if I did decide to leave, I have no idea where I'd go."

"So you'd consider staying with him just so you don't have to face a fresh start? I thought you were braver than that."

Well, *that* hurts.

When I don't say anything, he adds, "Where's the woman who faced a possible bear attack while locked in an outhouse?"

I want to laugh and cry at the same time. "Please don't hold that woman up as the gold standard. I nearly peed my pants when I saw that bear."

"Come on, Harper, you know what you have to do. If you stay with Brett, he's going to slowly suck the life out of you until there's nothing left. And eventually, when the kids get older, they're going to figure out what's going on. If they realize their mom agreed to live on those terms, when she had so many other options available to her, they just might repeat it themselves."

"So many options?"

He stares at me for a second, making me wonder if he might just consider himself as one of those options, but when he speaks, he quickly disabuses me of the notion. "It's not like you're going to wind up on the streets or something. You'll still have more money than most people ever dream of.

And it's not like you'll have trouble finding a better man than that turd you married. You know, if you decide you want to go down that road again."

"I can't decide my entire life this morning, okay? Especially not when my brain is this fuzzy."

"How can this even be a decision for you? It's so clear what you need to do."

"Nothing's clear when you have children," I tell him, tears springing to my eyes. "Do you know how awful it felt to have to send them off with their dad like that? Knowing that this is just the beginning of every moment I'm going to miss with them for their entire childhood? I'm going to miss half of it, Digger. Half of everything." I try to choke back a sob, but I can't.

He lets out a long sigh, his face softening. "I'm sorry. I'm not trying to upset you. I'd just hate to see you sell yourself short."

"You mean like you're doing?" I ask, keeping my tone gentle.

"This isn't about me," he answers, picking up his pace. "I'm living the life I want. You aren't."

Shaking my head, I tell him, "That is such crap."

"Excuse me?"

"You heard me. That's just a lie you tell yourself because you're scared. You won't even consider getting married because of what your mom did. It seems to me like if you're not willing to practice what you preach, you might want to get off the pulpit."

He spins around so fast, I stumble backwards. "My mother deserted me. She walked out of my life, making it clear that my sister and I were not a factor in the choices she made. My situation is a world apart from yours."

"I'm telling you that *as* a mother, I want what's best for my kids. One would think that given your situation, you could respect that." If I weren't suddenly ravenous for pancakes and eggs, I'd turn around and go back to my cabin.

We walk in an angry silence for a minute, until he sighs and says, "Look, Harper, I'm not trying to upset you. You're a great mom, a *wonderful* mom. But your kids won't always be this young, and they're eventually going to hear about the kind of man their dad is. By staying with him, you're training your son to think it's okay to cheat on his wife, and you're telling Lily it's okay to stay with an unfaithful man. Is that what you want for them?"

"I hadn't really thought of it like that." My voice is no more than a whisper. "I guess I'm damned if I do and damned if I don't."

He shakes his head. "It may feel that way now, but that won't last forever."

"You never healed from your mother's desertion," I challenge him.

The look in Digger's eyes is full of pain. "You're better than I am, Harper. You're stronger and more courageous. You can do anything and succeed."

"I think the same thing about you."

He shakes his head sadly. "You barely know me."

"You're wrong, Digger. I do know you. I know what's going on inside that head of yours. And that's a fact that scares you to death." I stare him straight in the eyes, holding my ground.

Digger McKenzie is no mystery to me. He was hurt as a child and as a result he's refused to let himself have the life he deserves.

A life I suddenly want to be a part of.

Chapter 28

Digger

Once we get to the lodge, my morning fills up quickly—cooking breakfast for our lodgers and preparing the fishing gear to take a group of guys out on the lake. I normally love to fish, but my heart is not in it today. Not after an uncomfortable night in a chair, followed by an even more awkward conversation with Harper.

Instead of feeling at ease, I'm short-tempered and not in the mood to play host. I certainly don't have the patience to deal with five dentists who are sport fishing during their corporate retreat. I don't even bother to learn their names, instead assuming at least one of them is a Todd. After four hours with Todd and Co.—'cause, let's face it, if the shoe fits—I pull the speedboat up to the dock. It's three in the afternoon and they're already sloshed.

I eye the float plane, wanting to grab Moose and head back out into the wild where I can be free of any responsibility. Which includes being free of a certain woman telling me she knows what's going on inside my head. *What in the hell was that all about?*

I scan the deck for her, not that I really expect to see her down here without the kids. I look for her on the path. And finally, after rushing up the steps to the lodge, I push open the door and peer into the restaurant. She's not there either. I'm left feeling oddly disappointed.

The door opens behind me and when I turn, I see a couple who look exhausted and out of place. They're wearing clothes that, while a bit rumpled, appear to be far too chic for Gamble, Alaska. Their matching grimaces have me saying, "You must have driven up here."

"My God, that road should come with a warning..." the man says. "I thought we were going to fall off the edge more times than I could count."

"I take it you guys took Poker Creek Road to get here." Total amateur move.

"I told you we shouldn't have gone that way," the woman says, pursing her lips.

"Oh, for ..." The man sighs. "We saved over an hour."

"Yeah, and look at us," she says, pointing to herself. "It's going to take me two hours to get this dust out of my hair."

"You wouldn't be covered in dust if you hadn't insisted on leaving the window open," he tells her.

"I was going to blow chunks if I didn't get any fresh air!" she yells.

"It wasn't all that fresh ..."

"You must be the friends of Marge Simpson," I interrupt them, hoping they'll start to settle down.

Their faces light up, and the man takes off his sunglasses. Extending his right hand in my direction, he says, "Ethan Caplan. I'm *Marge's* lawyer."

"Digger McKenzie." I shake his hand while sizing him up. He's roughly the same height as me and looks as though if he hadn't decided to go to law school, he could have made it in Hollywood as a leading man.

The woman is dressed in jeans and a T-shirt with a quilted vest over it, even though it's a hot day. Her long black hair is almost gray from all the road dirt. "Prisha Choudree, Marge's manager."

"You two look like you could use a drink," I tell them.

"I've never needed one more," Prisha says.

"Don't you think we should find Har … Marge first?" Ethan asks before glancing nervously in my direction.

"I'll get you something for the road then," I tell them.

Following close behind me, Prisha says, "Please don't tell me there's more driving involved."

"Just a nice stroll along the lake to the cabin. Water, soda, beer?"

"Beer," they both answer at the same time.

I grab two bottles of Stella from the bar fridge and crack them open. Handing them each one, I say, "I'll show you the way."

Once we're outside, Ethan looks around and inhales deeply while Prisha takes a long pull on her bottle. "The air up here is wonderful," he tells me. "It's so fresh." Then he turns to his traveling companion and asks, "It's nice, isn't it, Prish?"

"Meh, it's air," she answers as we start down the path.

There's something about her I instinctively like. I'm pretty sure it's her no-nonsense grumpiness. Glancing over at me, she asks, "How's Marge doing anyway?"

"I … um …" I'm not sure how to answer this.

"She told me that you've been a life saver and a confidant."

Nodding my head, I answer, "She's a strong woman in a tough situation."

"Good answer," Ethan says. "Positive but vague. You could work in the biz."

"I'd rather be waterboarded for a month of Sundays," I tell him.

Prisha laughs. "I think I'm going to like you, Digger. But seriously, how is our friend? Has she slept at all since Super Douche showed up?"

I can't help but laugh at her very accurate description of Brett. "She had a hard night last night," I tell them. "But with any luck, she's sleeping right now."

"Hard night?" She eyes me with a gleam in her eye.

"She was over at my sister's place last night. They had a few too many."

"Sounds like our girl is making herself right at home."

"My sister's a single mom too. Not that Marge is single yet, but …" I trail off, my gut aching at the thought of her going back to that asshat.

We're just about to round the last corner where the cabin will become visible to us, when I stop. "Look, it's none of my business, but I've spent enough time with Harper and her kids to care about how this all shakes out. If you two are really her friends, and not just more people out to manipulate her, you need to make sure she doesn't go back to Brett."

Narrowing his eyes, Ethan says, "Digger, is it?" He shoots me a look meant to put me in my place. "We've been part of Harper's life for over ten years. You haven't known her for ten days. If anyone should be questioning anyone, it should be *me* asking *you* why it matters to you what she does."

Puffing out my chest like a frigate bird, I tell him, "It matters because she's a good person who deserves a hell of a lot better than that bastard."

"Clearly, you've met him," Prisha says wryly.

"Unfortunately, yes."

She nods, then puts her hand on my forearm. "Trust me,

we're all on the same team here. No one hates Brett more than we do. *No* one. If I could go all Texas Chainsaw on him, I'd do it in a second."

I offer her a smile. "I was thinking cement boots and a deep lake."

Prisha nods. "Yup. I'm gonna like you."

Glancing at Ethan, and back to her, I say, "The feeling's mutual."

When the cabin comes into view, we see Harper sitting on one of the Adirondack chairs on the covered porch. Her feet are propped up on the railing, and she's got a book on her chest. Her eyes are closed, which makes me wish we could let her be for a while. While I know Prisha and Ethan are her friends, they're here to help her strategize how to handle her divorce. It would be nice if she had a bit more time to just relax.

Harper's eyes open when she hears us. She quickly stands and waves. After sliding into her flip-flops, she hurries down the steps, and calls out, "You made it!"

She hugs Prisha first, then Ethan, who, after pulling back, rubs her upper arms. He asks, "You okay, tiger?"

My jaw tightens at the sight of him touching her like that. *What the hell is wrong with me?*

Harper tips her head from side to side in an undecided gesture. "You know … not great. This is day two without the kids." Her voice breaks and Prisha takes her into her arms again.

"I know, sweetie, I know."

Harper wipes fresh tears from the tops of her cheeks. "It's so much harder than I thought it would be." Taking a deep breath, she adds, "I'm just so glad you're both here."

"There is no other place either of us wants to be," Ethan tells her.

"Except maybe back home having this conversation," Prisha adds, slapping at a mosquito on her neck.

Feeling utterly out of place and unneeded now that Harper has her team here, I say, "Well, I'll let you get to it. How about if I send Evie down with some supper for you in a couple of hours?"

Harper offers me a polite but detached smile that I can't help feeling bothered by. "That would be lovely. Thank you, Digger."

And…I feel very much dismissed. "No problem. That's what I'm here for."

I turn and make my way back to the lodge, wondering if Harper's attitude is a sign that the woman I've come to know has disappeared behind her Hollywood façade.

Chapter 29

Harper

Dear Readers,

I have word from the land of the midnight sun. Harper Kennedy's team is rallying around her for a good old-fashioned planning sesh. Prisha Choudree and Ethan Cohen have boarded a plane and flown to rescue our heroine. It's like *Wonder Pets!*, Hollywood style.

I can only assume plans are being planned and decisions are being decided. So long as the bugs I planted in their suitcases keep working, I'll have dish to end all dish very soon.

In the meantime, the Māoris are coming to Venice for their annual massage tour. I've signed up with Poppa Joe for a full two hours of abuse. But my chakras will be aligned, and my chi fully charged, so I'll be in top form to bring you every juicy detail of the Harper files.

Love and Dish,
Ferris Biltmore

"So, what's with Paul Bunyan, anyway?" Ethan asks as I hand him another bottle of beer.

"Paul Bunyan?" I can't help but laugh at his comparison. "Digger is the owner here. He's been a good friend to me and the kids."

"He's hot," Prisha says while kicking off her shoes.

"I didn't think he was your type, Prish," Ethan interjects grumpily.

"Dude, just because I'm gay doesn't mean I'm blind. That man looks like he was built to please."

I burst out laughing as my cheeks heat up at the thought. Ethan just looks annoyed.

"I'm guessing Sheila wouldn't like hearing you talk like that," he tells her.

Prisha scoffs. "Don't forget, my wife was married to a man for ten years. While she's not a huge fan of the lesser half of the species in a romantic sense, she's not a hater."

"*Anyway.*" I try to shift their focus back to the problem at hand. "Tell me more about Helioman and how Brett is in trouble."

"In *Helioman/Midnight Run*, Helioman falls in love with Rocketgirl and they get married," Ethan says. "The studio can't have the real life Helioman walking out on his own wife. It wouldn't sell to the fans."

"Galaxy has postponed the signing of Brett's contract, hoping he'll get his act together," Prisha adds. "Loosely translated, 'Get back together with your wife and family and we'll talk.'"

"His team has tried everything to get Galaxy to reconsider, but unless he can put this PR nightmare to bed, they're not budging," Prisha adds. "It turns out the American public isn't a big fan of his running off with his kids' nanny. Brett's people even reached out to me with an offer."

"What?"

"Get this, they're willing to pay you an advance on his contract if you'll agree to make a joint statement saying you're very much in love and committed to staying together for your family. They also want you to assure the public that Brett has never hit you."

A full-body cringe overcomes me at the thought of pretending to be "very much in love" with Brett ever again.

Before I can formulate an answer, Ethan says, "They're in talks with Oprah's people to see if they can get a Meghan and Harry-style interview with her for you two. The jackass would have to publicly apologize to you, as well. Which will include the standard BS, 'I almost lost everything that matters to me.' You get to hold his hand and pretend you believe him."

"They're going to Oprah before I've signed off on it? That's unbelievably presumptuous."

Ethan cringes. "The thing is, Harp, you've taken him back multiple times before, so …"

"So they just assumed I'd do it again," I answer. "Oh, my God, does the whole world think I'm a pushover?"

"No, definitely not," Ethan says at the same time Prisha shrugs and says, "Kind of, yeah."

"Listen, neither of us want to see you get back together with him. *At all,*" Ethan says, and I can tell there's a but coming. "But, if you are going to take him back anyway, do it now because you'll get half of his salary free and clear," Ethan says quickly like he's ripping off a Band-Aid.

"I couldn't care less about the money," I tell him, folding my arms across my chest. Digger's words about what my kids will learn from how I handle this situation pop into my mind. "And there's *no way* I'm going to agree to an interview my kids will be able to watch when they get older. I'm done lying to the world about him. I'm just done!"

"Good for you," Prisha says firmly.

I nod at her, then look at Ethan. He stares at me for a second and I know he's thinking about the millions of dollars I'm turning down. Finally, he says, "Screw it. Let's not insult the public by putting lipstick on a pig."

"Who exactly is the pig in this scenario?" Prisha asks, narrowing her eyes at him.

"Their marriage," he says as if it should have been obvious.

"I want to be offended, but at this point, I'm too tired to care," I tell them while leaning against the porch railing. "I just need this all to be over with so I can try to create some sense of normalcy for the kids."

"Here's what I propose," Prish says. "We go back to Brett's people and tell them you're willing to make a public statement to the effect that while you and Brett are separating, you're going to work together to co-parent your children as seamlessly as possible. You'll have to tell them the photographer who took the photo misunderstood what you said, and that Brett has never been violent."

I stare out to the lake, watching two loons as they swim along with their family in search of dinner. Smug loons with their perfect unions. "How the hell did Brett's contract become *my* responsibility? I'm not the one who was servicing the nanny."

"It is not on you at all. We're just trying to make things as simple as possible for the kids," Prisha tells me.

"The easiest way to do that is to show some level of cooperation," Ethan says. "Like it or not, if you make an enemy out of Brett, he'll bend over backwards to tarnish your reputation along with his. We don't want you to get blacklisted too."

Rolling my eyes, I tell him, "I don't care if I ever act again. I just want to do what's best for Lily and Liam."

"You may not want to now, but who knows how you'll feel down the road," Ethan says. "My job is to protect you today *and* in the future."

Glancing toward the trees, I see Evie driving up the path in a golf cart. I wave to her. "Supper's here," I announce. "What do you say we don't talk about Brett while we eat?"

"As his very name nauseates me, I'm in full agreement." Prisha makes a face like she's about to barf.

"Hey, Evie," I call out. "Thanks for bringing supper."

She hops out of the golf cart and picks up a large picnic hamper. "Digger put together a fish fry for you. Homemade tartar sauce, slaw, the works."

My stomach grumbles noisily. "Yum."

She walks up on the deck and hands off the basket before nodding to Prisha and Ethan. "I'll leave you to it. Let me know if you need anything else."

"Thanks, Evie. I'm sure we'll be fine." I watch as she walks back to her ride before I start to unpack our food.

"Digger cooks the meals, too?" Prisha's eyes pop open with interest. "What a Renaissance man. Maybe you should marry *him*."

I know she's joking, but her words hit me like a punch to the solar plexus. "He's not the marrying kind." I hand out individually packaged foil containers.

"And just how would you know that?" Prisha asks.

"His mom ran away from home when he and his sister were kids. She went to Hollywood to make it as an actress but wound up dying from a heroin overdose."

"Oh, my god, that's horrible." Ethan looks rightly appalled.

"According to Moira—that's Digger's sister—he's decided that marriage is the devil, and he doesn't want any part of it."

"That's like blaming forest fires on birthday candles." Prisha picks up a lightly battered fish filet and takes a bite. "Sweet Jesus, I've found religion!"

The food is so good, we feast in silence. By the time we're done, I'm too full to move.

"So, where are we sleeping tonight?" Ethan asks. "'Cause I'm about ready to pass out."

Prisha yawns loudly. "Me too."

"I got you a couple rooms in town staying with Digger's sister. It's not the Ritz, but it's better than all of us cramming into my little cabin." I stand up and stretch out. "Let's walk back up to the lodge and then I'll drive over with you."

Leading the way up the path, Ethan asks, "Any bears in the area?"

I startle, realizing this is the first time since getting here that I haven't worried about a bear attack. "I haven't seen any down here. But I almost got killed in the outhouse while we were up at Copper Creek."

"Is that so?" Ethan asks, clearly trying to sound casual, even though he's upped his pace to one that causes Prisha and I to have to run to keep up.

When we get to the lodge, I say, "I better run inside and let them know I'm going to borrow the pickup to show you the way." I really hope I run into Grandpa Jack and not Digger.

But Evie is the first person I see when I open the screen door. "Can I borrow the pickup for an hour?" I ask her.

She shakes her head. "Digger took it into town. He said something about needing to get out of here for a while." She offers me a curious look, like I'm the reason he had to leave.

"No problem," I tell her. "I'll just bring my friends' car back and pick them up in the morning."

As we drive through town, I spot the Toyota in front of a rundown looking place called The Steel Trap. I'm sorely tempted to pull in, but that would be stupid. There's enough on my plate right now without complicating matters with Digger.

Taking a left onto the dirt road that leads to Moira's place, Ethan says, "I feel like we're in the middle of a horror movie."

"What? No, it's beautiful out here," I assure him.

"Uh-huh." He doesn't offer more than that.

Moira's kids are running around the yard with Juno when we pull up the drive. I park and open the door. "Hey, guys, how's it going?"

They all come running in our direction. Colton asks, "Are Liam and Lily back?"

Ash says, "We didn't get a chance to play those fancy video games with them yet."

Wyatt adds, "Mom's in the house. You want me to go get her?"

"I know the way," I tell him. "My friends here are going to stay with you guys for a few days.

Colton eyes Ethan curiously. "You any good at baseball?"

"I haven't played since I was a kid, so I'm guessing no."

Prisha raises her hand and announces, "I was known for my triple plays on my college team." Then she smiles at Ethan and teases, "But I bet this guy here can show you how to make an origami parrot."

Ethan grumbles, "You make one paper bird, and it follows you through life."

"What's origami?" Ash asks him.

"It's the Japanese art of paper folding," Ethan tells him. "I spent a year in Tokyo, and I learned all kinds of interesting things."

"No way!" Wyatt gushes. "That's really cool."

We hear Moira before we see her. "Boys, the peach cobbler just came out of the oven! Get in here and wash up."

We're instantly left in a cloud of their dust.

Moira steps out on the porch and calls out, "Hey, you're here just in time. I just took dessert out of the oven."

She walks down her front steps and smiles at Prisha and then Ethan. "Hi there, I'm Moira."

"I'm Prisha and this is Ethan." She gestures toward Ethan, who gives Moira a lopsided grin I've never seen out of him, before saying, "Thanks for putting up with us for a few days."

"My pleasure," she says. Their eyes lock on each other for a second too long before she glances at the ground, then back up at him. "It's not fancy, but I hope you'll find your room comfortable enough."

"I'm sure it'll be great," he says, suddenly seeming a lot more on board with the idea than he was before he saw his host.

"Come on in and get settled before the boys eat all the cobbler," Moira says before turning around and heading back to the house.

Prisha walks next to her, while Ethan comes over to me. "Last chance to change your mind about things," he tells me. "As soon as I get in my room, I'm calling Brett's team to give them the bad news."

My heart pounds in my chest and I feel like I'm going to vomit, but I manage to say, "Do it."

"Good job," he says, wrapping an arm over my shoulder and giving me a kiss on the forehead. "You've got this, Harper. And Prisha and I have got you."

I nod and force a smile as I stare up at him.

"Having said that, prepare yourself because the storm is coming. I have a bad feeling it's going to be unlike anything we've seen from Brett before."

A few minutes later, I'm on my way back to the lodge, my head spinning with both fear and excitement at having finally pulled the trigger on ending my marriage once and for all. As I near The Steel Trap, I'm overcome by the urge to share the big news, and I know exactly who I want to share it with first.

Chapter 30

Digger

A priest, a rabbi, and an actress walk into a small-town bar … Okay, so it's just an actress, but there's still a punchline and I have a feeling I'm it. All eyes in the place immediately land on Harper, and the place goes quiet, save for the Dwight Yoakam song playing over the speakers. She chews on her bottom lip, scanning the room until her eyes land on me.

Standing next to the pool table, cue in hand, I watch as she walks directly toward me, ignoring the men trying to get her attention.

"Umm, Digger … is that the woman from *Conspiracy*?" Timmy Two-Toes asks me.

He's who I'm playing pool with, and yes, he only has two toes after an ice fishing trip gone horribly wrong. The good thing is, they're his big toes so he can still balance pretty well.

"Not that I know of." I'm not about to add to her troubles by ratting her out.

"Whoever she is, she's a looker, huh? Do you suppose she's coming over here to talk to me?" he asks while scrambling to tuck in his t-shirt.

She arrives in front of us, looking a good deal better than the last time I saw her. I'm guessing my fried food hangover remedy did the trick. "Can I talk to you?" she asks me.

I smile at Timmy and shrug my shoulders. "Looks like it's my lucky day, bud. Not yours."

"Talk away," I tell her, picking up the chalk and screwing it over the end of my cue. "I'm just finishing up my game."

"It can wait," she says, glancing at Timmy.

"Ah, don't worry about Tim. He's real discreet. Aren't you, Timmy?"

"I never told a soul about the time you slept with that busty Fish and Wildlife officer," he answers with a wry grin.

Shooting him a look, I turn to Harper. "See? Real discreet."

"Even so, I think I'll wait until your game's done," she says, plunking her purse on a small round bar table nearby. She hoists herself up onto the stool and sits down, looking agitated.

"Suit yourself," I answer, still stinging a little from how she was acting earlier.

I take my time lining up my shot, then when I sink it, I slowly make my way around the table to line up the cue ball with the eight ball so I can finish the game. It's a shot I could make in my sleep, but I'm kind of enjoying the fact that Harper is waiting on me. Also, that everyone in the entire place is watching her do just that.

Once I tap the cue ball, I straighten up. Before the eight ball sinks into the corner pocket, I tell Timmy, "Good game."

He scowls at me. "I hate it when you do that."

"Win?"

"No. *Assume* you've won before the game's over. That's plain cocky and no one likes that."

I glance back down at the table. The eight ball has already disappeared, and the cue ball is making a return trip toward the center of the table. "I could see how it might be annoying if I was wrong …"

Timmy looks at Harper and says, "I don't know why you want to talk to this guy. He's full of himself."

Harper smiles. "He made a good point though. He did make the shot."

Setting down his cue, Timmy grumbles, "I'm gonna wipe the floor with you next time, Mr. Cocky. Just you wait." Then he shuffles off.

Once he's gone, I pick up my bottle of Bud that was waiting for me on the side of the pool table and sit down across from Harper. "Beer?" I ask.

She winces, clearly not quite ready to drink just yet, then says, "Thank you, no."

"So? What's up?" I ask, taking a sip.

"Are you mad at me for some reason?" she asks.

"Nope," I answer. "I just realized I should extricate myself from your current situation."

"Why is that, exactly?" she asks, but before I can answer, Cecily, the only waitress at the Steel Trap, interrupts.

"What can I get you, hun?" she asks Harper.

"Do you have club soda?" Harper asks her.

"Sure do. Lemon?"

"Yes, please."

Turning to me, Cecily says, "Another beer, Digger?"

"You know it, Cecily." I look back at Harper, trying to remind myself we are not an item and never will be. "What were we talking about?" I ask even though I know.

"I was asking if you're mad at me for some reason."

I shrug my shoulders noncommittally. "Your friends are

here now, and your life is pretty complicated, what with you considering getting back together with that lying, cheating—"

"I'm not getting back together with him," she says firmly.

My head snaps back and my heart picks up its pace. "You sure?"

Nodding, she says, "Positive. You were right. I'd be sending completely the wrong message to my kids."

Relief washes over me, and I'm sure she can see it on my face. "Good for you."

"Thanks," she says. "I know it's the right thing to do, but it's scary, you know …"

I nod, even though I can't imagine what she's feeling. Cecily returns with our drinks, dropping them off quickly without a word.

When she's gone, Harper glances up at the ceiling. "I've had enough humiliation to last a lifetime."

I shake my head, hating like hell that she was ever treated like that in the first place. "You never should have had to put up with that crap. Not for a second."

"Brett's going to be furious when he finds out I'm not going to let him come back." She leans closer to me and adds, "He's going to be dropped by his studio and he's going to blame me."

"He'll get over it," I say, trying to look casual even though I'm fuming at the thought of that jackass blaming anything on her. He's the one who can't keep it in his pants. She's still working that bottom lip of hers and I can't look away. "You're lucky you've got good people on your side who will help you out."

Nodding, she gives me an intense look, her eyes searching mine. "Are you one of them?"

"I am," I tell her, feeling that all too familiar urge to kiss her. "I'll do anything I can to help you, Harper."

She swallows hard and licks her lips. "Really?"

"Just tell me what you need," I say, my voice growing thick with longing.

Etta James takes over the speakers and the most romantic song in the history of music starts to play—"At Last."

"Dance with me?" Harper says, getting up.

"Really?" It's like Christmas and my birthday, times ten.

Nodding, she holds out her hand. "Dancing seems like the right thing to do when you're starting over in life."

I stand and take her hand in mine, then lead her to the tiny, empty dance floor, knowing everyone in here is pretending they're not watching our every move.

Pulling her close, I wrap my left arm around her, then place my hand on the small of her back. We move slowly together, our bodies pressed against each other. A warmth grows between us as we sway to the music. Having her in my arms feels more right than anything I've ever experienced. Her cheek rests against mine and I can smell the scent of her skin and her shampoo. She's like a spring morning right after the rain. She's freshly baked bread. She's every good thing I've ever wanted.

"Harper, I don't know about this ..." I whisper, knowing that she has to be feeling the same things I am.

"Let's pretend we know it's going to have a happy ending for both of us."

I close my eyes, wishing harder than I ever have before that will be the case. Steering her toward the wall, I lean down until our mouths are inches apart. "I think I might just like a happy ending this time," I tell her.

Our mouths find each other. I brush my lips against hers, like I did that night by the fire. But tonight, I don't stop myself. I don't tell her we shouldn't. I just let it happen. I kiss her with urgency, forgetting where I am or who she is or how this will end. I kiss her like my life depends on it. I kiss her like she's my future. I kiss her like she ought to be kissed.

Harper presses herself closer to me, welcoming everything I have to give. After a few more delicious seconds, she pulls back and whispers, "I want you, Digger. I need you."

Her words almost do me in. I'm so caught up, I'd agree to damn near anything right now. "I'm here," is all I manage to say.

She presses her lips to mine and the entire world disappears again, only to reappear at the sound of Brett's voice from across the bar.

"Get your hands off my wife!"

Chapter 31

Harper

Dear Readers,

I was raised on a strange combination of musical tastes. My mom was a fan of folk music a la Peter, Paul, and Mary; angsty chick singers like Alanis Morissette; and good old-fashioned disco. My daddy was a rock man. Give him some Mellencamp, Bon Jovi, and Aerosmith, and he was set.

Where am I going with this? I'll tell you. Every life needs a soundtrack. Every journey needs a theme song.

I've taken on the task of putting together the playlist for the Harper/ Brett Netflix movie that is surely already in the works. It's only a partial, but I'm going to my bi-weekly hypnotherapy session later today where my spirit guide will help me flesh it out.

"Jack and Diane"—sweet blush of first love
"Walk this Way"—courting like a boss
"Lemon Tree"—when love gets sour
"You Oughta Know"—bitter breakup

The final go-to-curtain scene has yet to be written, but I can tell you this, it's either going to be "Livin' on a Prayer" (we can get through anything, baby, as long as we have each other) or "I Will Survive" (that's my boot on your butt kicking you out).

I'm on pins and needles as I eagerly await the outcome!

Dish,
Ferris Biltmore

"Brett, what are you doing here? Where are the kids?" Panic washes over me as sure as if I've been hit with a bucket of ice water.

"The kids are fine. They're up at the house sleeping. I just came down to grab a quick drink." He insinuates himself in between me and Digger.

"You don't leave children alone in a house while they're sleeping—especially a house they don't know. What were you thinking?" I demand.

"I was thinking my wife just screwed me over in the biggest way possible and I could use a drink," he hisses, narrowing his eyes at me. "You just cost me twenty-six million dollars, you know that, right?"

I straighten my spine, too angry at him for leaving our kids alone to care what accusations he lobs at me. Scoffing, I tell him, "You cost yourself that money. Don't you dare blame me for neglecting our kids. This is all on you."

"'Cause you're so worried about them. You're here sticking your tongue down some local yokel's throat?" he sneers, getting right in my face.

Digger pushes him away from me with a flick of his fingers. "Back up, pal, or you and I are going to have a problem."

"Stay out of this, you dumb hick. This is between me and *my wife*."

I'm not going to stand here while they fight. Not while my kids are all alone God knows where. "Where is the house, Brett?"

"I told you, it's just up the road." He drops his phone and the keys on the bar and signals the bartender. "Boilermaker."

"Give me the address right now," I yell at him, snatching the keys off the bar top.

"I know where it is," Digger says, grabbing my purse for me. "Let's go."

I rush out, with him right behind me. My hands are shaking so badly, I can barely hold onto the keys.

"I'll drive," Digger says, seeming to understand I'm too upset to manage it.

By the time I open the passenger door and get in, he already has the car running. "It's going to be okay, Harper," he tells me.

"He left our children alone in a strange house in a town where they barely know a soul. Who does that?" My heart is beating triple time.

Digger throws the car into reverse and circles around so he's facing the road. Then he takes a hard left and guns it. "I'm guessing Brett didn't have much to do with child rearing."

"Nope. That was my domain. I took care of the household and Brett took care of himself. Dear God, what was he thinking coming down here?" I turn and look behind us, but it seems my husband has decided to stay and have his drink.

Digger takes a sharp left up by the Jiffy Stop and we start to climb a hill. "Brett's staying at the Halloways' place. They built their dream home and then their daughter got married and had kids, so they moved to Fairbanks to be near them."

He pulls into a driveway with a steep incline. I have a horrible image of my kids waking up and not knowing where they are. I open the passenger door before the car even comes to a full stop. Racing to the entrance of a large two-story log house, I immediately ram the key into the lock. I'm inside the house in seconds.

Standing at the foot of the steps, I listen for any signs of distress. Digger follows me in. "You check upstairs, I'll look downstairs." As we part ways in search of my kids, I'm once again hit by the fact that Digger would be an amazing father. I know he wouldn't abandon them to go out drinking.

As I hit the top step, I hear quiet sobbing coming from down the hall. I move as fast as my feet will carry me. Outside the door at the end of the hallway, I hear Liam consoling his sister. "It's okay, Lily. I'm here. Did you have a nightmare?"

"I dreamed I was flying in a plane, and I fell out," she hiccups.

With my hand on the knob, I hear my eight-year-old tell her, "You're okay now. I'm here." My heart cracks in two that he has to be the adult in this situation.

I turn the knob and walk in. "I'm here, too." I hurry to her side.

"Where's Daddy? I called and called him, but only Liam came," Lily says as Digger walks in.

Thank goodness he does because I don't know how to answer her question.

"Digger!" my daughter squeals. "I had the worst dream. I fell out of your plane!"

He walks over to her and sits on the side of her bed. "That sounds more like a nightmare," he tells her gently. "But it'll never happen in real life because I'd never take off if you don't have your seatbelt buckled tight. There will be no falling out of my plane."

I sit on the other side of the bed and pull my children into my arms. "I love you both so much."

"I love you too, Mommy," Lily says. "Can we go back to the cabin with you tonight? I need to sleep in your bed with you."

I look over at Digger and feel the heat of what we almost shared. "How did you know I came to take you home? What a smart girl you are," I tell her soothingly.

Liam leans closer to me and whispers, "I don't know where Dad is. I came running when Lily called out in her sleep, but he didn't."

"He called me to come get you," I lie. "He had to go to a meeting."

"A meeting, at night? Here, in Alaska?" Liam is clearly not buying it.

I swallow hard and try to sell it. "He's a really busy guy, isn't he?" Deciding a change of subject is in order, I say, "Guess what? Aunt Prisha and Uncle Ethan are here. They got here this afternoon."

"Are they at our cabin?" my daughter asks.

"They're staying with my sister and the boys," Digger tells them. "I can take you all down to see them tomorrow."

Liam scoots out of bed and leaves the room, returning with his backpack in record time. Then he starts packing Lily's. "Let's hit it," he says. He looks at Digger, and adds, "Thanks for bringing my mom." His voice is laced with emotion.

I'm sure he knows I'm covering for Brett about something. But there's no way I'm going to tell him that his dad left him to drink in a bar. I can't even wrap my head around that.

"You're my main guy." Digger ruffles the back of Liam's hair. "I mean, who else can I trust to drive the golf carts as carefully as you?"

Liam sighs like he's trying to fill a balloon. "No one, I guess."

"Will you carry me, Digger?" Lily asks. "My feet are cold, and I didn't bring slippers."

"You bet, little lady." He picks her up, wrapping her in a blanket off the bed. He smiles at me. "You ready to go?"

"Yeah. I'm ready." Liam and I follow behind. The kids doze off in the car on the way back to the lodge. Liam wakes up long enough to get into the golf cart. Digger puts Lily on my lap, and we continue on, the air around us humming with contentment.

My plans for a romantic night are stalled, but it's probably for the best. I have enough complications right now without adding one more. One more long overdue, really incredible complication … One more sexy-as-sin complication …

Once we tuck the kids in, Digger builds a fire in the living room. "You okay?" he asks.

"I just can't believe Brett would have done something so stupid. He knows so little about our kids that he clearly doesn't even know that Lily has nightmares all the time. *Or* he doesn't care …"

He reaches his hand out to me and sits down on the couch, pulling me next to him. "He just can't seem to stop proving how unfit he is to be a father or a husband, can he?"

"No, he can't." I'm ashamed to have built a life with someone so horrible. My stomach churns with what's coming. People can't seem to get enough of ugly celebrity divorces. My heartache is about to become entertainment for the masses. "This is all going to get so much worse before it gets better."

Digger puts his hand on my cheek and gently rests my head on his shoulder. "But then it *will* get better, Harper. You'll be free of all of it someday."

"I wish that day was today," I say, inhaling the scent of him. "I want it all to be over so I can give the kids a normal, happy upbringing. Some stability."

"If that's what you want," he says, "I'll help you."

Lifting my head off his shoulder, I search his eyes, hoping to find a promise. "You will?" *Is he declaring himself?*

"I'll do whatever it takes to protect the three of you."

Leaning in, I close my eyes and kiss him on the lips, then wrap my arms around his neck and hug him tightly. He hugs me right back. "I feel so safe with you," I whisper.

"You are," he answers, dropping a kiss on my temple. "Why don't you get some rest? You must be exhausted."

Nodding, I snuggle into him again. "Thank you."

He pulls a plush throw off the back of the sofa and covers me with it. "Just sleep. I'm here."

I lie against him, listening to the sound of his heartbeat and let the rise and fall of his chest lull me to sleep.

Chapter 32

Digger

I wake with a start as soon as I hear Lily and Liam's voices. Quickly getting up off the couch, I straighten myself out and do my best to make it seem like I just got here. The last thing I want to do is confuse them.

Lily appears first, her blonde hair resembling a bird's nest in the back as she pads toward me in her long, pink nightgown. Her eyes light up when she sees me. "Digger? Did you bring us breakfast?"

Before I can answer, Harper bolts upright and says, "Hey, baby, good morning."

"Morning, Mommy." Lily hurls herself at her mom for a big hug.

"You hungry?" Harper asks.

"Starving like a big lion!"

"Well, we should feed you then," I answer. "I didn't bring breakfast because I need your help at the lodge."

"We need the big grill for all the pancakes I'm going to eat."

Harper stands up. "Let's get you dressed and brush your teeth, okay? Then we'll go see what Grandpa Jack's got going on."

I wait in the living room, listening to the sounds of Harper and the kids in their morning routine. I hear her say, "You have to brush *all* your teeth, Lily," then, "Okay, I better do the ones at the back for you."

I smile to myself, realizing that for the first time, maybe in my entire life, there's a chance I could let myself want more. Marriage, the kids, the whole thing. I know how crazy this sounds but maybe one of our own if Harper is up for being pregnant again. But if not, Lily and Liam are enough for me. It's nothing I've allowed myself to want because I never believed it could happen.

I've only known Harper for a number of days, but we've already gone through so much together, it feels like years.

Somehow, deep in my bones, I know there's a future here for us. At least I hope there is. The fact that I'm even thinking such a thing is enough to shock the hell out of me.

Harper and I are from two vastly different worlds. I'd never fit into hers, and I'm afraid mine will be too small for her. But maybe, just maybe, it won't be.

When the three of them finally appear, Liam rushes ahead calling, "I'm driving!"

We're almost at the golf cart when I first notice them. I hear the clicks of their cameras before I see the reporters hiding in the trees. Then one of them comes rushing out of the woods, shouting questions at Harper while a man with a video camera keeps pace next to him. Before I know what's happening, we're being swarmed.

"Harper! Is this your new leading man?"

"Did Brett really knock him out at the bar last night after he caught you two making out on the dance floor?"

"Are you ending your marriage for this guy?"

"Brett says you've been coming up to Alaska for a long time to be with Digger. Is that true? And if so, how long has this been going on?"

I freeze, not having the first clue what to do. Harper moves on instinct. She spins around, grabbing Lily and Liam. She tells them, "Get inside. Now."

I follow them, but she turns to me with wild eyes. "Not you. You have to go. Just say no comment. Nothing else."

As she ushers them inside, I hear Liam's voice. "Mom, why would they say that about Digger?"

I get in the golf cart and take off, feeling utterly helpless. Just last night, I promised to protect them, and the first chance I get, I fail miserably. The reporters run alongside me, shouting questions.

"How long have you and Harper been lovers?"

"We know you and Brett had words last night. Are you the real reason their marriage is over?"

By the time I pull up to the lodge, even more reporters appear. I'm surrounded as I get out and try to make my way to the steps. My lips are sealed, but my heart is pounding while rage courses through my body. Brett better not show his face around here because I'm afraid I'll kill him with my bare hands if he does.

The reporters form a circle, making it impossible for me to get through unless I'm willing to shove one of them out of the way, which I'm not. I let out a deep sigh and say, "No comment. Please leave."

But they don't. They keep peppering me with questions as I slowly push through them. The sound of a shotgun stops everything. Most of them flinch. One of them screams, while another hits the ground. Most of them scatter which clears a path for me to get through.

Grandpa Jack stands on the porch with his gun aimed at the sky. "Now, that'll be enough of that. This is private property, open only to guests of the lodge and the restaurant. We don't have any rooms available, so you either leave or you come inside and buy breakfast. I've got a special deal for reporters today. A thousand dollars a plate."

I use the distraction he's creating to get inside, and once the door is closed behind me, I turn and look out. The rats are scurrying toward their vehicles. I watch as they pull out of the lot, but they don't go far. Instead, they park on the road. Grandpa Jack walks in and hands me the gun. "I gotta go punch down the dough. You got this?"

"Yeah, I think so," I tell him as Evie rushes over to me.

"What the hell happened last night?" she asks. "I saw the footage at the Steel Trap. I can't believe you shoved Helioman!"

Crap. Someone was filming us.

"And that was some kiss, boss," she adds with a big smirk.

I shut my eyes and rub my forehead with my fingertips, feeling every muscle in my body tense up.

"It's a long story that I don't have time to tell," I say, walking into the office.

Evie follows me. "Are you and Harper an item now?"

"I … can't really talk right now, okay, Evie? Can you handle the restaurant for me?"

She nods, but before she leaves, I tell her, "Harper and the kids'll need some breakfast. Obviously, they can't come up here to get it."

"I'm on it," she says, shutting the door behind her.

I sit down at my desk, dumbfounded by what just happened. It looks like that bastard has made Harper out to be the bad guy in this whole situation to try to save his sorry ass.

I'm tempted to go out to the road and tell the reporters the truth—that Harper and I just met, and that Brett's not only a cheater, but he left his kids alone last night to go drinking. But I can't do that. It would only make things worse than they already are, and there's no way I want to add fuel to the inferno.

Grabbing my phone out of my pocket, I call Harper's number, but it goes straight to voicemail. "Dammit," I mutter.

If only I knew what to do to make this better. If only I could talk to Harper. If only I hadn't let myself get dragged into this mess.

Chapter 33

Harper

Dear Readers,

I've revised the Harper/Brett playlist to include "Dirty Laundry" by Don Henley. We are positively lapping up the tidbits leaking out of Alaska!

This morning Harper Kennedy walked out of her rustic lodgings with her kiddos and—drum roll, please—a man! A man that was not her husband. A man I wouldn't half mind seeing in a pair of red polyester gym shorts.

Needless to say, the press went wild. Harper sent Hunky Pants on his way, alone, and within an hour her "team" showed up. They have sequestered themselves.

I should probably point out that Harper was caught kissing her Alaskan hot potato in a bar last night. (The video is posted below.) I'm all kinds of aflutter over it, let me tell you. While the words, "She cheated first," are being bandied about, I'm giving her the benefit of the doubt.

After all, this is my girl's first hint of infidelity, but it's certainly not Brett's first rodeo.

Dish,
Ferris Biltmore

~

What are all those reporters doing here? Did they follow Brett? I push my kids through the front door of the cabin before hurrying around to make sure the blackout curtains are pulled tight on all the windows.

"Mommy," Lily calls from the living room. "I'm scared."

"There's nothing to be scared about, Lil," Liam tells her. "Those are some of the same worms that were at our house in California. They can't hurt us."

"That's right, no one can hurt us," I call out while hurrying into the room to join them. I open their iPad and pull up *Lilo and Stitch*. "You two hang out here for a few minutes. Mommy has to call Auntie Prisha."

Closing the door behind me, I hit the speed dial for Prisha's number.

"Oh, my God, I slept like a baby! And not a colicky, pain-in-the-butt teether, either. I closed my eyes last night and boom! I was out. I'm still in bed …"

Before she can keep rambling on and on about her amazing night's sleep, I tell her, "My cabin was swarming with reporters this morning. They saw Digger leave the house with me and the kids."

"He spent the night?! I'm not judging, but honey, this

isn't the time to get involved with a new man. At least not publicly." I hear her scurrying around. "Digger is a fine specimen, and I would heartily condone a hook-up there, but you've got to wait until the storm clears, or the press will eat you alive."

Panic causes my throat to constrict. "It's too late, Prish. I stopped to see Digger last night at The Steel Trap after dropping you off. Brett showed up and he saw us kissing on the dance floor."

"Shiva, Vishnu, and Ganesha …" That's Prisha's Hindu version of the Catholic Jesus, Mary, and Joseph. She must move the phone from her mouth because my eardrums don't actually break when she screams, "Ethan, get your ass up! Red alert! The mongoose is out of the barn!"

I'm not quite sure what a mongoose has to do with this, but it's clear she's as freaked as I am. "Prish, what do I do?"

"You do nothing until Ethan and I get there. Keep the door locked and hide under the covers. Help is on the way!"

I put my phone down and, when I walk back into the bedroom, I force a smile for the sake of the kids. "We'd better call up to the lodge and see if they can bring us breakfast, huh?"

"I want waffles and sausage and eggs and a muffin and cereal …" Lily starts naming every breakfast food she knows.

Liam on the other hand says, "I'd better have a poached egg on toast." My little old man. It certainly hasn't been a carefree childhood. No kid should have to dodge skeezy reporters and photographers.

I call the lodge, hoping and praying that Digger doesn't answer. I have no idea what to say to him. I'm absolutely mortified that he's gotten caught in the middle of this nightmare. "Whistler Lake Lodge." Oh, thank God, it's Digger's grandpa, Jack.

"Jack, this is Harper Kennedy."

"How you doin' this morning, hun?"

"I've been better," I tell him. "I don't know if Digger said anything but …"

"He didn't have to say a word. The crowd we had up here was like nothin' we've ever seen before. I had to get out my shotgun."

Holy crap. "You didn't shoot anyone, did you?"

"Well, my eyesight isn't what it used to be, but my aim is still good."

"Meaning?"

"Unless one of them was directly above me, I didn't kill anyone." He starts to chuckle so hard, he wheezes. "They all scattered pretty fast when the gun went off."

"Jack, I'm really sorry to get your family caught up in all of this."

"Don't mention it. I haven't had that much fun in years," he answers. "Now, what can I do for you?"

"Listen, do you think you could ask Evie to bring some breakfast down for me and the kids?"

"Food is already on the way," he says.

I consider asking him who's bringing it, but don't bother. Digger would know better than to come back here right now. "Thank you. I really appreciate it."

"No problem, sweetie. You take care of you and those two darlings of yours and let us know if we can do anything to help."

I hang up the phone feeling a mixture of fear and rage. I should have known Brett would tell the world that *I'm* the cheater. That bastard. I pace in the living room for a minute, then peek out the window. I don't see any paparazzi, but that doesn't mean they aren't there. I do spot a golf cart coming down the path though. As it gets closer, I see Digger is behind the wheel. What in the heck is he doing? I told him to stay out of sight.

He waves when he gets out of the cart. He looks right and left like he's going to be jumped at any moment. As soon as I open the door, I whisper-yell, "Why did you come?" sounding as angry as I feel.

"I brought breakfast ..." He looks confused. "I thought you'd want something to eat."

"I do. I mean, we do, but I told you not to come back. It's not safe here."

"I don't know if you remember this, Harper, but we don't have a lot of extra hands on deck. Grandpa Jack is in the kitchen baking, and Evie is waiting tables. That left me."

"Just hurry up and bring the basket." My head pivots right to left, looking for trouble.

As Digger climbs the stairs to the deck, we both hear another vehicle approaching. "Shoot." I grab him and pull him into the cabin. "No one can see you here."

"I *do* own the place, you know." He's mad, but I can't concern myself with that right now

"I can't be seen with you, Digger. It looks like Brett is playing hardball and that means I have to stay above reproach at all times."

As soon as he's through the door, I slam it behind him.

"Digger! You brought food!" Lily runs at him and gives him a big hug. I imagine that might have been the reception he expected from me too.

"Did you bring any poached eggs?" Liam asks, walking into the kitchen with a concerned expression on his face.

"Ew, no. I brought waffles and sweet rolls, fruit and yogurt." He ruffles my son's hair. "How does that sound?"

In lieu of answering, Liam merely nods his head.

The knock on the door startles us all. I call out, "Get out of here you scum-sucking losers!"

"That's a welcome for you." It's Ethan.

Yanking the door open, I motion for him and Prisha to

come through. Prisha takes one look at Digger and says, "I thought you left."

Digger crosses his arms. "I brought breakfast. I thought Harper and the kids would be hungry." He takes a step toward the door. "But don't worry, I'm leaving now."

"Don't go yet." Prisha raises her hand to stop him.

"He shouldn't stay," I warn her.

"While he's here, I might as well give him my crash course on what comes next." She takes Digger's arm and pulls him toward the living room.

I tell the kids, "Go on in and eat on my bed. You can play some video games too." Allowing them to eat in bed while playing games is akin to my telling them that I grew wings and can fly. Neither is a happenstance they've heard before.

Once the kids are out of the room, Prisha says, "I looked online before we came over. Someone at the bar filmed the two of you on the dance floor acting all lovey-dovey. Then they filmed an altercation between Brett and Grizzly Adams here." She gestures toward Digger with a frown on her face.

"This has nothing to do with me," Digger moves to stand up, but Prisha pushes him back down.

"It has *everything* to do with you," she tells him. "Up until the news of this little flirtation broke, Brett was the bad guy. But now, thanks to the two of you needing to suck face in public, he's working hard to convince the press his marriage ended because Harper was having an affair with you." She points at Digger.

"That's a load and you know it," Digger answers with a leveled rage.

"What I know doesn't matter," Prisha tells him. "The tabloids aren't exactly known for searching out the truth. The more salacious the story, the more often it's repeated. The thought of America's sweetheart here, getting it on with you"

—she points at Digger again—“is like Fourth of July fireworks at the Capitol. Everyone wants to watch that explosion.”

Ethan doesn’t say anything. Instead, he stands menacingly at the front door, acting as sentry. No one comes or goes without his say so.

“Look,” Digger says. “I’m not going to say anything. I’m not going to do anything. Just let me go back to the lodge.”

“You’ve got to stay away from her,” Prisha tells him. “I’m sorry about what happened last night, but it escalated the ugly and that means Harper has to forget that you exist.”

He looks at me with hurt in his eyes. “Harper?”

Shrugging my shoulders, I tell him, “It’s not what I wanted to have happen, Digger, but I have no control over the press.”

“So, what are you going to do now?” he demands heatedly. “Just walk away with your tail between your legs and let Brett win?”

“We’re going to do our best to clean up this mess,” Prisha says. “And you can believe me when I say that I will bend over backwards and do the splits naked in the middle of the I-5 if it means that Brett won’t come out on top.”

Ethan calls out, “Dear God, Prish, keep it PG, will ya?”

Digger looks at me. “What about you?”

Before I can answer, Prisha says, “She and the kids are leaving here today.”

Digger jams his hands in his pockets while shaking his head. “You’re going to leave? Just like that?”

“Just like nothing.” Once again Prisha answers for me. “She wouldn’t have had to go if you two hadn’t made such a public display.”

“That was my fault,” I tell her. “I shouldn’t have gone into that bar, and I shouldn’t have danced with Digger. I sure as hell shouldn’t have kissed him.”

"Nice to know how you really feel about things," Digger scoffs. "But while you're regretting knowing me, you might want to remember that the only reason you knew that Brett left the kids alone last night was because you were with me."

I reach out and touch his arm. "I don't regret that it happened. Just...*where* it happened. I've really enjoyed getting to know you ..."

He shifts away from me to get my hand off him. "Getting to know me? Oh, is that where we're at now? I promise you I'll take care of you and the kids, and the next morning you're telling me it was nice getting to know me?"

My head is pounding with the stress of it all. I want to cry and scream and curl up in a ball until it's all over, but I can't do that. I have to stay calm and level-headed. My reputation and my children are depending on it. Sighing, I say, "Look ... this whole situation is already out of control. And being with you is just not possible. Not right now. You must be able to see that."

"What I see is a woman who's spent years playing the victim and letting everybody else make her decisions for her. And now when you have a chance at real happiness, you're going to let it slip through your fingers, so you don't wind up looking bad. Who cares what a bunch of strangers thinks about you?"

"You don't understand what my life is like, Digger," I say. "As a mother, I don't have a choice."

"Yeah, like how you had no choice but to put up with Brett's shit for all these years."

"I was trying to protect my children!" I yell.

"You know what? I don't know if that's even true. I think deep down you're terrified of not being America's sweetheart anymore. There's a part of you—the part that took you to Hollywood in the first place—that still needs to have an adoring public. And you can't stand the thought of giving that up for anyone. Certainly not for me."

"All right, Digger, that's enough," Ethan says.

Ignoring Ethan completely, Digger says, "You're going to cut and run to save your own hide. Forget what happens to anyone else. So long as you don't look bad. You're exactly who I thought you were the day I met you—a Hollywood princess who only cares about herself."

He's lumping me in with his mom and it feels like a knife to my heart. "Digger …"

Spinning on his heel, he stalks to the door. Ethan steps aside to let him go, and over his shoulder, Digger says, "Goodbye, Harper. Have a nice life."

He's gone before I can say anything else.

Chapter 34

Digger

Harper, the kids, and her entourage got on the first plane out of Alaska this afternoon. Gone forever, never to return.

I tried to keep as busy as possible at work, but as soon as I finished up, I went for a long drive that wound up on my sister's doorstep. We're sitting out on her back porch having lemonade. Moira's munching on homemade chocolate chip cookies while I pour my heart out. She listens to the whole awful story without saying a word.

When I'm done, she demands, "So, *that's* how you left things?" Her face wrinkles up in disgust.

I nod and let out a long sigh. "That's how we left things."

"You don't … maybe think you were a teensy bit hard on her?" she asks, picking up another cookie off the plate. "I mean considering everything she's going through …"

"No, I don't," I answer, wishing I hadn't stopped here in the first place. "Everything I said is true, and if you ask me, she needed to hear it."

"The truth according to Digger, anyway," she says, raising her eyebrows.

"What's that supposed to mean?" I ask, irritation scratching at my insides.

"It means, you have a tendency to see things through poop-colored glasses, always assuming the worst of people, especially people like Harper," Moira tells me. "I mean, seriously, Digger? How could you tell her she's been playing the victim all these years, just for trying to keep her family together?"

A wave of guilt hits me again. I try to rid myself of it by reminding myself of the logic of my argument. "I could see a woman who has no education and no resources staying with a terrible husband, but someone so rich that she never has to work again? That's a woman who has options, Moira. A woman with choices."

"You don't get it." Moira sets her glass down on the table. "When a woman has kids, those little people come first, no matter what. The only choice is their happiness."

I scoff. "Yeah, like our mother?"

"Harper is *not* our mother. She's nothing like her and you know it. She puts Liam and Lily first every chance she gets. Having to spend two nights away from them nearly did her in," my sister tells me. "You must have been able to see that for yourself, unless you're totally blind."

"I didn't come here to be lectured." My eyes narrow in annoyance.

"If you came here to hear 'well done,' you stopped at the wrong house. You messed up, Digger. Big time. Telling Harper she's selfish was not the way to go if you ever want to see her again."

"She's the one who doesn't want to see me again. You didn't hear how dismissive she was, telling me she really 'enjoyed getting to know me.'" I emphasize the last bit with air quotes. "Who says that to someone they care about? Someone who basically told you he'd do whatever it took to protect you and your kids, and to help you start over."

Moira's mouth drops open. After a second, she says, "You told her that?"

I nod while trying to push aside the pain I'm feeling. "And the worst part is, I meant it." Scrubbing my hand through my hair, I add, "I'm such an idiot, falling for her act."

"What makes you think it's an act?"

"Isn't it obvious? She left the first chance she got."

Moira shakes her head. "She's in an impossible situation. Her life was already a hot mess, but with the press getting a hold of the video of the two of you, it pretty much imploded. Ethan told me that her being here with the kids had become a situation they could no longer control. There are too many ways people could get to them, now that they've been discovered."

Even though I'm listening, I don't want to hear it. I want to stay angry. Making Harper the villain is the only way to protect my heart.

Moira continues, "Do you know what her life is going to be like now?"

"Back to living life as a Hollywood princess, I suppose."

Rolling her eyes, my sister tells me, "They're posting security guards outside her home. She and the kids will be prisoners there for weeks. Ethan's already working on getting her the best divorce lawyer in the country so she can fight for full custody of the kids. Her entire life is going to be doing whatever it takes to make sure Lily and Liam get through this with the least amount of damage."

"I still say she didn't have to go back."

"She couldn't stay here. Not if she's going to shield the kids from all of this."

Listening to the sound of the frogs croaking in the creek nearby, I sit back in my chair and let out a long sigh. My body aches like I've gone ten rounds with a grizzly. I'm so twisted up, I don't know who's right and who's wrong. All I know is this hurts like a son of a bitch. I never should have ignored my instincts and let myself fall in love.

Holy hell, I'm in love.

"Look, you can sit here feeling sorry for yourself, but it's not going to get you anywhere," Moira says. "You need to get your head out of your backside and go apologize to her. See if there's any possible way that she'd want to see where things would go if you two gave it a real shot. In the future, I mean. After her divorce is final."

Shaking my head, I quietly tell her, "No way. We could never make it work. It's best if I accept that now and not open my life to a world of pain."

"Loving someone does that, idiot. The whole point is to trust somebody enough to be vulnerable with them."

"That's not how I roll, Moira, and you know it."

"Fine, take the coward's way out." Moira stands up to collect our dishes. "Go back to the same lonely life you've always had."

"I like that life," I tell her, watching as she stalks to the back door and yanks it open.

"Good night, jackass."

She's inside with the door shut before I answer, "I'll have you know I was happy on my own." As I stand up and walk down the steps, I add in a whisper, "It didn't hurt as much."

Chapter 35

Harper

Dear Readers,

Word on the street is that Miss Harper has decided to play hardball. And really, who could blame her? She's reached out to Madame Gloria Woodsworth, divorce lawyer to the stars, to ask her for representation in the big showdown.

For those who don't know, Gloria handled all of Jenny from the Block's divorces, Jen from Bennifer 2, and our dear "*Friend*" Jennifer when she and Brad parted ways.

If I were Brett, I'd be shaking in my Calvin Klein undies, because when Gloria comes for you, you are screwed. And not in a pleasant date-night sense, either. We're talking a prison shower and Brett just dropped the soap.

Miss Harper has made her decision and has finally cracked the whip like I knew she could.

Go, girl!

Today's dishes are officially done!
Ferris Biltmore

We don't try to hide on our way out of town. There's no point. Instead, we keep Liam and Lily inside while we make a big show of packing all our things into the trunk of Ethan's rental. Then, we whisk the kids into the backseat, careful to shield them from the cameras. The windows have a dark tint, so once we're safely inside, no one will be able to get a good picture.

We're leaving to draw the media away from the lodge. As hurt as I am by what Digger said, he's not wrong. This is my mess to clean up. Evacuating Gamble is just my first step. I don't want Grandpa Jack and Evie to have to deal with the paparazzi climbing around in the shrubbery for the next few days.

Liam and Lily have been non-stop complaining that their vacation got cut short. Lily's devastated that she didn't get a chance to flip pancakes with Digger, and Liam is sporting that worried look that breaks my heart. He knows I'm not telling him something, and even though he's too wise to ask me about it in front of his sister, I know I'll be facing a lot of questions from him when we're alone.

The crappiest part is that I can't tell them why we're leaving without them learning more than they should. Protecting a man who's actively trying to hurt you is the absolute worst.

As soon as we get on the private jet, I let the kids play on their iPad. With their headphones in place, they won't hear the grown-ups talking. But just to be sure, I've got them snuggled into comfy chairs near the front of the plane so I can see if one of them wanders back here.

Ethan called a friend of his who's a high-powered divorce attorney. Since we've got a thirty-minute delay before the plane can take off, we're going to make good use of that time. Gloria Woodsworth is going to walk us through the next steps.

"Harper, how are you holding up?" my new attorney asks me after Ethan makes introductions.

"I'm all right. I feel like a complete idiot about the video that got leaked though," I tell her.

"A judge won't care. It's not like it was a full-on sex tape." She sounds so confident, I almost feel better. "Trust me, *those* are hard to come back from. Unless of course, you're Kim Kardashian and Paris Hilton. But still—ew."

"That stupid kiss was the only thing that happened," I say.

"Honestly, it's none of my business. Ethan has filled me in on Brett's … transgressions. The judge will care *a lot* about his repeat offender status, so it really puts you in a power position. Having sex with the nanny while the children were playing nearby was a huge misstep. Leaving them alone to go to the bar—unforgivable. That's your ace in the hole."

A wave of anger comes over me when I think of the kids at home alone, and Lily having woken up from a nightmare. Tears of rage fill my eyes and I blink them back, unable to find my voice.

Prisha fills in the silence for me. "How do we stick it to him?"

"If there weren't children involved, I'd tell you to go public with everything, really let the world see his true colors," Gloria answers. "But as it's Harper's goal to protect the kids from as much as possible, that means we need to use the leverage we've got without actively smearing Brett's reputation. More's the pity."

"He deserves to be drawn and quartered," Prisha mutters, sitting back.

"Definitely not the most satisfying strategy, but it yields the best outcome," Gloria says. "We go to his attorney with the threat of including those incidents in the petition for divorce. Being that all documents filed with the courts become public record, his only shot at protecting what's left of his reputation will be to agree to Harper's terms. Harper, what's your best guess about him fighting for joint custody?"

I swallow hard. The truth hurts like hell to voice. "I think he'd rather protect his career."

If Gloria is shocked by this, she doesn't let on. Instead, she says, "Ethan, thoughts?"

"I agree. I think if Harper's reasonable about the money, Brett will be quick to give up the kids."

I let out a sob, then cover my mouth and try to regroup. The truth of that statement breaks my heart more than anything else that has happened.

Gloria's voice becomes gentle. "It's so hard, I know. You had a family with him because you believed you both wanted a family."

"Exactly," I whisper. "And there are two innocent little people who think the world of him, who will one day realize he never fought for them."

Prisha rubs my back while Ethan rests his hand on mine. "They've got you, Harper, so they're always going to know they're loved."

Nodding, I sniffle and look out the window for a second. Seeing the mountains in the distance makes me wish I wasn't going home.

"I'm going to let you go," Gloria says. "I have enough to get started, but there will be lots of back and forth before we file. Harper, your job is to maintain a squeaky-clean image until all is said and done. That means no contact with your lumberjack."

"That won't be a problem," I tell her, thinking of how much Digger must hate me. I hate myself for how I treated him.

The trip home is exhausting. It's nearly midnight by the time we're finally at the house. Prisha already has a team of security guards patrolling the perimeter, a fact that makes me feel simultaneously safe and sick to my stomach. How is this my life?

After getting the kids in bed, I make myself a cup of Sleepytime tea, then wander around the house while I sip it. I stare at the space that was once my refuge, my haven. But it isn't anymore. The whole place feels foreign to me. It's too big, too decorated, too … much. I've grown comfortable living in a small and simple cabin. I know the kids loved it.

When I get to the living room, the image of Brett with a bent-over Justine flashes through my mind. The first thing I need to do is get rid of that damn couch. In fact, maybe I'll redecorate the entire house. But somehow even that doesn't seem like enough to make this feel like my home again.

This was our family home. The place Brett and I were going to live out the rest of our lives. I was so bright-eyed and naïve, I believed every lie he ever told me. *I'm sorry, Harper. I love you, Harper. This is the last time, Harper.*

I need to move on, which means moving on from this place. Burning the couch will be a symbolic end for this chapter in my life.

I finally drag myself up the stairs, but instead of going to my bedroom, I walk to Lily's. Standing in the doorway, I watch her sleep for a minute. The pressure on my chest is unbearable. Crawling into bed next to her, I smell the top of her head and immediately feel the comfort of my sweet, innocent little girl. Instead of falling to sleep, I proceed to toss and turn the night away. I think about Gamble and Brett and Digger. I think about all the choices I made that have led me to where I am now.

What would have happened if I'd never got that commercial in college? I wouldn't have had enough money to comfortably move to LA. Would I have done it anyway? What if I'd never met Prisha? What if I'd never met Brett? What if I hadn't been cast in the starring role of *Conspiracy*?

The what-if game is the enemy of sleep. One question leads to another and before you know it, you're a tightly wound ball of anxiety. Snuggling closer to my baby, I force my brain to count my blessings. Nothing in this world would have been better than having my kids, and in order to have them, I needed Brett.

I try to be grateful for him in that regard, but the question that keeps popping in my brain is, why wasn't I enough for him? What did all those other women have that I didn't?

When I finally detach from reality and let my brain rest, I dream about Digger. I dream that I'm lying in his arms, safe and secure. Loved and appreciated.

Why couldn't I have met him first?

One Month Later …

The last few weeks have been an endless cycle of meetings that I didn't want to attend, angry calls from Brett at all hours of the day and night, and more sleepless nights than my body can tolerate. The longer this drags on, the more positive I am that I'm completely done with Hollywood.

I can count my only friends in this town on two fingers (middle fingers, which I'm holding up to the rest of the people parading around as my close personal confidants—the ones who only call to get the inside scoop).

I do my best to avoid social media, entertainment news, and any online articles about Brett and me. But I still know my name is being dragged through the mud by his people. And all they've got is me kissing Digger. How they feel that's on par with the Manson murders is beyond me.

The clock is ticking because school starts in a few weeks, and I know once the kids go back, there will be no hiding the truth from them. They'll be surrounded by classmates whose parents want the gory details. They'll be prodded, questioned, and they'll hear far too much. At after-school pick-ups, I will be barraged with a slew of inquiries about Brett, Justine, me, *and* Digger.

I'm going to have to tell the kids just enough, so I don't break their trust, but not so much that their view of love and marriage is forever tarnished. It's a tightrope I'm not sure I can cross. But if I fall, the consequences will last a lifetime.

On top of all of that, I ache for Digger. The look on his face the last time I saw him, the pain and disappointment. All I want to do is pack our things and rush back up to Gamble to be with him. The kids were happy there. I was happy there. And it was because of him. I've never felt so safe or adored in my entire life than I did when I was with him. Everything was better with him.

Not being able to contact him until the divorce proceedings are final is killing me. I want him to know the truth. That I'm in love with him, and even though I don't know how to make it work, I want to find a way.

Chapter 36

Digger

Summer is finally drawing to a close. The night skies are starting to make an appearance every evening around nine p.m. They bring cool air and the promise of change. Winter means that Evie, Grandpa Jack, and I get a well-earned break from being run off our feet.

Thanks to the whole world hoping to catch sight of Harper, the lodge has never been busier. It's by far been our most profitable season yet. A season that, according to our upcoming bookings, is uncharacteristically carrying over into the fall. I'm saving up to build a large gazebo for hosting special events, which should help draw even more business.

I'm also back to my preferred state of being alone. No romantic entanglements for this guy. The only problem is nothing feels normal, like it did before. And all because I was fool enough to let myself fall for someone I had no business falling for.

Having said that, Harper is the reason we can afford the

gazebo. We've been booked solid every night and the restaurant has become a tourist destination for those who want to "sit where Harper sat." The chaos of it all is exactly what I've needed to get through the last few weeks, but the constant stream of people asking me about Harper hasn't exactly made it possible to forget about her and move on.

Every night when I flop into bed, I find myself looking her up online. I pretend I'm just checking to make sure nothing bad has happened to the kids, but of course, that's just a load of crap. As pathetic as it is, I'm really hoping to see some sort of sign that she's thinking about me (even though she's not) and that she's changed her mind and is coming back (which she won't).

Neither of us have tried to contact each other since she left. But the truth is, she's the one who left, so it's really up to her to make the next move. If there is a next move to make, that is.

Today is Grandpa Jack's seventy-ninth birthday, so we're at Moira's for some whiskey and cake (his preferred way to celebrate). We've already sung the song, Jack opened his gifts (the same thing he asks for every year—wool socks, a new plaid shirt, and a three-pack of Hanes white cotton T-shirts), and we've had cake and ice cream. He and Moira are sitting in her kitchen visiting while I read the twins a bedtime story.

I've just closed the book and my eyelids are growing heavy. I'd like nothing more than to drift off to sleep right here so I can avoid …

"Uncle Digger," Ash says, waking me up. "You're snoring real loud."

"Sorry, buddy," I tell him, rolling off his bed and standing up.

"That's okay," he says, grinning up at me. "But, man, you are a loud sleeper. It's like a chainsaw was going off."

I ruffle his hair, drop a kiss on his forehead, and wish him a good night's sleep. Turning to Colton's bed, I see he's already out cold, so I tuck his blanket up under his chin and sneak out of the room. When I get to the kitchen, Grandpa is on his second drink (at least I hope it's only his second one) and Moira is standing by the kettle, waiting for it to boil.

"Would you like some herbal tea?" she asks.

"No, thanks," I say. "We should probably get going. I'm beat."

"Sit down," Jack tells me. "I only have a few more birthdays left in me."

I do as he says, but not before I point out that he's been saying that since I was a teenager.

"And every year I get closer to being right," he says with a gleam in his eye. "Now, what are we going to do about you?"

"What do you mean?" I ask, even though I'm pretty sure I know what he means.

"Well, from where I'm sitting, you're miserable, and I don't see it getting better unless you do something about it."

"I'm fine," I tell him, looking over at Moira for support.

She joins us at the table, but instead of taking my side, she reaches out and puts her hand on mine, patting it like she does the boys'. "You're anything but fine."

"Don't start," I tell them angrily.

"Digger, did I ever tell you about my friend George?" Jack asks.

Oh, here we go. Pursing my lips, I shake my head. "No, but—"

"—George was a real stubborn ass. You never could tell him anything. This one time, he figured it was still cold enough to take his skidoo out on the lake for one last run before the ice melted."

"Let me guess, someone tried to tell him not to, but he wouldn't listen, the ice cracked and he died."

My grandpa looks offended, as he probably should. I'm being rude. "Nope. *Nobody* told him that. Not even Kitty, his wife of thirty-six years, because they all knew he wouldn't listen."

"Oh, plot twist," I say, raising my eyebrows. "But he ended up dead, right? And George is just a metaphor for the fact that I'm dead inside without Harper and the kids, and that I should hop on the next flight out of here and apologize and tell her I love her and that I want to spend the rest of my life with her?"

Jack looks at me for a second, then makes a clicking sound with his tongue. "The ice didn't crack, George made it home safely. But that night, Kitty added rat poison to his spaghetti. Finished him off right there at the table. She just couldn't stand the thought of living another day with a man who wouldn't listen to reason."

He takes a sip of his drink while Moira and I give each other the "what the hell was that?" look. When he sets his glass down, he says, "But you're right. You're also a stubborn ass and you should go find the woman you love and tell her how you feel."

I open my mouth to protest, but Moira beats me to it. "Don't waste your breath, Grandpa. There's no reasoning with this one," she says, pointing to me with her thumb. "He's going to say he's not in love with her and that it would never work anyway, and that Harper left *him* so there's nothing he can do about it. Oh, and he's also going to say that she never loved him in the first place because she said that thing about"—and here's the bit when they both start talking in unison—"'it was nice getting to know you.'"

"Yup," Grandpa says. "Obviously, it had nothing to do with the fact that she was just about to embark on a very public, nasty divorce and that the timing was all wrong …"

"And everything to do with her, meaning she didn't give a crap about him and never did," Moira continues.

"Did you two rehearse this when I was putting the boys to bed?" My eyes narrow at them.

They both wear innocent expressions that display the family resemblance to a tee. "We'd never do something like that," Moira says, lifting her mug to hide her face.

"Look," I tell them. "For a brief time, I thought I might not mind going down that road. But that was when I figured there was a chance Harper wanted to be with me. But I was wrong. She doesn't, and it's definitely over." I turn to my sister. "And you're right, Moira, she is in the middle of an ugly divorce. Now, if in the future, she were to come back up here, I might be willing to see how things pan out. But since that's highly unlikely, I'd appreciate it if the two of you would just leave it the hell alone already so I can get back to pretending I never met her."

Standing, I look at Grandpa Jack. "If you want a ride back, you'd better get up out of that chair and start moving to the door, because I'm leaving."

I walk to the front entry and tug my boots on. Grandpa is on his feet, making his way over as slow as a two-hundred-year-old turtle. Moira puts his gifts in a bag and passes him. Handing it to me, she says, "She's not going to come back if you don't give her a reason to."

"She's not coming back, no matter what I do."

Shrugging, Moira says, "I guess you'll never know, will you?"

"I guess I won't." Dammit. She's right.

She and Jack look at each other.

"Sounds like he can live with the idea of having chased off the love of his life," Jack says to her.

"Too bad. He's been a real bear since she left."

"Like a grizzly after winter," Jack adds.

"Could you two please stop talking about me like I'm not here?" I ask, feeling completely irritated. "It's not as cute as you think it is." Pushing the door open, I walk out onto the porch. "Thanks for the cake," I tell my sister while jogging down the steps to the driveway.

"It's not the cake that's going to change your life. It's the advice."

God save me from everyone who feels driven to stick their nose in my business.

Chapter 37

Harper

Dear Readers,

The popcorn is popped and I'm ready to roll. I'm so excited I've even pooh-poohed my traditional spray butter for the real stuff, and a lot of it.

I'm nestled under my faux fur throw on the couch eagerly awaiting Harper's interview with Sophia Sato.

Word is that Oprah wouldn't do the interview unless Brett was in on it. But the truth is, I love Sophia like she's my second mother. I think it's because she's kind of maternal looking with those tunics meant to hide her midsection—I say "meant to," because, hello? No one with an actual waist wears those things.

She also has a way of getting the good stuff out of the

celebrities she interviews. She lulls them into a sense of calm and then bam! They spill the beans all over the table. She calls people dear and sweetheart, so they start to feel like they're talking to their grandmother.

And my hairdresser's half-sister's milkman heard from Sophia's people that Harper is expected to spill like the Exxon Valdez.

I'd better hurry up and eat this popcorn before I'm too riveted to chew and swallow.

All the dishes,
Ferris Biltmore

~

The Penninsula Hotel is known for the high-class sex workers who display their wares at the bar while looking for their next hourly boyfriend. Prisha and I used to come here and nurse one twenty-dollar martini while enjoying the show.

"You okay?" Prisha asks. She's holding onto my elbow, moving me toward the elevator.

"As good as can be." I fake a brightness I do not feel.

Ethan rushes ahead and pushes the up button. Once we're in motion, he says, "Today should be the last of it. Just stick to vague answers and try to be as likable as you can. Not that you need to pretend to be likable. You're very likable …"

"Calm down, Ethan," Prisha tells him. Turning to me, she says, "Remember: you're grateful for your fans, your support team, and all the opportunities you've had in life. You've been blessed with a wonderful career and two amazing children who are your everything."

Ethan interrupts, "You're focused on creating the best future possible for your children, and someday, when *they're* settled, you look forward to resurrecting your career. You wish things had turned out differently, but you've fully embraced your new path and are excited for the tranquility that a fresh start will bring."

"I remember the lines," I say, irritation edging out my anxiety.

"We're just doing our jobs," Prisha says, before taking on a kindergarten teacher tone. "When she asks about Digger, you remember what to say?"

Letting out a sigh normally reserved for only the most hormonal teenagers, I robotically answer, "He was very kind to me at a time when I needed kindness. Unfortunately, that moment was caught on film and blown epically out of proportion. Blah, blah, blah…Brett and I had already been separated for several weeks."

The elevator stops with a ding, letting us know we've reached our destination. The door to the penthouse opens and we're greeted by Sophia's producer. She's got a clip-board in hand and she's wearing a headset. Sticking out her hand, she rapid-fire says, "You're here! Hair and makeup are in the bathroom. Sophia is just running over her questions in the living room. Sound check is in thirty. I'm Liza. Frankie will bring you water, but no nibbles once your lips are done. Okay? Good. Let's get this show on the road!"

My heart rate accelerates with every word.

"Come on." Prisha pulls me along like a lamb to the slaughter.

Hair and makeup take a grand total of twenty minutes as I arrived ninety percent ready. I just needed the final blush and brush. I'm wearing a conservative, short-sleeve twinset with a knee-length navy skirt, which is the opposite of sexy.

If anything, I'm showing the world the very reason my husband looked elsewhere.

"Harper." Sophia approaches me with a big smile on her fifty-something face. "You look lovely."

I sit across from her. Crossing one ankle over the other like I'm the queen mother, I say, "You mean I look unoffensive."

She lets out a chuckle. "You look like you know how the game is played." She glances behind me. "You ready, Mario? One, two, three, and all that good stuff?"

"Just keep talking," the director calls back. "We'll make adjustments as needed and then we can start."

A sound person approaches and wires me up while Sophia and I make small talk. "How are the kids handling everything?"

She's just warming you up for the real interview, putting you in an emotional frame of mind. Do not fall for it. "Divorce is hard for young people. I'm doing my best to protect them, but I'm afraid they're hearing more than they should at school."

"Comes with the territory, huh? Hollywood kids grow up *so much faster* than normal ones."

Normal ones, ouch. "Yeah, I suppose so."

One of the producers rushes over and starts to go over the timeline with Sophia. I take a moment to process her words about my children—the phrase "normal ones" bouncing around until my head hurts. My gut reaction was to feel defensive, like I'd made the choice to have abnormal kids, or something.

But then my mind flashes to hiding under blankets in the back of cars with darkened windows to evade the press, my son mooning a strange man hiding in our tree, the hurt in Liam's eyes when he asked me to tell him the truth about Justine and Brett. Like a bomb going off, I suddenly know what I have to do. I have to get them the hell out of this town before it chews them up and spits them out like it's doing to me. I'm not just going to sell my house. I'm going to leave LA.

The director tells Sophia it's go time, and she smiles at me. "We're not going to do a lot of stopping and starting. Don't worry if you stumble over words, we can fix things in editing if necessary." The reason they don't do a lot of stopping and starting is because she wants me to be comfortable so I say more than I would if I had time to think about it.

I take a deep breath, then nod. "I'm ready."

Sophia looks at the camera and smiles. "Good evening and welcome to *Sophia Talks*. Joining me tonight is a very special guest who's been making headlines around the globe. You know her as Emma Jones from *Conspiracy* and more recently from the cover of every tabloid in the nation. I'm speaking to the very talented and lovely Harper Kennedy about her extremely public break-up from super-star husband Brett Kennedy.

"Harper has agreed to an exclusive interview with me. Once tonight is over, she won't be talking publicly about it again. So, keep it right here for the next forty-five minutes, because you won't want to miss it." Pausing, she looks at me. "Harper, welcome."

"Thank you for having me, Sophia." Small smile punctuated with a head tilt.

While flipping index cards in her lap, she says, "I'm sure you'd rather be anywhere but here."

I laugh delicately. "I almost scheduled a double-root canal instead."

"I don't think there's any reason to beat around the bush. You and Brett have been Hollywood's 'It' couple for years now. No one thought it would happen to you two, and yet, here you are, in the midst of a scandalous divorce. Why don't you walk us through the moment when you discovered your husband was cheating on you."

"Which time?"

Her eyebrows shoot up to her hairline in excitement. "Let's start with the most recent. I believe her name is Justine?"

Nodding, I do my best to keep my face neutral, even though every muscle wants to wrinkle up in disgust. "That's correct. She was our nanny who worked four days a week and lived in our guest house."

Another key Sophia move is to not talk too much and wait for the person she's interviewing to start to ramble. So, I do. "I came home from a lunch out one afternoon to discover Brett and Justine in the middle of … you know … it."

"Sex?"

"Yes."

She throws a bejeweled hand over her heart in shock. "That must have been so painful. What did you do?"

"Somehow, I managed to remain calm, although when I think about it now, I don't know how I did that. I fired Justine and told Brett he had to leave. My children were in the backyard, and I didn't want to make a big scene in front of them."

"What a betrayal," Sophia says, making a tsking sound. "A young woman who knew you and actually lived in your home with you and your children."

"Let's not forget about my husband," I tell her. "He's the one who stood up in front of our family and friends and vowed to be faithful."

"But he struggled with that particular vow, didn't he?" Sophia asks. "Over the years, Brett has been linked with dozens of women, several of whom he had alleged relationships with *during* your marriage." She stops and stares at me intently, which means she's going in for the kill. "Why did you stay after all that? I mean, you're a beautiful, talented woman who would have had no trouble finding someone else."

"I stayed for the same reason most women in my situation do—for my children. I wanted so badly to give them a stable, loving home. I also hoped that each time Brett cheated, it would be the last time." I pick up the bottled water sitting on the side table next to my armchair. Taking a small sip, I manage a slight smile. "He didn't get an Oscar because he's bad at acting."

"So, you stayed for the kids."

"Hollywood kids don't always have the easiest time, and I guess I overcompensated. I now see how naïve that was."

"Let's talk about your children, Liam and Lily. You do your best to keep them out of the public eye, but it's not always possible, is it?" Sophia says.

"No, it's not."

"How are they handling everything?"

"How do kids ever handle divorce?" I ask. "It's never easy for them."

"Yes, but for it to be so public … That must surely make things harder." She gives me a sympathetic look.

"Of course it does. That's why I took them away on vacation when the story broke." I can see Prisha nodding out of the corner of my eye. So far, so good.

"Right, to Alaska!" *Oh, she's salivating now.*

"I figured it was the last place we would be found. Obviously, I underestimated people's interest in my heartache."

Sophia leans forward and touches my hand. "People are interested because they care about you."

Inhaling deeply, I look from Prisha to Ethan. This is where I'm supposed to humbly mention how nice it is to be so well thought of and how grateful I am to have so much support. Several seconds pass and I don't say a word. The tension palpably builds. Sophia sits expectantly but quietly. It feels like we're in the middle of a gunfight waiting for the first bullet to fly.

Fine, let 'er rip. "I think people love gossip. They like to see someone they once put on a shelf, fall off that shelf."

That was not what Sophia was expecting to hear. "Interesting."

"Is it?" I ask. "Divorce is unimaginably hard. Everyone in the family suffers. And at a time where all you want is peace and quiet, the world feels entitled to kick back and enjoy your pain."

Behind Sophia, I can see Prisha doing the "cut it out" sign with her hand raking across her neck.

Sorry, Prish. I have to do this.

Setting my gaze on my host, I say, "I know I'm in a position of great privilege, and that a lot of people will say you can't have fame without putting up with everything that being famous includes. I don't expect anyone to feel sorry for me. But couldn't we all agree to leave the children out of it? They didn't ask to be born to famous parents."

"Is that why you came to me, to beg people to leave your children alone? I think there's something else on your mind." Sophia Sato's success is not a fluke. The woman is a barracuda dressed as a middle-aged mom.

"I have a lot to say." I turn to the camera. "I genuinely appreciate the fans who have had my back and supported me. I can't tell you what that means to me. I'm so grateful to the people who have spoken out for me and those who have simply given me my space. But for those of you who stalked me and my children, took our pictures while we bought ice cream, and followed us on vacation—you should be ashamed of yourselves."

"Let's talk about your vacation. You met a man there, didn't you?"

My heart aches at the thought of Digger. I hope he'll watch this so he can see who I really am. "I did. I certainly wasn't looking for one, and I wasn't looking to pay Brett back for his betrayals, but you know what *they* say, don't you?"

She shakes her head. "Tell me."

"Love finds you when you're not looking."

"Are you saying that you *fell in love* while you were in Alaska?" Sophia is so excited she looks like she's about to launch off her seat while Prisha's eyes are open so wide I'm afraid she's having a stroke.

"Love is a gamble, Sophia. It's never a sure thing. There are no guarantees. When Brett and I got married, I was certain we would be in love forever. But we weren't married long when his eyes started to wander. Then, the rest of his body followed."

She laughs like it's the funniest thing she's ever heard. When she's done, she gets right back to being serious. "All you had left of his love was a taunting memory of what could have been."

Drama Queen party of one. "You could say that."

"Let's talk about your divorce. You filed for sole custody of the children and Brett is not contesting that," she says. "What does it say about a man who doesn't want his own children?"

And here's the only moment in my entire life when any of my acting training will ever matter. Because someday, Liam and Lily will watch this interview and I never want them to know how little their dad cared about them. "Brett loves our children very much, enough to realize that his lifestyle and filming schedule would make it difficult for him to provide them with the stability they need. He's making the ultimate sacrifice for their good."

"That's certainly an unusual way of looking at it."

Shrugging, I say, "I choose to focus on the rainbow, not the clouds."

"Let's get back to this Digger McKenzie fellow. He's a pilot who owns a lodge up in Alaska? Sounds like he's as far away from Brett Kennedy as you can get."

I will not pick up the gantlet she just dropped. "Digger is an amazing man. He's honorable and trustworthy. Nothing is for show with him. He helped me and the kids at a time when we needed a soft place to land."

"Tell me about that kiss because"—she fans herself with her cue cards—"wow!""

"I kissed *him*. He didn't initiate it. The truth is, that when you're neglected for long enough and someone finally shows you a little affection, it's hard to keep your focus."

"You make it sound like you regret that kiss."

Shaking my head, I tell her, "I have plenty of regrets, but that's not one of them. I regret staying in a marriage for so long when it had clearly ended years ago. I regret not understanding what was truly important and seeking out a simpler life sooner. I regret caring so much what other people think about me that I walked away from what might have been the best thing in my life."

"It sounds like you're thinking of moving out of the spotlight …"

"My house is on the market," I tell her.

"Where are you planning to move to? Are you going back to Alaska?" She's trying to look empathetic, but I can tell she's inwardly rubbing her hands together in glee.

"I haven't decided where we're going yet. I don't think it will be Alaska though."

"Why is that?"

"I bring a lot of unwanted attention wherever I go and

the last thing I'd want to do is hurt the people there any more than I already have."

"You mean Digger."

"Yes."

Sophia shuffles the cards some more. "And what about Brett?"

"What about him?"

"I know he says his relationship with the nanny is over, but do you believe it?" She tilts her head down so she's looking at me above the rim of her glasses.

"It's none of my business," I say shortly. "Brett Kennedy is his own man. He's free to date whomever he pleases."

"You're a bigger woman than I am," she says. "If Brett was my husband, I'd want revenge."

"Believe me, if Brett were your husband," I tell her, "all you'd want was your freedom."

Ethan throws his hands up into the air out of desperation while Sophia laughs.

"I've always liked you, Harper," she says. "I'm glad to see how maturely you're handling this situation. I know it can't be easy, but there's a grace about you that is going to make you come back stronger than ever."

"I appreciate that very much, Sophia. Life has a way of giving and taking when you least expect it. It's not a journey for the faint of heart, but luckily my heart is pretty strong."

"But your heart isn't in Alaska?" She's tenacious.

I've already said more than I should but, in the moment, I decide to keep going. "My heart is most assuredly in Alaska, but sometimes you have to make decisions to protect the people you care about. Right now, I'm going to focus on my kids and help them heal in any way that I can."

Sophia nods her head. "You are a class act, lady. I have nothing but the greatest respect for you." She turns her head to the camera and continues, "We'll be right back with more Harper Kennedy."

When the director calls cut, Ethan and Prisha storm the set like a pair of Navy Seals. Ethan gets here first. "You went rogue. What were you thinking?"

A sense of calm comes over me. It's a feeling I haven't had in years. "I was thinking that I don't care about this town anymore. The dreams that brought me here are all dead. It's time for something new."

"You can't just … decide to end it all," Ethan says. "I mean, what if you change your mind?"

"I won't."

"You better not, because you've insulted a lot of people today, including the viewers of this show. Insinuating that people have enjoyed watching your pain."

Prisha, who has been suspiciously quiet, scrolls through her phone while listening. Then she looks up and says, "I don't know, Ethan. Social media is loving our girl right now."

The director calls out, "Thirty seconds!"

"You sure this is what you want?" Prisha asks, tears forming in her eyes.

"I need this, Prish."

She smiles while she shakes her head in disbelief. "In that case, just keep on keeping on and this should be over soon."

This will be over soon, and I'm not just talking about the interview. This chapter of my life is ending. And while I'm excited about what comes next, I'm also terrified.

Chapter 38

Digger

Evie and Grandpa Jack are sitting on either side of me on the couch in the lodge, presumably so I can't get up and walk away. Moira rushes in just as the interview is wrapping up. "Did I miss it? Edna was late getting to my house to watch the boys."

Keeping his eyes on the television, Grandpa Jack waves her off. "Shh!"

Sophia Sato turns to the camera. "Well, there you have it, folks. When one door closes, another one opens. I'd like to thank our guest, Hollywood ex-pat and all-around wonderful woman, Harper Kennedy." Then she turns her death stare into the camera, and adds, "Digger McKenzie, if you're watching tonight, I think you better hurry up and walk through that open door!"

Evie squeals, Jack claps his hands, and Moira yells, "What open door?"

I sit, not daring to move a muscle while I watch the

credits roll over Harper and Sophia, who are still chatting. As the show's theme song replaces the audio from the studio, I have no idea what they're saying. If only there had been a Boy Scout lipreading badge.

"Digger's famous," Evie tells Moira. "Like, super famous. Harper said he's honest and amazing and that she fell in love with him."

"And her heart's in Alaska," Jack adds with a huge grin.

My own heart pounds in my chest as I scramble to process what just happened. Did Harper just admit she's in love with me on national television?

"Did she say she's coming back?" Moira asks, looking like she might hyperventilate.

"No, she said the exact opposite," I tell her, getting up and clearing the glasses off the coffee table.

Evie follows me toward the kitchen. "But that's only because she'd be bringing unwanted attention with her."

"Which she would," I answer, pushing the swinging door.

Of course, the trio are right on my heels. "Are you nuts? We're swimming in cash from her short stay. Imagine what would happen if she *lived* here?" Evie says.

"She said she *wasn't* moving here," I remind her. "She was pretty damn clear about that."

"I can't blame her if that's the attitude you have. The ball is in your court, mister. You need to go to LA," Moira insists.

"I can't just show up on her doorstep and say, 'Hey, since you're moving, why not move all the way to Alaska?'" I gently place the milk glasses in the sink.

"Why not? She said she loved it up here and she's looking for a simple life for her kids," Jack says. "What better place to do that than right here? With a man she called amazing, kind, and honest?"

"She also called you exactly what she and her kids need," Evie makes sure to say.

"She said that?" Moira clutches her heart.

I shake my head. "She meant what she needed at that moment. Not now."

"You're not going to even try?" Jack wants to know. "What kind of knucklehead did I raise?"

"My showing up there will only complicate things for her. She needs to figure out her next move based on what's best for Liam and Lily," I say, even though my heart is begging me to go directly to the airport, do not pass go, do not collect two hundred dollars.

Autumn is short here. It comes and goes in a blink. One day, the leaves are just turning, then the next, winter blows in full force. It's been ten days since Harper's interview. Ten long days and nights with my stomach in knots. Evie, Jack, and Moira are so mad, they're barely speaking to me. Evie's taken to calling me "Inaction Man," which she's sure to tell me is much nicer than what she really wants to call me.

The rollercoaster of emotions never seems to stop. I constantly question what I should do. I spend an hour convincing myself I'm doing the best thing by leaving Harper alone and not putting any pressure on her, then the next hour, I'm absolutely positive I'm dead wrong. Every instinct is telling me to go to her.

I'm just heading out of the office for the day when the phone rings. "You got that?" I ask Evie, who rolls her eyes at me.

"Why? You heading to California to go get the love of your life or something?"

"Just answer the phone, Evie." I push the door open and walk outside.

Taking a deep breath, I let the cool air fill my lungs. I'm on the verge of relaxing a little when Evie comes running out. "Digger! It's Harper's friend on the line!"

Freezing in place, I ask, "And?"

"She says she needs to talk to you. It's urgent."

I hurry back inside, worry replacing any peace I'd started to feel. Please don't let anything be wrong with Harper or the kids. Grabbing the receiver off the front desk, I say, "Digger here."

"Digger, it's Prisha, did I catch you at a bad time?"

"Is everything okay?" I demand, my heart in my throat.

"Harper and the kids are fine, but I need you to settle a bet."

A bet? "What?"

"Well, I've been saying you'd gladly spend your life with Harper, if only she would tell you that she's in love with you and wants to make a life with you. But *she's* sure that if you really cared about her, you would have contacted her by now—you know, especially after she declared her feelings for you on national television." Prisha takes a break before asking, "So, who's right? Me or her?"

Every muscle in my body comes to life like I'm about to shoot out of the runner's block and sprint to California. A huge grin overtakes my face. "I … well … are you sure? Is she sure?"

"She's *so* sure, Digger. She hasn't been eating or sleeping because she's so tied in knots that you haven't contacted her. She just sold her house. I figured I'd better call you and tell you because she's about to make a huge mistake."

My heart is pounding so hard, I can barely hear her over the rush of blood in my ears. "What kind of mistake?"

"She's talking about house hunting in Illinois, where her

parents live, but honestly, they drive her nuts. Also, you're not in Illinois so …"

Jamming one hand in the front pocket of my jeans, I say, "She shouldn't go live there. Not if her parents drive her nuts."

"Are you saying you think she should go to Gamble?"

Swallowing hard, I say, "I'd like nothing more."

"Good stuff. Book yourself on the next flight here, then text me the details. I'll come pick you up and take you to her place so you can tell her the good news yourself."

"Okay," I say, shock vibrating through me at what I'm agreeing to. "I'll be there."

"Oh, and … maybe wear something nice for a change," Prisha adds. "She seems to like that Brawny paper towel guy thing you've got going on, but … you know … a little effort will go a long way."

"Good tip, thanks."

When I look up, I see Evie and Jack both staring at me, wide-eyed.

"Can you two hold down the fort for a few days?"

"I'll need a raise," Evie says jokingly.

"How about I don't fire you for calling me Inaction Man?"

She tilts her head from side to side as though considering it. "Sounds fair."

"You … uh … got plans there, son?" Grandpa asks.

Grinning, I tell him, "Thought I'd go to LA. Soak up some sun, maybe see if I can get myself a wife and some kids while I'm there."

Chapter 39

Harper

Dear Readers,

Word on the street is that Harper Kennedy sold her house for a cool six point eight million dollars. Damn, girl, that's loads of cash! You could buy a whole town for that kind of money.

While I'm sending my girl all the love and light, I'm pretty devastated. Being a Hollywood insider like I am, I happen to know where Harper lives. I hope this doesn't sound too stalkery, but I've driven by several times in hopes of seeing her.

I don't plan on stopping and bothering her, I just want to yell out words of encouragement. "I adore you! Stay strong! Ride that cowboy!"

Alas, I haven't spotted her. But on the very off chance the

divine Miss H reads my blog, here it is—Go forth and make a happy life, lady. You deserve it!

Crying in My Dishes,
Ferris Biltmore

I've lived in this house for a decade. For ten years, I've nested and nurtured here. I've also stuck my head in the sand and pretended my life wasn't a melodrama of epic proportions. But either way, this has been my home, my sanctuary.

"When are the movers coming?" Prisha walks into my living room, looking over a stack of boxes blocking her view of me.

"Four days," I tell her. "Their first stop will be Goodwill."

"Buck up, friend. You look like a puddle of sadness over there."

I look up at her with tears in my eyes. "I'm going to miss you so much, Prish. You're not only my best friend and godmother to my kids, but you're like a sister. I'm nothing without you and Ethan. Come with me," I beg.

"Wish I could, but Tanya Freeport just broke parole—she was found at Club Cool with a needle in her arm. While par for the course with that one, this is particularly bad as she's got a world-tour booked. Ethan and I need to work our magic and get things on track."

Nodding my head, I say, "Just because I'm leaving the business, doesn't mean everyone else is, huh?"

"Well, I'm not. This town's inability to behave is going to pad my bank account with enough cha-ching to retire by fifty. But remember how Ethan was planning a sabbatical to write that book on the celebrity legal battles?"

"Yeah. He said he was going to do that next summer."

"He's starting as soon as we figure out how to fix Tanya's latest leap off the wagon."

"Maybe I can talk him into doing it in Illinois. We could set up an office for him in my parents' barn or something." I'm joking but I'm not joking. I need my friends.

Prisha laughs. "Yo, Bessie, can you hand me the printer paper? What about you, piggy wiggy, want to eat lunch together? No BLT's, I promise."

"What am I going to do without you guys?" While I know the best thing for me and the kids is to move away from here, it's going to be the hardest thing I've ever done. My mom will spend every waking moment trying to feed us, my dad will talk endlessly about corn rot and the demon corporations who are trying to make small farms extinct. Even worse, I just know they won't be able to stop themselves from criticizing Brett in front of the kids. I'm going to have to put my foot down on that one though. Criticizing him is like rejecting fifty percent of my children's DNA. That can't happen.

If that's not bad enough, every time I go into town, someone is going to stop me to lament my tragic life. *Poor Harper, getting cheated on by Helioman and having to come home.*

"I've got to head out for a couple hours," Prisha interrupts my pity party. "I'll be back with supper though. I'm ordering Thai."

"Can you get something not so spicy for the kids?" I ask.

"Sheila and I thought we'd take them to In-N-Out for their last double-double in a while. Then we thought we'd stop by Brett's place so they can spend some time with him."

"You're the best, Prish. But don't order food just for me. I can make a sandwich or something."

I watch as she walks out the front door, leaving me alone in my malaise.

Finally peeling myself away from the living room, I go

upstairs and help the kids pack their rooms. Liam greets me with, "Are you sure we have to go to Illinois, Mom?"

Neither of the kids are excited about the move, which makes it harder to go through with. "I know you're going to miss your dad," I tell him. "But he's going to be in Latvia for several months, so he won't even be here."

After Galaxy let Brett go, he jumped at the first offer he got: playing the villain, Sir Dickle Buttmunch, in an Austin Powers reboot. Oh, how the mighty have fallen …

"I'll miss Dad for sure …" He hems and haws for a minute before adding, "But it's not that. I don't mind leaving, I just don't want to go to Illinois."

"You think we should tell the movers to take our stuff to the Bahamas?" I tease him while pulling him into my arms.

I feel his head shake against my chest before I hear his muffled reply. "How about Alaska? We liked it there, didn't we?"

Lily chooses this moment to walk into the room. "Yeah, how about Alaska? That would be the coolest! I could finally flip those pancakes and we could go fishing, and skiing, and camping, and …"

"I already told you guys. It wouldn't be fair to Digger. I've caused him enough trouble."

"But Digger loves us!" Lily maintains. "He gave me all those piggyback rides and was teaching us all kinds of cooking things."

"I can help him out by driving the golf cart," Liam adds quietly.

Digger McKenzie stole my children's hearts in record time. He stole all our hearts. "Why don't you guys write to him?" I shouldn't encourage a deeper connection, but I hate to see how they're yearning for him.

They've known their dad their whole lives, but due to Brett's schedule, they've barely spent any time with him.

Digger represents more than a father figure to them, he represents stability.

It's been almost two weeks since my interview with Sophia Sato. Almost two weeks where Digger could have contacted me and told me if he still had feelings for me. No news means no feelings.

"Hey, guess what? Auntie Prisha is going to take you to In-N-Out Burger for supper tonight!" Changing the subject is my only option.

"Can I have a strawberry milkshake?" Lily asks quietly.

"You can have anything you want," I tell her. "What about you, Liam? Are you going to get a shake, too?"

He nods his head sadly. "Vanilla, I guess."

"After supper Aunt Prisha and Aunt Sheila are going to take you over to see Dad. That'll be fun, won't it?"

"Daddy's learning his lines for his new movie," my daughter announces. "He doesn't have a lot of time to play with us."

Typical Brett. He can't "Dad" while he's learning lines, he can't do it while he's getting into character, he certainly can't do it while he's filming. That leaves the short time between projects for him to show some interest in his kids. This is the very reason we need to get the heck out of Dodge.

"Your dad is working hard," I tell them, hoping to instill a small amount of respect in them. Not that Brett deserves it.

"He has a new girlfriend," Liam announces.

"Really?" I try to feign excitement like my son just told me that Santa Claus was moving in with us. "Well, good for him."

"I don't like her," Lily says. "She's got huge boobies and barely wears any clothes."

"She's really young," Liam says.

I hate that Brett is already parading his hookups in front

of our kids. It's another nail in his coffin, as far as I'm concerned. "You don't have to go if you don't want to, but you should get that double-double for sure."

The next two hours are spent half-heartedly cleaning out drawers and cabinets. We all work like automatons, but our hearts aren't in it. I'm relieved when Prisha finally gets back.

"Hey!" she shouts from the front door. "I brought a surprise!"

The kids run down the stairs like a herd of buffalo are after them. After a few minutes without her saying anything else, I call out, "Is it Thai food?" My stomach rumbles at the thought. I can't remember having eaten today.

"I hope it's a little better than Thai food," comes the deep, sultry voice I feared I was forgetting.

My body fills with chills that grow from tiny little goosebumps to ostrich eggs.

Digger McKenzie is in my house, in California.

Chapter 40

Digger

Liam and Lily both launch themselves at me like a couple of baseballs out of a pitching machine. I catch them, one in each arm, and pick them up, my heart spilling over with happiness at their reaction to me. Tears fill my eyes, but I don't even care. I feel pure joy seeing them again after so many weeks of believing this moment would never come.

"Hey, you two," I say as Lily presses her cheek to mine. "I missed you."

"Are you here to make pancakes because I really want to flip pancakes," Lily tells me, pulling back and taking both my cheeks in her little hands.

"Well, that's not specifically why I came, but I'm sure we can manage some pancakes while I'm here," I tell her with a wink.

Crouching, I set them both down. Ruffling Liam's hair, I say, "You went and got taller after you left."

He smiles proudly, straightening his spine. "I'm pretty sure I shot up a couple inches."

"Good thing you showed up in time because we're moving out of this house and you wouldn't have found us," Lily says, grabbing my hand. "We're moving to Ill Annoyed, but Liam and me want to move to Alaska instead."

"It's Illi-NOY, not Ill Annoyed," Liam corrects her.

"Well, I don't care. I'm calling it that because I'm *annoyed* we have to move there," Lily says haughtily.

I tuck my teeth between my lips so I don't laugh. I lift my head to glance at Harper who's just walked down the stairs. Her eyes are shining as she smiles at the three of us. We stand, staring at each other without saying anything for long enough that Prisha decides to take charge. "Listen Liam, Lily, your mom and Digger need to have a grown-up talk, so why don't we go pick up Sheila and hit In-N-Out Burger now?"

Lily squeezes my hand. "I don't want to go. I want to stay with Digger."

Smiling down at her, I say, "How about if I promise to be here when you get back?" I hope like hell it's a promise I can keep.

She screws up her face as though trying to decide, then nods. "Okay, I guess I do really want a milkshake."

Prisha ushers them out the door, then turns back and says, "You two sort this out. There's a happily ever after waiting for you, but I've done all I can. The rest is up to you."

Once the door is closed and the house is quiet, I'm torn between wanting to rush to Harper and taking her in my arms and knowing I have absolutely no right to do that.

I'm more nervous than I've ever been. It was one thing to hear about her Hollywood life, but it's another thing entirely to see how she lives. She's in a mansion with guards posted outside and all I can offer her is a modest cabin in the woods.

I open my mouth, then close it. Finally, I take a deep breath and just let the words spill out. "Harper, I am so sorry about what I said to you the day you left. It was cruel and … unfair of me, and I didn't mean any of it. It's been haunting me since you left. The last thing you are is selfish and you're sure as hell not some princess. You're an amazing woman, an incredible mom, and …" *And just say it, coward.* "And I want you to know that."

Nope. I missed. Dammit, Digger. Say it.

She nods, tears filling her eyes. "I know why you said what you did. I hurt you. I made you feel like you didn't matter to me, but you do."

A lump forms in my throat, but I let her hear the emotion in my voice. "The last thing I'd ever want to do is hurt you or complicate your life. I … just want you and the kids to be happy and to have the life you deserve, but I can't offer you this," I say, pointing around at the enormous kitchen.

"I don't want this," she whispers. "This is … just … stuff. It's a life that'll wind up screwing up my kids permanently. I'm done with it. We need a fresh start."

"I can do fresh starts," I say, my heart pounding in my chest.

"Can you do happy endings?" she asks, smiling through her tears.

"Absolutely." I finally rush across the room to her. Taking her in my arms, I stare into her beautiful blue eyes, and let the truth come out for the first time. "I'm in love with you, Harper. You're the person I want to spend my life with. You, and Liam, and Lily. I want to be the man who takes care of you and protects you. I want to make you laugh and hold you when you cry. I want to build a life with you, wherever that takes us. If you don't want to spend it in Gamble, I'll happily go wherever you want to be, because if there's one thing I figured out after you left, it's that my future is wherever you are."

Lifting herself onto her tiptoes, she plants a big kiss on my lips. I kiss her back. It's a promise that I mean what I say that I will be there for her, wherever she is. Holding her tightly, our bodies feel like one as the entire world seems to melt away. Finally, I pull back and look down at her. "Is that a yes?"

Nodding, she says, "It's a yes."

I grin, love and joy radiating through me, then kiss her some more. "I've had a lot of time to think about it, and I think we should take it slow. The kids'll need time to adjust to having me around and the last thing I want to do is insert myself in your lives before you're all ready to have me."

"Agreed. We take it slow," she says. "But let's rush back to Alaska."

"You sure?" I ask, afraid it's too good to be true.

"I am. Gamble feels right to me. To the kids too. It's the perfect place to raise them. Somewhere that they can just be kids, you know?"

"It's the perfect place to raise a family," I tell her. "And if it gets too cold in the winter, I'll be there to keep you warm."

"Or we can hop on a plane and go south for some sun," she offers.

"Or we can do that," I tell her, chuckling.

She reaches up with both hands and pulls my face back down to hers. "I'm so glad you came."

"It's the first smart thing I've ever done in my life."

"Well, I'm glad I could be your first," she teases.

"You're my first, last, and only," I tell her, giving her a lingering kiss. "How long do you think the kids will be gone?" I ask.

She raises an eyebrow. "What did you have in mind?"

"Oh no, not that, not now," I tell her. "When we do that, it's going to be the right place, the right time, and it's going to require all night."

Her cheeks turn pink, and she fights a grin. "Then why did you ask how long the kids will be gone then?

"I just can't wait to tell them the good news."

Tears spill down her cheeks as she smiles up at me. "What do you say? Should we go meet them for milkshakes?"

"Let's go."

And that's just what we do. We set off on our very first adventure as a couple, knowing it's the start of a lifetime of love, happiness, and being a family.

Dear Readers,

I'm trudging through life, clinging to every sex scandal/drug problem/botched Botox debacle, in hopes the sparkle will come back to my life. But the plain truth is, just knowing there's no chance of running into Harper Kennedy at Whole Foods is really messing with my equilibrium.

After all, what is Hollywood, if not the dream of something bigger and better happening? For me, that was the hope Harper and I would finally become besties who spend our afternoons shopping for lawn furniture while sipping pink drinks from Starbucks. Lemon drops after hours.

Alas, my girl has left me for greener pastures—mountains, igloos, and bears! Oh, my!

I take refuge in the fact that Brett Kennedy's career path has taken a nosedive. The bad guy in an *Austin Powers* reboot in Latvia? What's next, a *Saved by the Bell* reboot in Rikers?

BIG sigh. I can only hope the void in my heart will one day be filled by another up and coming starlet of quality and grace. In the meantime, pray for me.

Tired of dirty dishes,
Ferris Biltmore

Coming Soon: A Hate Like This (A Gamble on Love Mom-Com, Book 2)

Single mother Moira Bishop hates when her family interferes in her love life. If life as a young widow isn't hard enough, just add three boys, a slew of unruly pets, and ownership of Gamble, Alaska's only diner. The last thing she needs is a man to look after too.

Entertainment lawyer to the stars Ethan Caplan hates his clients. There's only so much coddling and placating a man can do in a lifetime. He's finally decided he's had enough, so he escapes to the tiny no-horse town of Gamble to work on the novel he's always wanted to write.

Positive that Alaska will be distraction-free, Ethan's sure he can pen a bestselling legal novel. That is until he lays his eyes on Moira Bishop. Suddenly he finds himself having five meals a day at the diner, just so he can talk to her for a few minutes.

When Moira's son wins tickets to the Galaxy Studio Theme Park in L.A., Ethan jumps at the chance to play host to the family. He's sure he can win her over by showing her how glamorous life could be with him. With the help of his friends, he plans the date to end all dates, hoping one incredible night will change her mind about giving love a second chance.

Will Moira open her heart to Ethan? Will Ethan do what it takes to prove that he can be the man Moira and her boys need in their lives? Will little Colton be tall enough to ride the Galactic Mindbender?

Find out in the deliciously fun second installment in the Gamble on Love Mom-com series.

Pre-order today!

About the Authors

WHITNEY DINEEN

USA Today Bestseller Whitney Dineen is a rock star in her own head. While delusional about her singing abilities, there's been a plethora of validation that she's a fairly decent author (AMAZING!!!). After winning many writing awards and selling nearly a kabillion books (math may not be her forte, either), she's decided to let the voices in her head say whatever they want (sorry, Mom). She also won a fourth-place ribbon in a fifth-grade swim meet in backstroke. So, there's that.

Whitney loves to play with her kids (a.k.a. dazzle them with her amazing flossing abilities), bake stuff, eat stuff, and write books for people who "get" her. She thinks french fries are the perfect food and Mrs. Roper is her spirit animal.

MELANIE SUMMERS

Melanie Summers lives on Vancouver Island in Canada with her husband, three kiddos, and two cuddly dogs. When she's not writing, she loves reading (obviously), snuggling up on the couch with her family for movie night (which would not be complete without lots of popcorn and milkshakes), and long walks on the beach near her house. Melanie also loves shutting down restaurants with her girlfriends. Well, not literally shutting them down, like calling the health inspector or something. More like just staying until they turn the lights off.

Made in the USA
Las Vegas, NV
18 September 2022

55566375R00173